BAYEUX

Bayeux

Published by Headford Ridge Press, 2024

ISBN: 978-1-0686390-0-5

Copyright © James Farnham, 2024

The right of James Farnham to be identified as author of this work has been asserted by him in accordance with the Copyright, Designs and Patents Act 1988.

www.jamesfarnham.com

This book is sold subject to the condition that it shall not, by way of trade or otherwise, be lent, resold, hired out, or otherwise circulated without the publisher's prior consent in any form of binding or cover other than that in which it is published and without a similar condition, including this condition, being imposed on the subsequent purchaser.

Bayeux is a work of fiction. Names, characters, places and incidents are the product of the author's imagination or are used fictitiously. Any resemblance to persons, living or dead, events or locales is entirely coincidental.

https://bayeux.blog

All rights reserved.

A CIP catalogue record for this book is available on request from the British Library

Typeset in Adobe Garamond Pro 11/15 pt by The Book Typesetters
thebooktypesetters.com

Printed and bound in Great Britain by Clays Ltd, Elcograf S.p.A.

MIX
Paper | Supporting responsible forestry
FSC® C018072

BAYEUX

JAMES FARNHAM

1

She choked in the fug of smoke. Her eyes smarted, and she couldn't shut out the roar because her arms were pinned above her by the crush of bodies.

Yet Elizabeth forced her way through the crowd in the drawing room bearing a silver salver of canapés, which people reached up to pick from as she went, smiling and praising her hospitality. 'The best hostess on the Holt,' someone bellowed above the noise, which was what Magnus said too, occasionally.

As she reached the middle of the room, she came to a stop. People were pushing in from the other side of the drawing room to dance, or flail more like, which had recently become the way the world spun now that the Beatles had redefined it.

She stood under the chandelier, fixed with the smile she had cultivated to conceal her distaste for these endless entertainments Magnus demanded. Two birds with one stone, he always said, keeping his advertising clients happy and impressing everyone on the Holt at the same time. She had learnt to appear content while shutting out the deafening madness around her, retreating into her inner stillness.

She froze as she saw, through the haze of smoke, a face she hadn't seen for over twenty years. Surely it was Ralph reincarnated, an apparition from the past.

Nobody could have heard her gasp above the din, and somehow she hid her panic amid the mayhem. She wrenched herself round and started burrowing her way through the crowd towards the door that led to what had once been a service corridor; there she would be able to breathe and regain her composure. She managed to keep her smile set as she pressed through the sea of people nodding at her appreciatively – as if respecting her urgency on some errand to keep the party rolling, keeping everything going for Magnus and his magnificent parties, instructing the staff to bring out more food, more Scotch, more ashtrays, her demeanour rigidly efficient.

Once in the corridor, she banged down the salver onto a side table. The noise of the party faded behind as her heels clicked along the parquet in step with the thudding inside her. She darted into the linen room and closed the door, finally in the dark and the silence, and sat on one of the laundry baskets, breathing in deeply the freshness of the linen through her hands that covered her face.

A few minutes of calm to recover, that was all that was needed. She knew this because she had almost perfected the art of oblivion, erasing memories of her life before Magnus – 'BM' she called it, in an effort to make light of it – another of her strategies to compartmentalise the past, to lock it away. During the twenty years since then, these episodes had become less frequent. Last year, at Christmas, someone had dusted the cuff of their jacket with the back of their hand as if shooing away hens, just as Ralph once had, and she ran from the room then too. This time, it was the glimpse she caught of the young man smiling with exactly the same tilt of the head that Ralph used to have when surveying a room, his face lit up with a smile, standing tall above the crowd, with the same sandy hair and the same amused expression.

Even the shirt was like the one Ralph had worn at that Oxfordshire garden party by the Thames, May or June 1944 it must have been, not long before he was killed. She ground her fists harder into her cheekbones, willing the spectre to pass; she would flick the switch and restore herself.

As she was about to get up to rejoin the party, she heard footsteps approaching along the corridor. The door sprang open and the light clicked on. Helena.

'Mother! What on earth ... Are you all right? Everyone's asking where you are and the staff don't know what to do. And there are no fresh napkins. Is that why you're in here?'

'Yes ... yes, I just needed to rest for a few moments, that's all. These shoes are killing me. And you know how bad I am with all the noise and the smoke and the braying.'

'You always say that, don't you? The *braying*! Have you seen Adam yet?'

'No, I haven't spoken to anybody – I've been swept off my feet. And how would I know? All you've said is that he's tall. There seem to be more young people than usual tonight. Magnus must have invited some of his account managers and creatives from the agency, which is a nice change for you, not having everyone three times your age.'

'I'll make sure he comes and talks to you. He's the one with the blond hair and the parting.'

'The sky-blue shirt with the dark stripes?'

'So you *did* see him!'

'Yes, it seems I did. Anyway, we'd better get back to the

party. We can take a pile of napkins each.'

Back in the riot and the jostling of the drawing room, Elizabeth was herself again and started her journey towards the kitchen at the other end of the house to deliver the napkins.

She reached Wilbur in his white dinner jacket, shaking cocktails, his sonorous Caribbean patois rumbling above the din.

'I'll have one of your special daiquiris please, Wilbur, if you don't mind.'

'Ma'am doesn't usually go for cocktails.'

'You're quite right, but I think I'll have one this evening, it's so hot.'

They laughed together while Wilbur shook and served the daiquiri, which Elizabeth drank quickly so that she would have both hands free to carry the napkins. Feeling light-headed, she thanked Wilbur, her dear friend, and started off again, forcing her way through the crowd and the clamour. She glided through the chaos while people waved at her or shouted above the noise, trying to attract her attention, complimenting her on her dress, her hair, the fun of it all. But it was just a game, because everyone knew she could never be distracted from her duty or her sense of decorum. Passing each knot of people, she heard snatches of conversation as if she were turning a dial on a radio: *Petrol at five-and-six a gallon, disgraceful!* ... The Frost Report, *yes, very clever ... Enoch Powell, he'll stir things up ...*

Her eyes watered in the haze of smoke mingled with Chanel No.5 and the fumes of whisky and gin, but she made it to the arch that led into the morning room – always a tricky place, she thought, as people crammed their way through; it was here at the last party that there had been a hand where it should not have been; she knew it was the lawyer Julian because he was looking up at the ceiling at the time.

She arrived in the kitchen to find Magnus asking one of the helpers, very loudly, whether there were any more napkins. Standing in the doorway, she watched him turn round.

'Ah, there you are, dear ... but you have them, more napkins, how clever!'

Laughing, he took some and bore them like gifts back to his huddle of clients.

Another two hours before she could retire to bed. Everyone knew her rule – she always excused herself at midnight, her duties done. But despite her tiredness and smarting eyes, she pressed on. She passed Shirley, Penelope and Celia, who were gushingly courteous as usual. Elizabeth knew they thought her sanctimonious because she made obvious her disapproval of the adulterous flirtations, and worse, that were rife on the Holt.

She'd forgotten the name of the large man who parted the crowd for her and said loudly, 'Please make way for Magnus's adorable wife.'

She walked through and thanked him, regretting her excessive politeness, which she hoped would not be misconstrued as sarcasm. Behind her, she heard someone mumble in a low growl, 'Adorable, yes, but unavailable, sadly.' It had often fascinated her, the way a voice of low or high pitch could unintentionally be heard above all the others; it was like eavesdropping on a whisper. She was certain it was Jeremy, who was in the motor trade and lived at the top of the Holt. He was usually very civil.

Onwards she swept, looking straight ahead amid the shouts: *I was at the launch party ... Twiggy was there ... yes, well above the knee ... what a killjoy that Barbara Castle is with her breathalyser ... Conran, yes, with his shop in Chelsea, so fresh, so swish ... and Wimbledon this year on colour TV!*

All this echoed in her ears, then immediately was dulled as Adam came towards her, striding confidently, his arm outstretched.

Yet she would be steadfast. She would not suffer another relapse; her strength would shut him out. He belonged to Helena.

'You must be Adam, how do you do?'

'How did you know it was me, Mrs Fortescue?'

'My lovely Helena described you – most favourably. She says you are to be with us for the whole week, but I fear there is less to do here than in London. There's tennis and the swimming pool, of course, but please, you must make yourself at home, and I do hope you enjoy your stay. But look, you have no drink. Let's go over to Wilbur who's making cocktails over there. He's very good, you know – Magnus pinched him from the Connaught.'

She wouldn't detain Adam for long, she thought as she guided him through the crowd with the tips of her fingers on his elbow. Once Wilbur had given Adam his daiquiri and Elizabeth had declined a second one, she and Adam talked for a few minutes – the usual politenesses: where he lived (he was shortly to move into a terraced house his parents had bought in a rundown part of Kensington), how he had enjoyed his first year at Durham (he was studying engineering, but wanted to switch to an arts degree), and the weather of course (he must only have mentioned that because he thought her old, she concluded).

He thanked her again for allowing him to be her guest and melted back into the roar of the crowd.

She had got through it; she had survived. It had been a momentary aberration, that was all, a temporary onslaught. He was Adam, not Ralph; it was foolish to have been ambushed by the resemblance, or to be duped by the baritone, or the chop of the hands for emphasis, or the quizzical look in the eyes when some question was asked. She was safe.

Helena approached, forcing her way through the crowd. 'I'm glad the two of you have met at last. I was watching you talking. You looked as if you'd known each other for years.'

'Yes, we've met,' Elizabeth said. 'I'm going to bed now. It's well before midnight, but I've had enough. Will you take over, Helena? You can bring out the last of the canapés, and check that Wilbur has enough supplies, although surely everyone's too drunk to ask for anything more. I'll be going over to Miranda's early tomorrow to get my sanity back. Will you be able to supervise Mrs Longworth and the cleaners in the morning?'

'Yes, of course, provided you tell my wonderful godmother that the reason I'm skipping church is that I'm on clearing-up duties.'

'She'll forgive you, I'm sure. She's too kind.'

* * *

For Elizabeth, the day was done. At last she was in the sanctuary of her bedroom. She turned off the light and felt the pillow's silk folding around her ears, causing the boom of the party below to fade. She felt invincible now as she drifted away with comforting thoughts about Helena, who was rapidly becoming so mature. Adam was the first person Helena had ever invited to stay, apart from her school friends. But she hadn't been sheepish at all when she informed Elizabeth that she wanted Adam to visit. There was no suggestion that the invitation had any particular significance – that one thing might lead to another – Helena was far too sensible for that. Of course there would come a time when she applied the same amount of determination to some boy as she did to her studies and her music. Surely Adam would not be the one for that. True, he had very good manners, but he was too reflective and solid for Helena's exuberance, sawing away beautifully at her cello. But he seemed quite sensible and might be a steadying influence, which would do no harm at all. Yes, perhaps they were strangely suited.

2

Despite the wrecked state of the house the morning after Magnus's parties, Elizabeth welcomed its stillness when she was the first to get up, walking through the aftermath, every surface littered with discarded plates and greasy glasses, the acrid reek of ashtrays and stale whisky, the furniture askew, the crumbs trodden into the carpets. She ran her finger along the Queen Anne sideboard and held it up to the morning light, wincing as it glistened in the sun.

The house was silent because everyone was sleeping it off. They would all be in bed: Magnus, Helena – and Adam, who had been given a guest bedroom at the far end of the house. The other spare rooms would all be occupied by those who had found themselves incapable of driving home. She strained her ears now because she thought she could hear the distant sound of someone snoring above, which reminded her of a time when Helena was very young; it must have been about a dozen years ago, when Helena would have been five. Entering Helena's room to wake her in the morning, she heard snoring. It came from a vast mound under Helena's pale blue candlewick bedspread. Two feet in grey socks protruded from the end of the bed. In her panic she nearly snatched the bedclothes away, but saw Helena curled up in her old cot in the corner of the room – the cot in which she now kept her dolls and cuddly toys. Oliver, the huge prop forward, presumably worse for wear, must have manhandled the girl out of her bed and laid her in the cot with a blanket neatly folded over her. But all was well; Helena explained later that she had not woken in the night at all, had suffered no fright, indeed thought it very funny to wake staring into the eyes of her favourite dolls, who she always arranged very precisely in the cot before she went to bed. Bath time revealed no marks, no bruises, and Elizabeth had felt very guilty for thinking Oliver remotely capable of impropriety; he was a gentle giant of a man, beyond suspicion, and it was wrong to have cast doubt upon him.

She walked over to the large refectory table in the corner of the drawing room and looked at a pagoda of playing cards that had been built high, presumably by some drunk trying to prove that he was not. She smiled as she pushed the tower over, the cards cascading over the mahogany tabletop and onto the carpet below.

There was a thud upstairs. Someone was getting up. She needed to make good her escape. She would scrawl a note for Helena with household instructions for Mrs Longworth and her three friends, who would be arriving at ten to do the house. She wanted to be with Miranda now, the only person on the Holt she could fully trust, her closest companion other than Helena.

* * *

'How lovely to see you, Elizabeth. So you managed to break free?'

'Yes, it's a relief to get out of the house and away from the wreckage.'

'I know you hate all the parties, but last night was wonderful – people have such fun at yours. Coffee?'

Miranda went out to the kitchen in her dressing gown and shawl, and Elizabeth could see she had already been in the conservatory for some time; the Sunday papers lay scattered on the floor next to a discarded breakfast tray.

'You've been up a while, I see,' Elizabeth said when Miranda came back.

'Yes, I haven't been sleeping very well these last few days.'

'Is there something the matter? You haven't been quite yourself. I noticed it at the flower show last week.'

'I lost the baby.'

With a sigh, Elizabeth got up and stood behind Miranda's chair and ran her fingers through Miranda's hair, soothing her in the silence.

Eventually, Elizabeth said, 'You're younger than me. You must keep trying. Everything will be all right in the end. Does Duncan know?'

'I haven't told him yet, you're the only one who knows.'

'It will stay that way, of course.'

Miranda nodded and said, 'You told me that you lost a baby once.'

'I did. But it wasn't a miscarriage. I gave him away.'

'Your life before Magnus, the one you never talk about?'

'Yes.' It was all Elizabeth could say because she ached with sorrow for Miranda, who was desperate for a child; it seemed unjust.

'Tell me about it,' Miranda said. 'It will do me good.'

Elizabeth finished smoothing Miranda's hair and went over to the conservatory door to stare out at the red and yellow torch lilies, vibrant against the green of the lawn and the trees behind. She breathed in deeply, wondering how much of her story to tell Miranda, who was clearly heartbroken by her loss.

Elizabeth turned from the window and came back to sit silently in the wicker armchair next to Miranda. She brushed her dress several times over her knees. 'It's difficult, you see. I've never told anyone, not even Magnus or Helena.'

'But you know you can be safe with me.'

It was true, Elizabeth thought, she had complete faith in Miranda; she was like a sister and could not be refused.

'I told you about Ralph, who died soon after D-Day, when I was seventeen.'

'That's all you've ever said. You never talk about it.'

'After he was killed I realised I was carrying his child. I was very young and confused. That wild first love, that ridiculous bliss suddenly ripped away. At first the very thought of the child was the only way out of my grief – that having lost Ralph, I would find comfort through a form of him still living, something that was ours. I was completely alone, working for the ATS in Normandy. I couldn't tell my parents back in England about it – they would have disowned me for the shame of having a child out of wedlock. And I couldn't turn to Ralph's parents because I had never met them. We were only together a few months while we were both stationed in Dorset preparing for D-Day. After the landings, I was stationed in Bayeux, and he was in the parachute regiment, pushing into France as part of the advance forces.

'After Ralph was killed, I immersed myself in my work as a supplies administrator in an attempt to displace my misery. The strategy worked at first, I suppose, because I was very good at my work and became obsessed with it, so they gave me more and more responsibility. But gradually everything got worse. As winter approached, I was able to conceal my pregnancy by wearing heavier coats, and then everything spiralled out of control. I was frequently very ill and exhausted with work, still in grief, utterly alone for the shame of telling anyone. Towards the end, the people at work thought I was suffering trauma, but I refused to be sent home so they insisted I went into a convent to recover. When the time came to go into hospital, I finally broke down in despair and realised I would never be a capable mother and said I wanted the child to be adopted. They have a different system in France, where a mother can remain anonymous, handing her child over to state control before it's placed with a family that wants to adopt.'

'What did you call your child?'

'I called him Raoul, the French name for Ralph. I was more sentimental then. But the French family that adopted him would have given him a different name. He would be twenty-two now, a fine Frenchman five years older than Helena. I often wonder about him. It seems very callous, very cruel, that you should not have a child while I gave one away.'

'You mustn't think that, Elizabeth! What happened to you sounds far worse than anything that's happened to me. I can tell because you've described it so plainly as you always do. In fact, I don't think you've told me the whole story at all – it was probably even worse. But I'm grateful. You've made me feel better.'

'How so, Miranda? How can it possibly have made you feel better?'

'I don't know. You've given me hope, I suppose. All that resilience. It sets an example – the fact that in the face of all that adversity you found the strength to start your life again when you came back to England. Yes, it gives me hope …'

Miranda changed the subject. They talked about the party, the things they'd heard, the way Elizabeth had looked like a queen, bearing her pile of napkins through the crowd. They lay back in the wicker chairs, laughing at the blue sky through the conservatory roof, at the inanities of the Holt, the conspicuous consumption, with the Bentleys and the Jaguars and the second homes on the Côte d'Azur, the infidelities, the urgent revelling, as if the rationing and the bleakness of war were still to be expunged by sheer excess.

Miranda said, 'It's a wonder how you do it, Elizabeth, your marvellous parties. Unfortunately some of Magnus's friends were completely out of order last night. Felicity complained of being groped, rather intimately, she said. And someone tried to unzip Penelope's dress as a joke. Of course the pranks are unforgivable, but Felicity, Penelope and all the others simply don't help with their double standards. I also learnt last night that you and I are known as the prudes. They think us aloof. I can see the scorn on people's faces: they expect me to be staid because I'm married to a brusque insurance broker who plays golf. They don't realise that I'm actually very happy, thank you very much.'

Miranda got up and stood behind Elizabeth's chair, resting her hands on Elizabeth's shoulders. 'I'm sorry. I didn't mean to be smug. Did you see Magnus last night with his new secretary?'

'Yes, I did.'

'You deserve better, Elizabeth, you deserve to be happy.'

They fell silent, looking out over the emerald lawn, its dew glistening in the dazzling sun as Miranda kneaded Elizabeth's shoulders.

Elizabeth had no word for it, this bond of comfort she and Miranda shared. It was platonic, not erotic. People used these words as if they defined some scale, as if one thing eventually became the other. But their mutual sincerity was nothing on that stale scale at all; their closeness was a companionship of tacit understanding. It was far beyond anything crude or carnal; it was worthy, and its worth far nobler than that. It was the running of hands across a shoulder in the perfect knowledge that it would pacify completely.

Eventually Miranda continued. 'Anyway, the younger members of the party behaved perfectly, unlike the Holt contingent. Adam and Helena seem very well matched. When I saw them together last night I thought they were like peas out of a pod. Helena's chosen well, hasn't she?'

'I'm not sure *chosen* is quite the right word, but we'll see. She and Adam are certainly good friends, but I wouldn't put it more strongly than that. I think it's primarily a musical connection. Every time they've been together since they met at that Easter music school in Somerset it's been for some concert or musical event. It's obvious Helena's not in love with him or anything like that. We were talking the other day about our favourite colours, and I asked her what Adam's favourite colour was, and she didn't even know. I suspect they'll go their separate ways when Helena starts at university and meets new friends. All the universities she'll be applying for are in the south, so she'll be quite far away from Durham where Adam will be continuing his studies – assuming she gets in somewhere, that is.'

'Oh, there's no question she'll get in,' Miranda said.

'I hope so, but I'm worried she's not revising enough, what with all these distractions, with her cello and now with Adam. Do you think you could give her some godmotherly advice and get her to knuckle down? She always listens to you.'

'Yes, of course. But you mustn't worry about her. I know she can be impetuous, but underneath it all she's very determined and can be remarkably level-headed. I'll tell you something else that will also make you very proud. Last night I overheard Suzanne talking to Jerome, the man who runs the theatre. He said, and I quote, "Helena is clearly going to be as beautiful as her mother." Isn't that nice?'

'Oh, you mustn't pay any attention to what Jerome says. He knows you and I are close friends, so he probably said it loudly so that you would hear it and pass the flattery on, which in fact you have.'

Miranda laughed. 'I had quite a long chat with Adam last night. He was very complimentary about Helena's cello playing but rather dismissive about his efforts on the trombone. Perhaps he's naturally modest, just like you. Did you see Celia and Tamara and the others finding excuses to talk to him? Queuing up, they were, the poor boy. But you were different, of course. I saw you from the other side of the room talking to him, very calmly, as you always do.'

* * *

Crossing the common back to the house, Elizabeth felt completely restored. She almost skipped through the long grass as she walked, taking care not to trample on any of the red campion – one of her favourite plants – its magenta bright in the sun against the fresh green of the meadow, which she breathed in, closing her eyes. Everything was solved. She listed her successes as she bounded along: she had succeeded in comforting Miranda for the loss of her child, even if it had been at the expense of confessing the loss of her own; she was pleased with Helena for taking charge of the cleaning of the house and happy that Helena was happy with Adam; and Miranda had agreed to have a word with Helena about her revision, so that would all be settled too. True, she had a tricky week ahead, preparing for her meeting in Whitehall on Thursday when she would attend the committee on which she sat as a lay member, but she always took such things in her stride. She strode on now, avoiding the orchids as well as the campion, and arrived back at the house fully content.

3

Adam and Helena had not been playing much tennis. They were lying on their backs on the grass of the court, Adam in his white flannel shorts and Aertex shirt, and Helena in her white dress, staring up at the white clouds marching in the breeze across the blue sky.

Helena found nothing romantic about it. The whole morning had annoyed her from the moment she had got up to help Mrs Longworth and her friends tidy the house after the party. Emptying the heaped ashtrays and clearing away the glasses and plates had made her wince, reminding her of the party, which she had not enjoyed, mainly because she had watched some of the Holt wives fawning over Adam, making her feel young and inadequate. It seemed impossible that Adam had not noticed the interest he had attracted, yet he seemed genuinely oblivious to it. She had asked him about it when they were walking up to the tennis court after lunch, but he merely shrugged. She was sure most of his friends at Durham would have basked in the glory of such attention; not that she had met many of his friends yet because none of them seemed interested in music, which was always the context in which she had been with Adam. They had often talked about each other's friends, but she found it irritating because all her friends were still at school and most of his were at university. It made her feel less sophisticated.

It wasn't the only thing that had made her feel unsophisticated. This business of Adam's parents buying him a house seemed grossly unfair, given that her own parents would never dream of doing such a thing for her, not for quite a few years anyway. She had asked Adam about his house in Kensington when they were winching up the tennis net, preparing for their first game. He had been very defensive, saying that while he called it 'his house', she mustn't get the wrong idea – his parents had bought it because they were certain that property in the dilapidated streets of Kensington would one day prove to be a sound investment. The dingy terrace was wholly owned in his parents' names, and they were paying for all the renovations. It was merely a convenient arrangement that Adam was allowed to live there during the vacations when he was not at Durham, provided he supervised some of the house improvements.

She lacked her usual energy for tennis. She just wanted to rest in silence and look up at the sky, but he seemed determined to talk, so she closed her eyes and listened.

He talked enthusiastically about music, which was one of the things she usually found appealing about him. It was perfectly logical to play Bach's cello suites on the trombone, he insisted – the two instruments were in the same musical range, and the maths of the music worked just as well for either of them. She was not in the mood for one of their playful arguments that often gathered momentum whenever he thought aloud, testing some point of logic or exhibiting one of his more fanciful reflections. On this occasion she knew their gentle sparring would merely annoy her, exposing their different perspectives; she was more interested in the spirit of musical performance than its analysis. A clash between art and science.

She closed her eyes and let him continue his musings. With gathering enthusiasm he talked about the second bourrée in the third cello suite and how the trombone was just as suited to slide the notes as any stringed instrument – the execution of the glissandos could be much the same, he contended.

He asked her what she thought about his musical theory, but she could only find a tentative groan as if she was thinking about it.

'I'm boring you, Helena. We can change the subject if you like.'

He tried to clasp her hand, which she snatched away. She knew what he was thinking because he had asked her earlier why her mother had given him a bedroom at the far end of the house.

It was hot and humid and the grass was making the back of her calves itch.

Now he was asking her about the plans for her eighteenth birthday in a few months' time. Which was to be the greater celebration, he asked – her eighteenth or her twenty-first? It was the same frustrating question she had recently raised with her parents, who had said emphatically that they disapproved of the new-fangled idea of eighteenth birthdays being celebrated as enthusiastically as twenty-firsts – she would have to wait until she was twenty-one for her big party, as dictated by tradition. She would have a very extravagant celebration then, they promised. Yet everyone always said she was already an accomplished adult, so it seemed unreasonable to have to wait for three years before being formally recognised as one.

She decided to humour him: she would carry on resting with her eyes closed, occasionally asking him short, simple questions, and he would then continue with his long answers, so she wouldn't have to speak very much.

'You've never mentioned what you did for your eighteenth birthday,' she said, 'so I assume your parents have decided the same, that your big day will be your twenty-first?'

'Will be? I had my twenty-first in January last year.'

'What?' Helena said, springing up onto her elbow and turning towards him. 'What do you mean?'

'I was twenty-one last year.'

'How can you be? You've only been at Durham for a year.'

'Yes, that's right.'

'But don't you remember, when we discussed your birthday – it was at the Wigmore Hall – we joked about your road to Damascus because the twenty-fifth of January is the conversion of Paul. I remember you teasing me because you'll be starting your third year at university when I'll be starting my first.'

'Yes, that's right, we did discuss the twenty-fifth of January and St Paul. It was when we were in the ticket queue. The conversation about being two years ahead of you was a completely different one – that was when we were having a coffee break during those rehearsals at Cheltenham. We were discussing your Cambridge exams and what fun it would be when we were both at university. We agreed that it didn't matter that I was ahead of you and that most likely we would be at different universities, because we would have the fun of taking it in turns to visit each other. Anyway, why does it matter?'

'So when were you born?'

'I was born in 1945. I still don't see why it should matter.'

'But I've told my parents you're two years older than me. What will they say when I tell them you're actually five years older than me? Of course it matters! Either they'll think I've lied, or that I'm ridiculously naïve for making such a silly mistake. And you should have mentioned it – you know these things are important.'

'I'm sorry, Helena, I really am, but I never seem to know what's important to you.'

'You know that I detest lying.'

'But I'm not! You've merely got to tell your parents you made some mistake, or that *I* made a mistake if you like, or that you made an assumption, but I haven't lied.'

'Well, it feels like a lie and that's what's important. It all feels wrong.'

For Helena, the day went from bad to worse. She interrogated Adam about how he had spent the years between his A-levels and starting at Durham. She had always known that his father had built up a successful civil engineering business and was keen that Adam should take over the running of it eventually after gaining his engineering degree. Adam had occasionally talked about the work he did for his father, but that had been another misunderstanding; whenever he mentioned it, she had always assumed he helped out from time to time, as a son might as heir apparent to his father's business. There had been no mention of Adam being on the payroll full time for a number of years, which apparently had been a requirement of Arnold's, who insisted that Adam should be immersed thoroughly in the practicalities of running the business before getting the relevant academic qualification.

'But why didn't you mention this before?' Helena said.

'To be honest, I got the impression civil engineering was not of much interest to you, which I can quite understand. I avoided the subject. I thought you might find it tedious.'

When Adam had finished explaining everything, he said, 'I can see you're upset about my age, Helena, and I'm sorry if you think I've misled you.'

'I suppose you're not to blame, but this changes things. I need to think about what to do. I'm sure we can be perfectly civilised about it.'

4

Elizabeth lay in bed thinking about Helena, who would be bounding in shortly for their early morning chat as she had always done since she was very young, gushing about her dreams while she slept or her plans for the day, waving her arms in the air as she flitted from subject to subject. Elizabeth thought Helena a little too old now for this early morning ritual, but it was the indulgence of an only child and would not last forever. And besides, their little early morning conversations were useful. It was the time of day when Helena was at her most receptive to those little things that needed to be mentioned from time to time. A few weeks ago, Elizabeth had taken Helena to task about her occasional lapses when eating at table, particularly her infuriating habit, when eating something like a syllabub, of turning the long spoon upside down after each mouthful, usually when she was contemplating something deeply and wondering what to say next. It had been a great success because ever since, Helena had eaten all sorts of custards and crumbles very decorously.

Something was amiss with Helena, Elizabeth thought. They hadn't had much opportunity to talk to each other since Helena's tennis match with Adam the previous afternoon. At dinner, the glances between her and Adam had seemed different, self-conscious in fact; Helena would turn her head away if Adam caught her eye, whereas the day before, they had that momentary coy glow of a smile, a slightly reverential dip of the head, perhaps. It was a strange relationship, which seemed to be built on mutual respect and trust, such as a brother and sister might have. How lovely it would have been for Helena to have had a brother.

Of course, it was a relief that Helena was so sensible and there had never been any danger of her losing her head and rushing headlong into anything reckless with the various young men who had taken an interest in her. But Elizabeth wondered whether her parenting had been too stringent; at what point did someone strong and independent become distant and aloof?

Here she was, padding along the corridor, rather sloppily because it was impossible for her to pick up her feet properly in those ridiculous pink slippers that looked like balls of fur.

Once they had embraced, and Helena's legs were properly tucked under her as she sat on the bed facing Elizabeth, she said, 'Mother, I have something to tell you. Adam will not be staying until the weekend. He will be leaving on Thursday.'

'Why, what's wrong? Have you had an argument?'

'Not exactly. I just don't think we're compatible.'

'Do you want to talk about it?'

'No. Not now anyway.'

'I'm not going to be a bore, Helena, and say that one should never be too quick to judge. I can see you've made up your mind, so I'm not going to argue. I happen to think you're both rather suited – you're both quite mature for your age.'

'Yes, perhaps ... But you're right, I have made up my mind.'

'Have you considered how he might feel? You can't go round breaking hearts, you know.'

'Would you be able to run him to the station after breakfast on Thursday?'

'No, I don't think I can. I've an important meeting in London. And what are we to do with him for three days in the meantime? It's not going to be awkward, is it?'

'Certainly not. Adam and I will continue to be friends, that's all. Everything will be perfectly civilised.'

'So you'll carry on playing tennis and swimming with him and practising your music together until Thursday?'

'That's one possibility, but I wanted to ask you a huge favour. Would you be able to keep him occupied while I do my revision? He likes gardens and that sort of thing. He could potter about with you today, and I'm sure he'd love to visit somewhere tomorrow or Wednesday – the weather's meant to be fine. A while ago, you said you wanted to go to Blenheim again. And then you can take him to the station on Thursday morning.'

Elizabeth sighed. 'It's extremely inconvenient,' she said, 'and I will only do as you ask if you promise to do some serious revision. And your room is a complete disgrace. You must promise to make it clean and tidy.'

It seemed unlikely that Helena had heard Elizabeth's last demand because she had already kissed her mother, pecking her on the forehead and calling her an angel, no less, and had leapt down and whooped from the room.

* * *

Waking up at his end of the house, Adam groaned as the events of the previous day flooded in. On one level, everything would be fine. Everybody would be perfectly considerate and polite. Those were the very words Helena used during the stroll she had suggested up to the summerhouse after dinner the previous evening. She had smiled and tapped his shoulder, reassuring him that there was nothing dishonourable about the situation, no loss of pride.

As he rubbed his eyes and went to open the curtains, he tried to come to terms with his new status – that instead of being the subject of Helena's special attention, he was now consigned to the role of a house guest. He felt as if he had failed an exam, or as if a judge had handed down a sentence. It was an injustice, a summary execution without a shot being fired.

When Helena had said that there would be no embarrassment, she was speaking for herself, surely, because for him the embarrassment was likely to be acute. It was all very well her saying there would be no reference to their rift, but that didn't mean everyone wouldn't know there had been one. Helena and her mother were so close that they were bound to find the opportunity to discuss his fall from favour. It was uncomfortable, this sense that his suitability would be assessed in hushed whispers behind closed doors. Helena was a riddle. Most of the time she possessed an effortless confidence that she must have learnt from her mother; her warmth was infectious and welcoming but simultaneously kept at a safe distance.

While there had been no lie, not even a fib, maybe Helena was right about their age difference being important for some reason. Perhaps he should just accept that their split was irreparable because anything else he may not have mentioned would be held against him. His difficult time at school had never arisen in conversation. She would definitely not have approved of that, and not having referred to it would certainly have stored up some future trouble.

It was very disappointing, but he would have to get used to the idea of Helena quietly drifting apart from him. They had discussed the previous night whether he should go home immediately but agreed it would look as if some scandal or disgrace had occurred – and besides, it was impossible for him to go back to his parents' house because they had given over his room to guests who had come to stay until Thursday morning. 'It's a pity you haven't moved into the Kensington house yet, Adam, because you could have gone there,' Helena had said. 'Shall we agree then that you stay until Thursday? Everything will be good-humoured and I'll think of a plan.'

5

The morning was breezy and overcast, so Elizabeth put on her sheepskin jacket before stepping onto the patio with her coffee. Despite the wind, she could hear the sweep of the cello from inside the morning room, which Helena preferred to the music room that had been set aside for her years ago. Apparently, the morning room's acoustic was far superior; it was the vibrato, Helena said.

Although life at home was always more relaxing when Magnus was away working in London, Elizabeth had feared that breakfast with Helena and Adam was going to be very strained, but everything had turned out perfectly. Over grapefruit, Helena had informed Adam of her emergency – that she was completely behind with her revision and had been unable to sleep for worry about her exams; she would be revising in Magnus's study every day but would join them both for mealtimes. To establish this fact, she laid out in the middle of the tablecloth the daily timetable she had written on a piece of foolscap with her favourite Parker pen. In fairness, Helena did acknowledge her cardinal sin – that the laying out of letters, papers or documents of any sort at mealtimes was forbidden – but she had apologised and pleaded special circumstances. She had insisted that her revision was absolutely vital and required several days of very strict routine: she would practise her cello for an hour and a quarter after breakfast each day, then she would revise for her English in the mornings, her French in the afternoons, and her history at the end of the day.

Then, while they ate their coddled eggs, Helena assured Adam that she was not acting on some whim. To show how seriously she was taking her predicament, she laid out another piece of foolscap that listed the syllabus items she would be studying for each revision session in her timetable.

Over the toast and marmalade, Elizabeth had been quite fierce with Helena for putting Adam in such a difficult situation, and Helena, to her credit, had appeared genuinely contrite. She apologised profusely to Adam, who took it all with commendable politeness. Indeed, he seemed resigned to the necessity of Helena's plan of action. The result was that he did not mope. He said, sanguinely, that it was disappointing but that he understood.

Before Helena and Adam left the breakfast table to go up to their rooms, Elizabeth had cheerfully told Adam her plans. 'Unfortunately, you'll have to put up with me until Thursday,' she had said. 'After breakfast I will phone Miranda and invite ourselves over to her house for coffee. She's a marvellous friend, and you'll be able to see Duncan's collection of vintage cars. In his garage he has an old Wolseley, a Sunbeam and a 1930s Lagonda. I like the Lagonda best. Then, this afternoon, you can help me in the garden. You said you were interested in plants? And if the weather is fine tomorrow or Wednesday we'll drive out to Blenheim. I haven't been there for ages. It's at its finest at this time of year.'

* * *

Having walked together across the common, Elizabeth and Adam arrived at Miranda's house. Elizabeth had barely shaken the heavy ship's bell in the porch before Duncan tore open the door and said to Adam, 'Hello. How do you do? Do you like cars?'

'Yes, I do,' Adam said.

'Then we can go straight out and leave the women to talk. I've decided to take the morning off. Come on through, the Lagonda's already out the back.'

Miranda and Elizabeth stood on the drive outside the front door and waved goodbye to them through the trail of blue smoke spouting from the Lagonda as it sped away.

'What a treat to see you two days running, Elizabeth! Now let's go through to the kitchen for coffee and you can tell me all about this business with Helena.'

In the kitchen, Elizabeth described Helena's sudden decision to concentrate on her revision. 'At first, I thought you must have spoken to her already about doing more revision, but you haven't?'

'No, not at all – you only mentioned it yesterday.'

'Then she must have finally realised for herself that she wasn't working hard enough.'

'You should be pleased that Helena has reached her own conclusion about needing to work harder,' Miranda said. 'It's very encouraging because once she's made up her mind about something she becomes very focused. She's just like you.'

'Perhaps, but I have my doubts on this occasion. I have a suspicion that her new-found enthusiasm for studying is merely a ploy to spend less time with Adam. Things have cooled between them.' After describing Helena's breakfast performance, Elizabeth said, 'I could tell Helena had written her revision timetable very hastily by the handwriting – it wasn't as neat as usual.'

'But if you're right and there is some other reason for her cooling towards Adam, surely she's being very considerate in taking the trouble to make a convincing excuse, allowing Adam to save face? It's very grown up of them to have settled things so amicably. But you have no idea what the real reason might be for them breaking off?'

'No, not at all, and it would be pointless to ask. I can tell this is one of those occasions when Helena has said all she's going to say and that's that.'

'So you've got to look after Adam until Thursday?'

'Yes, and it's infuriating because I've had to cancel my trip to London on Thursday. I've only been a member of this medical subcommittee in Whitehall for six months and it's the second meeting I've had to cancel. It's very embarrassing. They'll think I'm unreliable.'

'And what will you do with him?'

'Nothing. He'll just have to mosey about with me in the garden and in the house. Maybe we'll go out somewhere for the day. It'll be very boring for him.'

'It may not be ...'

'What do you mean?'

'Oh, it doesn't matter ... now, have you heard about Roland and Bethany?'

Elizabeth had told Miranda many times that she disapproved of gossip. But away Miranda went, talking first about

Roland and Bethany's pact to remain married despite each other's adulteries, and then about an even more bizarre arrangement by another couple on the Holt, a little ménage à trois described in too much detail for Elizabeth's liking. But Elizabeth allowed it all to wash over her. She would not criticise; everyone had a fault, and Miranda's was her fascination for the tawdry scandals on the Holt. And besides, she could listen to Miranda's sing-song voice all day long, sweeping up and down the scales like one of Helena's partitas.

It was nearly one o'clock and still the Lagonda had not rumbled up the drive.

'Will you wait for Duncan and Adam to return and stay for a bite of lunch?' Miranda said.

'No, thank you, I must be getting back. Mrs Longworth is making one of her fish pies for lunch today and I don't want to offend her by being late. I also need to check that Helena is actually doing her revision now that she's caused all this trouble. She needs my support. Will you tell Adam to follow me back? He knows the way.'

As Elizabeth turned to go, Miranda said, 'And don't forget, you're coming over here on Thursday at teatime to help me make those curtains.'

6

What Mrs Fortescue had said at breakfast was true, Adam thought. At the party he *had* mentioned an interest in plants. He remembered now that he had thrown the comment into the conversation out of politeness because she had been talking so enthusiastically about the years it had taken to create her garden. She should have used the plural, because since lunch they had already walked through the herb garden and what she had called the white garden, and now they had arrived at the arch into the rose garden, which was too narrow for them to walk side by side, so he fell behind to let Elizabeth go first, watching the flowers brushing against the side of her cream muslin dress.

As the brick path widened again and they resumed walking beside each other, Elizabeth said, 'I'm sorry about Helena changing everything and ruining your stay. You two haven't fallen out, have you?'

She spoke softly and glanced across at him, but he had to look away because her eyes were too commanding, as if she already knew the truth. He should have resented her directness, but instead he wanted to tell her everything. Being invited into her confidence seemed strangely safe. But he would resist; he hardly knew her. A strand of cobweb had stuck to his sleeve, so he fell back to pick it off before catching up with her again.

'No, we haven't fallen out exactly. We've decided to be good friends, more like a brother and sister, I suppose. I respect her very much, Mrs Fortescue. We hope to stay in touch.'

'Well, I'm very pleased to hear it. I'm so glad.'

Elizabeth stopped to cut a rose, holding the stem deftly with her left hand threaded through the handle of the trug hanging from her elbow and using her other hand to snip with her shears.

'I'm sure she can seem trying at times,' she continued. 'She's very determined that everything should be just right, just so. Well, not everything, of course, as you will have seen from the state of her room.'

'I haven't really seen her room. She opened the door briefly when she first showed me round the house, but maybe that's why she closed the door so quickly.'

'Well, there you are. She knows that the untidiness of her room is one of her few imperfections, so she closes it out. You will have noticed her correctness in everything else. If she makes up her mind about something or makes an assumption, it's cast in stone. She attended Sunday school until long after her confirmation. The vicar was most distraught when she stopped going, because her conviction about what was right or wrong was beyond challenge and set an example for everyone else. The poor man probably had a much tougher job after she left because Helena was apparently much more successful than him when it came to convincing the other children about the ten commandments. It's just the way she is, you see.'

Adam was not sure that he did see. What he could see was that Helena was her mother's daughter, or whatever the expression was. The pair of them seemed to speak in riddles much of the time. He remembered seeing Helena at the party kissing her mother goodnight. It was the first time he had seen them together, and it had explained Helena's earlier accounts of her relationship with Elizabeth, which had always confused him – the strange fusion of bluntness and deep reverence close to awe. But he had understood it perfectly in that moment, watching them through the haze and noise of the crowd as they stood and smiled at each other with their lips pursed shut; it was as if they had no need to speak because of the bond between them. Elizabeth merely palmed Helena's shoulder, giving it three little taps as if to say 'goodnight, dear' before she turned and walked away. It was something that he craved, to be part of that wordless understanding – some instinct that rendered language irrelevant. He adored his own parents, but the bond seemed less profound than the affection between Helena and her mother.

He had dreaded the prospect that Helena had handed him that morning – that while she revised he would have to traipse round with her mother. But it was not unpleasant walking with Mrs Fortescue; she seemed to be making allowances for his difficult situation by making her conversation more light-hearted than usual.

Elizabeth had walked ahead again, or glided more like, and was cutting another rose, straining upwards to reach it, but then it dropped to the path.

'Mrs Fortescue, while you cut the flowers, would it help if

I carried that basket for you?'

'The trug, do you mean? Yes, thank you, then I'll have both hands free.'

She handed him the trug and crouched down to pick up the rose. He looked down at the crown of her head while she delicately took up the rose, avoiding the thorns. He brushed the back of his neck; he felt foolish having never held a trug before, or maybe it was because the day was hot, shimmering with the intoxicating scents from the flower beds. She stood up, brushing a leaf from the side of her dress before relieving him of the trug, as if on second thoughts it would be better if she carried it herself.

They came to the end of the brick path that opened out onto an area of lawn with herbaceous borders.

'I think we have enough roses now,' Elizabeth said. 'Let's go over to that border over there with the delphiniums. We need to pick some for the dining room. You'll have to carry them because the trug is nearly full.'

As she stepped over the edge of the path onto the lawn, one of the bricks dislodged, causing Elizabeth's shoe to slip.

'Are you all right, Mrs Fortescue?' Adam said, steadying her elbow, which she snatched away.

'Yes, of course. This path needs to be redone, that's all.'

She seemed to regret her abruptness and said, as if it were a concession, 'I suppose if we're to spend some time together you may as well call me Elizabeth.'

He weighed the sound of the four syllables of her name, which seemed to chime; they matched her poise. *El-iz-a-beth*. The name suited her; she would never be a Lizzie any more than Helena would ever be a Helen. But Elizabeth had not finished with names, because now she stood back from the herbaceous border and was instructing him, as he had requested, with the names of the flowers she snipped, sometimes with their common names, sometimes with their Latin names and sometimes both. It sounded like a stream of song.

'There, I think we have enough. We can go in now,' she said, walking briskly ahead back to the house.

He stumbled along after her across the lawn bearing an armful of blooms, their names ringing in his head. He knew nothing of flowers, but he remembered how she had enunciated each name very precisely: euphorbia, campanula, alstroemeria, mullein, achillea. She had applied the same precision snipping away at the stems with her scissors, her eyes fixed on the task as if he was not by her side at all. He tried to keep up with her, tripping across the grass, not wanting to stumble and drop the flowers for fear of upsetting her or offending her curious wisdom.

7

Elizabeth drove back from the station with one hand held flat across her mouth in shock. It was no use; she was normally a good driver, but she felt unable to drive. She pulled into a lay-by.

Once she had turned the engine off, she sat there in the silence with her chin on the steering wheel, which she gripped with both hands, staring ahead at a bus shelter while her cheek still burned. Fortunately, nobody was waiting inside the shelter to see her in such a state. She was trembling, angry with herself for failing to notice the signals. She banged the steering wheel with her fist and leant back, screwing up her eyes.

She always did her best to acknowledge that she possessed certain faults – her perfectionism, her aloofness at times, even a degree of prudishness, but nobody could possibly accuse her of being naïve.

But she had been. She had assumed that Adam's clumsy behaviour while he had been with her was due to the humiliation he must have felt from Helena's refusal. She had great sympathy for him and had made allowances for his awkward situation. It was not nice to be palmed off with the mother of the person who had rejected him.

She struck the steering wheel again, then leant back in the seat with a sigh. God knew she had noticed his uneasiness – that was never in doubt. On their first day in the garden, for example, she had noticed Adam wrestling with his feelings and fumbling for opportunities to express them. At the beginning of their second day, he had seemed confused and constantly on the verge of making some blundering announcement. She had merely assumed him to be a little gauche, a little out of sorts.

And then at Blenheim they were leaning on the parapet of Vanbrugh's bridge, and he had stood too close to her, their elbows touching – by accident, she thought. She did not jolt hers away impetuously; it was wrong to upset people, especially when they were upset themselves – she realised that. No, she had detached herself skilfully, explaining the history of the Capability Brown landscape laid out before them, flourishing her hand expansively to the west, and as she did so, shuffling half a step to her right to restore the distance between them without it seeming deliberate or offensive, or even acknowledging that a touching of the elbows had taken place at all. Shortly afterwards, there was that dreadful incident in the restaurant when the woman in the green swing coat with the absurd buttons had said, 'Sorry to interrupt you and your son, but could I take one of these spare chairs?'

And she had replied archly, 'Yes, of course, though he's not my son, he's merely my daughter's friend.'

It had been hard to make out what Adam made of that; he just bit his lip in wounded disappointment, which she realised now was because it was not her daughter he wanted to be friendly with.

It all seemed so obvious now. What would she have done if she had spotted his infatuation? She would have scotched it straight away. She would have taken him to one side in the garden, out of earshot from anyone else, and given him the full flame of her disapproval. She might even have faced him and grabbed both his shoulders and hissed, 'Now listen to me, young man …' It would have been painful to watch. Once, she had brought a crowded party to a standstill by confronting someone who had been too familiar. It was a loud and excoriating tirade and the man, one of Magnus's friends, had slunk away never to be seen again.

She banged the steering wheel yet again, even harder this time, because now she had another problem. When she had first seen Adam across the room at the party, looking like Ralph reincarnated, she had succeeded in erasing the similarity from her mind; she had been able to shut it out. She was proud of her ability to compartmentalise her life, not least the past she had buried. Adam had been safely consigned to the compartment marked 'friend of Helena's' or 'house visitor' or 'passing acquaintance'.

She would be sure to keep it that way; he would send a letter of thanks for his stay, of course, and then that would be that. He would be gone for good. Many years later she would be able to laugh it off with Helena: *Do you remember that boy who came to stay …?*

Feeling more settled, she turned the key and started the engine; she would exorcise it, sweep it away and go home for a quick lunch before spending the afternoon at Miranda's to make curtains as arranged.

* * *

Miranda's sewing room was a large bedroom on the first floor of her house that had been set aside for the purpose because of its two sets of sash windows that filled the space with sun. She and Elizabeth had spent many an hour in this room laying out bolts of cloth and stitching hems, chatting and tut-tutting at the world while they fixed heading tapes and attached linings. It was therapeutic, and besides, they resented paying people for curtains that were simply not up to scratch these days.

Today, Elizabeth had not been talkative. When Miranda had asked her how her day at Blenheim had been, she replied rather curtly that it had been fine, and then concentrated even more closely on the hem she was stitching. She was annoyed with herself for refusing to say very much; it was unfair on Miranda, who was always buoyed up by their cheery conversation. She was also annoyed with herself for having knocked over a box of pins with the heel of her hand and pricking her finger as she picked them up.

After another long pause in their conversation while Elizabeth used the sewing machine, she shouted out and stamped on the floor; she had set the presser foot too tight and the cloth had ruched up and tangled the thread.

'Is there something wrong today, Elizabeth? Something you want to talk about?'

Elizabeth said nothing and shook her head, frowning and pursing her lips as she focused even more intently on untangling the thread, resetting the presser foot and starting the sewing machine again. She sensed Miranda staring at her occasionally while the machine rumbled away and her eyes were fixed on the needle flashing up and down. Finally, she capitulated; it was selfish to ignore Miranda's concern. She stopped the machine and leant back in her chair, throwing her hands up in the air.

'I said Blenheim was fine, but dropping Adam at the station this morning was not.'

And then it seemed a relief to pour out the details of the time she had spent with Adam – working in the garden, Blenheim, and the station; it was like a confession while Miranda listened patiently as she prepared the next set of linings.

When Elizabeth fell silent, Miranda finished measuring her lengths of fabric and said, 'I knew this would happen. When you told me that Adam was to be with you for a few days I was going to warn you.'

'I wish you had. Why didn't you?'

'I didn't want to interfere. I thought you must have considered the possibility of Adam taking an interest. Anyway, hindsight's a wonderful thing. Now let's begin at the beginning. When you were in the garden on the first day, was there anything that could have led him on?'

'Absolutely not! I never made any affectionate remarks, in fact I was quite blunt with him at times. I wore no make-up, I didn't dress up. I looked a complete frump. I did suggest he call me Elizabeth rather than Mrs Fortescue. Do you think that was a mistake?'

'Depends on how you asked it. Was it done with one of your bewitching smiles, for example?'

'Please be serious, Miranda. Certainly not. It was done

very matter-of-factly. His Mrs Fortescue-ing me all day got on my nerves.'

Next, Miranda asked a stream of questions about the day at Blenheim and thought there were perhaps some signals Elizabeth should have picked up. As for the kiss at the station, Miranda wanted to know its exact nature.

'I don't see the need for the lurid details. I stretched out my hand to say goodbye and as he took it, he drew me forward, placed his hands on my shoulders and kissed me very firmly on the lips. I shouted "What did you do that for?" and I looked up and down the platform to check there was nobody there I knew. Can you imagine if anyone from the Holt had seen it? Then, because I was speechless and embarrassed, he became so too, and turned to board the train. I just walked away without saying goodbye, which I admit was rather rude, but I was still in shock, you see.'

'Yes, I can imagine you were.'

Was Miranda smirking? Elizabeth wondered. No, surely not; she was far too kind for that. No, but it was a knowing smile. Miranda said she had many more questions to ask, but before that they needed to work out the plan for the next set of curtains.

Once they were both measuring, cutting and stitching again, Miranda resumed. 'So what will you do now – about Adam?'

'Rather than involve Helena, I'll get his address from the telephone directory and send him a very stiff letter so that everything is made perfectly clear.'

'Or you could just ignore the whole thing and forget it. It's probably just a passing phase. He's mature for his age, but still finding his way. It must have felt harsh being rejected by Helena and then by you as well. You don't dislike him, do you?'

'No, I don't dislike him. Apart from the nonsense at the station, he's pleasantly polite.'

'I feel sorry for him,' Miranda said. 'Think of it from his perspective. You and Helena are very alike, so he might have seen you as an experienced version of her. Men find that attractive, yearning for something maternal – you know how dependent they can be. You should be flattered.'

'*Flattered?*'

'Most people would be. It was only a kiss on the lips. When did you last have one of those?'

'Please, Miranda, it's not a laughing matter. You're making fun of me now, so it's time for me to go home and see Helena. I hope to God she's been revising flat out after I've been through all this.'

As Elizabeth walked along the path away from the house, Miranda called after her and shouted, 'And by the way, you never look like a frump. Buttoned up, sometimes, but never a frump.'

Elizabeth did not reply or look round, she just sliced her hand out sideways a couple of times while she walked, which Miranda would know was her light-hearted way of saying *Enough! Enough!*

She was pleased they had ended their conversation so cheerfully; the flippancy had done her good and she felt restored. In fact, she had already decided not to write a stiff letter to Adam; she would merely forget him.

8

Adam was at his parents' house, sitting at the desk in his bedroom overlooking Holland Park. Dozens of screwed-up balls of Basildon Bond writing paper lay in a horseshoe around his desk blotter. He was exhausted.

Normally, it took a couple of minutes to dash off a letter of thanks, yet it had already taken him an hour and a half. He didn't want to write a conventional thank-you note because he knew Elizabeth would simply read and discard it. He imagined her at the breakfast table opening his letter with the silver paperknife she kept to the left of her side plate. She would then read the note, perhaps remarking on it briefly to Helena, before adding it to the pile of other redundant mail, ready to be placed in the wastepaper basket after breakfast. He would be consigned to distant memory as one of the many suitors her daughter was bound to have in years to come.

He groaned at the thought of never seeing Elizabeth again.

His first few attempts had been full of clumsy hints to indicate that he was writing more than a letter of thanks – that something far more significant than customary politeness was at stake. He had tried several variants expressing his hope that they could meet again some time, that he admired her very much and had often thought about their conversations in the garden and at Blenheim.

Deciding to be bolder, he had then written more versions that described his feelings much more plainly, but the words seemed insipid, and he was certain that rather than placing the letter in the wastepaper basket, Elizabeth would thrust it in with the same indignation that had been on her face when he dared to kiss her at the station.

Remembering her subdued fury, he had thrown himself into more desperate efforts to express himself, even writing a couple of poems that were indeed, he eventually admitted, desperate.

To clear his head, he went for a walk in the park. He shuffled along a path, kicking stones, counting how many times he could kick the same stone before it rolled off the path onto the grass. He had already retrieved four stones and dropped them back on the path because he didn't want the blades of a lawnmower to be damaged, or a stone to be hurled by the blades into someone's face.

It was futile; nothing could distract him from thinking about Elizabeth, whose name kept whispering in his head each time he remembered their time together. The word *together* made him wince. He stood still in the middle of the path, looked up at the sky, spread his arms out, and let them flop down to his side.

He remembered walking next to her in the garden. She had asked him to cut a hellebore, and he must have looked blank because she said, 'Here, this one, it needs a long stem because it'll be positioned towards the back of the flower arrangement.' Another time, she had mentioned the phlox, and, amused by his confusion, she had spelt out the letters slowly. It was the first time he had considered deeper comparisons between Elizabeth and Helena, analysing their differences as well as their similarities. If Helena had spelt out the letters, there might have been a hint of superiority, but with Elizabeth the lesson was given with generous elegance; there was nothing didactic – she was simply sharing her knowledge and experience in effortless good humour.

Their farewell at the station haunted him constantly, heating his forehead one moment and making him shiver the next. He still clung to the hope that when she turned away to walk along the platform without looking back, she was merely stunned rather than repulsed.

The bitter regret for having appalled her alternated with the sweetness of having been so close – tactless to tactile and back again. He longed to catch a train just to root himself to the exact spot on the platform where the steel of the wheels had squealed on the rails. He had inhaled the air around her hair waving in the breeze, breaking in curls on her shoulders. It took his breath away.

He kicked his last stone and it stayed on the path; it was time to write the letter. He would not be distracted.

* * *

Elizabeth was not enjoying her Friday night dinner with Magnus and Helena because of the note Magnus had left on the kitchen table before he departed that morning for London. The note said that he expected to be back in time for dinner and that he would like 'to have a little chat' with her afterwards in his study. While the note itself was innocuous, she knew from previous experience that an unpleasant conversation lay ahead; the dread of it had made her uneasy all day. She would be tired by late evening and would have to respond to a long list of Magnus's demands.

Had she a right to complain? After all, it was part of the life she had chosen, rubbing along with Magnus. They had a long-standing arrangement. His preoccupation was building his advertising business in London, which kept him there for most of the week – along with his other distractions that she tried to ignore. For her part, she had the house to herself most of the time, with Miranda and Helena for her main company. It provided the freedom to pour her energy into her great vision for improving the house and landscaping its extensive gardens. Her project may not have been of Sissinghurst proportions, but everyone agreed that she was creating something very special. The price she paid was meeting Magnus's need to impress the world with a family life that matched his success in everything else.

She and Magnus had come to their understanding ten years into the marriage. Discovering Magnus's first infidelity was less of a shock than his denial of it – for her, the dishonesty was the worst sin of all. The very night she found out, she left the bedroom and slept in one of the guest rooms, and by the following night she had taken the large bedroom in the east wing with its four-poster bed and its adjoining bathroom; it had been her domain ever since. It took Magnus some time to accept the rift was permanent, for he wanted a son. But, gradually, he adjusted to the division in their sleeping arrangements and a lifestyle that became a division of labour as well, with Elizabeth devoting her attention to creating an impeccable family home and Magnus pursuing his advertising glory in Covent Garden. Their pact ran so smoothly that visitors to the house rarely had any idea of the underlying differences between them. Elizabeth didn't bridle at Magnus's boorish behaviour, which meant that he in turn tried to respect what mattered most to her. Occasionally, though, Magnus set about asserting his authority, probably in the same way that he did at work with the directors reporting to him. She knew many of them from various events over the years, and although they were confidently tenacious themselves, they seemed intimidated by Magnus, even servile. Maybe Magnus did the same to them – leaving little notes that said *I think we need to have a little chat*.

When they had finished their dinner, Helena left the table and Magnus did so at the same time, catching Elizabeth's eye as he went out with a nod in the direction of his study as if to remind her that he expected her there shortly.

She cleared the dinner table and made some coffee, which she made in mugs rather than cups in the hope of making the discussion she was about to have less formal and starched.

When she arrived at the study door, it was shut. It was as if she were back at school and would have to knock before entering.

She closed the door gently behind her. 'Here, I've brought you some coffee.'

'I don't want any. I'm going to pour myself a stiff gin instead, thank you very much.'

Magnus got up and went to his cocktail cabinet, while

Elizabeth sat in the chair opposite his. 'How did you find dinner? Did you enjoy it?'

'No, as a matter of fact. That was one of the things I wanted to talk about.'

'Oh?'

'The meat was tough. It's happened a couple of times recently. Is it the butcher? Do we need to find a new one?'

'I hadn't noticed. Let me look into it. Is that the important thing you wished to discuss?'

'No, I wanted to discuss Helena,' Magnus said, easing himself into the chair opposite. 'But since we're on the subject of housekeeping, I've been looking at your household accounts. Are you sure we need so many people helping out? I can understand some catering assistance for the larger parties, but do we really need this extra gardener three days a week? And the laundry bills look enormous.'

'The extra gardener is temporary, while we landscape the new area up by the woods. The laundry bill is indeed enormous – three baskets some weeks – but you insist on linen napkins, for example, when many people now find paper ones perfectly acceptable. As it happens, I also prefer linen, but how many napkins do you think are needed for a party of ninety people?'

'Shall we discuss Helena?'

Elizabeth sat still and said nothing because conversations with Magnus about Helena were rarely helpful.

He took a gulp from his tumbler. 'I know looking after Helena is your department, but is she all right?'

'Yes, everything's all right. I can assure you she's turning out to be a very fine woman.'

'Oh, I can see that! A little on the thin side, but that's the fashion I suppose. Is she eating enough?'

'Magnus, what's this all about?'

'Well, this business with Adam. He seemed a decent enough fellow and well mannered, but Helena was on edge when he came to stay. It's not the first time it's happened. The other fellow, Mark, who came to lunch a couple of times – he was perfectly OK and she chucked him in too. Is everything normal?'

'What do you mean exactly?'

'I mean does she have a problem with men? Or is she frightened about taking precautions or something? She'll need to settle down at some stage, won't she?'

'She's seventeen, Magnus.'

'Old enough to vote, nearly, according to the papers. I should have known you'd be protective. It's because she's the only child. If you'd produced a son …'

She surprised herself sometimes with her composure. After their conversation had ground to a halt, she left the room and closed the study door very calmly. She walked steadily to the other end of the house, breathing carefully, her shoulders back, carrying two mugs on a tray, one full, one empty. She had denied him the satisfaction of seeing her seethe. After his tirade, almost in the same breath, he had dared to discuss arrangements for the next party. As for mentioning her failure regarding a son, she could have fallen apart then, but Magnus wouldn't have known the wound he had inflicted there because he had never known much about her life before they married. Her past had rarely interested him, least of all when they first met, when she was a 'girl' in his typing pool.

* * *

Monday mornings were Elizabeth's favourite time of the week. She knew it was at odds with the rest of the world, but she could relax. Memories of the Holt's weekend debauchery faded; the tobacco smoke smarting her eyes was dispersed. The reek of stale alcohol was banished, along with the empty bottles piled in the dustbins. Above all, the deafening roar had ceased and she no longer had to feign happiness, gliding through the braying innuendos and insults of various parties.

The day had started pleasantly, eating kedgeree at the breakfast table with Helena, but at the moment they sat in silence because Helena had broken a rule. The postman had arrived later than usual, just after they had sat down to eat, and instead of waiting until after breakfast, Helena had gone out to the porch to collect the letters, which she brought in and placed on the table. Elizabeth felt no need to explain her silence, and Helena didn't look at her as they resumed their meal. The sliding of silver cutlery squeaking on the china seemed loud for a moment, but that was sufficient to remind Helena that leaving the table during mealtimes was forbidden. The point having been made, good order was restored, and they renewed their cheerful conversation as if nothing had happened.

Usually, the post arrived before breakfast and Elizabeth placed it on the table to her left, using her paperknife to open any letters that might amuse or interest whoever was eating with her. Today, because of Helena's faux pas, she gathered up the pile of mail after Helena had left the table and took it to her office, as she liked to call it. Originally, it had been

Helena's toy room, but when it was no longer required, Elizabeth had commandeered the dingy space, putting in an old desk and chair, a telephone and some shelving for lever-arch files. It was at best a makeshift office, but she liked it because it reminded her of the little office she had cobbled together while working in Bayeux during the war.

She had a system for organising the post. The brown envelopes marked with *Her Majesty's Service* would all be for Magnus, so they would go on a pile with his other letters, ready to be taken to his study, where they would be put in the in tray to await his return from London.

Her own pile of letters consisted of several bills, including those from the butcher, the greengrocer, the laundry company, the electricity board and Helena's cello tutor. Additionally, there was a letter from the medical committee she attended in Whitehall, some charity appeals, a sheaf of useless circulars, a couple of postcards from friends on holiday, and a Basildon Bond envelope written in a spidery hand she didn't recognise.

Then she realised the Basildon Bond was probably a thank-you note from Adam, and she pushed it away and off the blotter onto the varnished desk.

She hadn't been entirely successful in her resolve to forget about him because she knew a letter of thanks would arrive at some stage – out of nothing else than common courtesy. It had niggled her that the letter was to be expected because it prevented her from abandoning memories of him and his lunged kiss. It was like a circular argument, a cycle she wanted to break, which she would do now by reading and then discarding the letter. The matter would then be closed.

Reaching for the envelope with the spidery writing, she faltered for a moment as the thought crossed her mind that instead of containing a conventional letter of thanks, it might be more complicated.

Opening it cautiously, she was surprised to find two letters from Adam.

The first was a well-mannered letter of thanks for his stay, which conformed perfectly to the convention that it be short but not terse and light-hearted but not frivolous. It was signed 'Adam Matlock'.

The second letter was a much more serious affair, not just because it was signed without his surname. She crushed it tightly into a ball and left it in front of her on the desk. She should have hurled it into the wastepaper basket, but she left it there for now because she feared she might unravel it and read it again.

The room she called her office was stuffy and her neck felt hot.

At first, she was indignant about Adam's little ruse. He must have devoted considerable thought to writing one letter that would be fit for Helena's or Magnus's consumption and another that was not. He had obviously imagined her waving the innocent letter around at the breakfast table saying 'Oh, look! a little thank-you note from Adam, you know, who came to stay …'

It seemed to stare back at her, the second letter that was screwed up in a ball on the desk. It was a very alarming letter, but she had to admit it was well done; it had been politely insistent rather than plaintive and had come straight to the point. Adam wanted to meet her when she was next up in

London, merely, he emphasised, to explain properly what had happened between him and Helena and to apologise for his behaviour when they had parted at the station. He had not been himself – it was an unusual and momentary lapse – and it was always best to clear up any misunderstandings, he wrote. He ended his letter in a jocular tone as if he were an old friend sharing news from a distant country – jesting that he was looking forward to becoming a man about town now that he had the run of his own house. She knew it was a quip because he had used two exclamation marks, which people did these days – quite unnecessarily, she thought.

She ran her hands across the back of her neck again and took the ball of screwed-up paper and unravelled it, spreading out the creases on the blotter as if flattening aluminium foil.

Having read the letter carefully again, she realised she had overreacted. The letter was poised and courteous; it must have taken courage. She didn't want to be hypocritical – she had to remind Helena frequently about the importance of admitting one's mistakes and then taking steps to make amends. Adam was merely doing the same thing. He felt the need to explain himself – how could she refuse that? She had no right to be dismissive of someone who was much the same age as Helena, finding his way in life. He had clearly been upset by the way Helena had treated him and that of course explained his confused behaviour. He was suitably apologetic and deserved to be heard.

And besides, she was determined to find out why Helena had broken off with Adam. Every time Elizabeth had tried to wheedle out an explanation, Helena had been evasive. Furthermore, Magnus needed to be proved wrong that something was amiss.

She didn't crumple the letter this time but folded it over twice and slipped it into her pocket; she would keep it in the jewellery box in her bedroom, where it couldn't arouse suspicion.

As for Adam's other letter, she would leave that out later on the sideboard in the kitchen for Helena and Magnus to see, as was the custom for all letters of thanks received for the family's hospitality.

Consulting her diary, she saw that she would be up in London for a subcommittee meeting the following week. She scrawled a note to say that she did indeed want to know why he and Helena had broken off. She wrote that his letter had not included a telephone number to make arrangements, but that was no difficulty because it was a very confidential matter best discussed face to face. She gave the date of her meeting and the address of a little café she knew off Trafalgar Square, where she would be at two thirty that afternoon.

Having dashed off the note very quickly, she paused after writing 'Yours sincerely'. Since childhood, she had always placed her signature exactly in the middle of the page, so she needed to decide whether to include her surname before positioning the 'E' of Elizabeth. She pursed her lips, the nib of her pen hovering over the notepaper from side to side. The world was becoming less formal, she assured herself as she wrote 'Elizabeth' – precisely centred – without the 'Fortescue'. After all, she had suggested that Adam call her Elizabeth and consistency was important.

Now she wavered again as she remembered Adam's impetuosity on the station platform. What if he tried to phone or write again before they met – maybe to change the arrangement? She gripped the pen tightly, dreading the embarrassment of Helena or Magnus answering the phone or recognising an envelope with the spidery handwriting – it was quite distinctive and they would ask for an explanation or whether she was being pestered.

She didn't approve of postscripts; she thought them devious because although ostensibly they were afterthoughts, they often concealed a deeper truth.

After 'PS', she wrote that under no circumstances was he to phone or write before they met, and if he wasn't at the café, she would write again. It would be silly to set hares running, she wrote, trying to sound less fierce.

She sealed the envelope, applied a second-class stamp and put it in her posting tray, where it would soon be covered by all manner of other envelopes from her administrative tasks: the payment of bills, the letters and the charity donations. Then she would be free to enjoy the rest of the day in the garden.

9

Adam stepped closer to the sitting room window of his Kensington house to catch more light. He had already read Elizabeth's letter four times but wanted to examine the flow of the ink strokes, imagining her scratching the paper meticulously with her Parker pen. He could hear her fluency as he read her words. When she spoke, it was neither hurried nor slow; the sound was always measured and firm, possessing a softness at the same time. So it was also with her writing as he squinted at the words marching neatly across the page. Her 'g's and her 'y's had generous loops finished with a precise flick. The 't's were firmly crossed, but the 'i's were more lightly done, casually crowned sometimes with something more like a dash than a dot. He held the letter out at a greater distance in order to see its form as a whole, the straightness of the left margin, the perfectly spaced lines. It reminded him of the care with which she picked a flower or set down a vase, sending him off into yet another reverie, remembering her smile as they walked side by side through her apple orchard.

It was more than he had hoped for to have received a reply at all following her anger at the station when they parted, let alone that she had signed it without her surname; the plain familiarity of 'Elizabeth' was considered and softly whispered.

He tilted the notepaper again in the light, brushed its vellum and breathed it in. Sliding the letter back into the envelope, he contemplated how she would have performed the same action after putting down her pen. Would her elegant hands have lingered thoughtfully just for a second before she slid the letter in? Or would she have sat nonchalantly in that office of hers, despatching her letter with no more care than scrawling a cheque for the household bills or licking a stamp?

He crossed the room and sat down on a sofa he had known all his life. It was an antique curved sofa made by Howard & Sons of Berners Street, one of a pair that his parents bought second-hand for their drawing room when they settled into their new house in Holland Park shortly before the war. But only one of the sofas had made it into his new house because the sitting room was too small for both of them. He wondered which of the pair he was lying along now. Was it the one that had faced the grandfather clock in his parents' drawing room, or the one facing the overmantle mirror, the sofa on which he had spilt some cherryade when he was six? It made him sad, wondering whether it was in fact fair to separate two sofas that had been together for so long. Had his parents sold the other one? He didn't care if he was being sentimental. In fact, he embraced the idea, lying back on the sofa at full length with his hands behind his head. How would Elizabeth describe him now? He heard her whispering the word 'expansive' and smiled because that was how he felt as he rested.

Then he leapt up, determined to get a grip of himself and break out of his endless reflections. Otherwise his meeting with Elizabeth in the café would be an even greater disaster than the farewell on the station platform. Unless he curbed these intrusions, he would make another blunder and that would be the end of it. She was considerate and forgiving, but she would never give him a second chance. In fact his only chance was to fix his self-control by cultivating an air of polite maturity towards her when they met, to shield him from the possibility of making another error. He would learn from her wisdom and do nothing rash. He would imagine himself as her son, the male equivalent of Helena, polite but certain. That would impress her. He instilled this into himself as if it were a military drill – he would not fawn; he would not melt; he would be kind yet strong, affable but not overly eager.

* * *

He arrived early at the café near St Martin's and sat in the corner to gather himself and greet her unassumingly.

When she entered, he watched everyone turning to look at her, dressed very smartly in navy blue, some kind of suit with its matching jacket and skirt. He had never really noticed what she wore when they were in the garden or at Blenheim. His pride embarrassed him, sensing the admiration of her as she walked towards him. And then he would be stared at too by everyone wondering what it was all about. He stood up to greet her, shaking hands courteously and taking her coat. So now they knew, and the glances turned away. A woman meeting a nephew perhaps, something like that.

He blinked, seeing her again in startling reality, rather than recalling her from the memories that had flooded his mind for days. He thought her formal appearance might have been to signify a conscious distance she wished to place between them, but then remembered she had come from her morning meeting. She sat down opposite him, asking cheerfully whether he had been waiting long.

'No, not at all,' he said.

She looked at his empty cup and looked puzzled for a second before the waitress arrived to take their order for coffee and cake.

But after that nothing was awkward at all. Elizabeth was friendly. She couldn't possibly have forgotten their moment on the platform when they last met, so the fact that it was never mentioned was encouraging; it was gracious. They started chatting easily. She told him about her committee meeting, which had been a great success and how relaxing it was to visit London from time to time, free from her responsibilities at home.

'And how about you, Adam, how are you?'

He told her about his house and how it was not yet properly furnished or organised, and it led her to state that every house – regardless of size – required some basic rules or the place would degenerate into chaos. That was the very expression she used before joking that if you don't have rules of the house you'll end up with an unruly one. He hadn't seen her laugh properly before, and it seemed to surprise her as well because she tried to hide her laughter behind her hand.

When he suggested he might buy some style magazines to give him some inspiration for decorating his house, she seemed horrified and spoke excitedly for a long time about something he didn't fully understand – that it was vital to develop one's own style and work with the natural aspect of the house. She insisted on the importance of identifying the correct colour for the mood of each room and that the best strategy was always to paint a room with two things in mind: first, what kind of floor there was – wood, rugs and tiles for example – and second, what light was available in the room, both by day and by night.

'It's quite a simple matter,' she said, 'you have to remember that a room almost chooses its own colour. It's a matter of instinct.'

It shocked him to realise how much he had to learn. Perhaps the coffee had been too strong.

She said, 'Haven't you got somebody to advise you on doing up your house? It needs to be done properly. Your parents have been very kind to buy it for you. Can't they help?'

'You're right, they've been very kind, but I think they want me to become more independent. I haven't a clue where to start, to be honest. I need someone experienced to advise me.'

'I see …' she said, frowning briefly. 'Well, to business, Adam. We're forgetting the reason for meeting. The reason why Helena broke off. I know she can be rather testy sometimes. If she gets it from me, I apologise. Now, please, I want you to be quite frank – in absolute confidence, of course. Was there some kind of problem? Problems always occur from time to time, but once you know the cause there is some chance of preventing them from happening again. You do see what I mean?'

Now that she had asked him so directly, Adam thought it ridiculous to explain that Helena had fallen out with him because of a misunderstanding about his age. Not for the first time, he considered other possible reasons for Helena's change of heart. Had she found some other unmentionable fault in him and was merely using the embarrassing discovery of their age difference as an excuse to explain their rift to her mother?

Elizabeth sat patiently, waiting for him to answer. He leant forward to drink his coffee but found it difficult to pick up the cup. The handle was too small for his fingers, he thought.

Perhaps he could say that he and Helena had realised that their affection for each other was purely a musical one? Prior to meeting Helena, he had attended a summer school in Dartington, where he had met Susan and Roger who played together in a professional string quartet. He had assumed they were married, but it turned out their closeness was entirely due to the bond of music and practising together for countless hours. Susan had described the intimacies their quartet shared – the exact way in which an eyebrow might signal a minute nuance in the rhythm of the strings, or a painful confession to the others about a violin that was misbehaving because of the heat or humidity. The quartet inhabited each other's minds with these anguishes like lovers. When he asked Susan about her life with Roger, she said that other than the intensity of making music together, she didn't know him at all. He lived in Ealing and had an aunt in Kent, but that was almost all she knew.

Yes, he could tell Elizabeth that he and Helena broke off because they were like Susan and Roger. His grip on the cup slipped a little, spilling some coffee into his saucer. Elizabeth seemed to ignore it, taking a sip from her cup and placing it down noiselessly. 'It's all right, Adam. You don't have to answer. I know these things can be troublesome.'

She asked how his parents were. The sudden change of topic was bewildering. He said his parents had gone to Windsor for the day to watch some polo, which he realised was not what she had meant at all. However, she ignored his slip, and they started a conversation about horses, discovering that they had both found learning to ride when they were young very troublesome. They laughed at how many times they had fallen off because neither of them had mastered the essentials from their impatient riding instructors.

Elizabeth leant back, clearly still amused. 'Of course you know there's a very famous horse just over there,' she said, nodding in the direction of the National Gallery.

She seemed to spot his confusion and explained her little joke – that *Whistlejacket* was one of her favourite paintings. 'And it's certainly my favourite Stubbs,' she added.

'I'm sorry, I'm not very good on art.'

'Stubbs, you know, who painted *Whistlejacket* …'

But she was kind, and instead of being appalled by his ignorance, she insisted that he should see it, he really should. She looked at her watch and said, 'It's time for me to go and catch my train, but we just have time to walk over to the gallery and see *Whistlejacket* in all his glory. We really must.'

They asked for the bill and when it came, they both insisted on paying. He had seen people tussling in restaurants over the bill and thought it better to let her pay.

Walking over to the National Gallery, she looked at her watch and quickened her step, conscious no doubt of the train she wanted to catch. When they stood in front of

Whistlejacket, he wanted to say that he liked it, but all he could say was that the greyish-brown colour of the background was the same as the wallpaper in the entrance hall of his house.

'It's pale tan,' she said.

He didn't know how to react to her occasional abruptness, but he invented something to say, that the horse looked frightened, and she replied that it was always best not to frighten the horses. It was hard to read her sometimes.

And he certainly didn't know how to react when they walked past the *Rokeby Venus*. He dreaded her stopping to look at the picture next to him; she would know he was thinking about her. He would blush, not because of the picture, but because of the picture she would have in her mind of the picture in his. It would cause her offence.

In the gallery foyer, she extended her hand formally, saying it was time to catch her train. She said goodbye without mentioning when she would be in London again, or whether indeed they would ever meet again.

He stood still on the mosaic floor, watching her walk down the steps and through the door, the portico's pillars framing her exit. She didn't look back at him. He felt drained and unable to move, wondering whether he had overcompensated – that in his determination to appear relaxed in her company he had been too cautious and distant. She would be crossing Trafalgar Square now, towards Charing Cross. He tried to summon the energy to run after her, to search frantically for a blue figure in the crowd. Finding her, he would apologise for being so faint-hearted, for avoiding her question about Helena, for his clumsiness with the coffee cup. But he remembered the sternness of Elizabeth's face on the station platform. It kept him rooted to the mosaic under the dome. He turned away from the glass door to look back at the steps up into the gallery, scratching his head.

'Do you know where you're going sir?' the steward said.

'Oh, yes, thank you. I was wondering whether to go and look at *Whistlejacket* again, but perhaps some other time.'

Out in the square, he couldn't bear to follow the route Elizabeth would have trodden to Charing Cross, so he walked in the opposite direction to Leicester Square to catch the Piccadilly line to Gloucester Road. The fresh air would do him good. As he walked, he thought about her travelling home and hoped that she was safe. He already missed the sound of her voice and wanted to telephone her as soon as she was home. Helena had previously given him her home phone number, but he shuddered at the suspicions he would raise if Magnus or Helena answered the phone. Why was that boy who came to stay phoning Elizabeth late in the evening? The idea thrilled him for a second, but he would never want to cause her trouble and her anger would be too much to bear.

* * *

In the days after they met in London, the possibility that he would never see her again hollowed him out. At times he was reconciled to it – she was a busy woman, she had been pleasant to him, she had even humoured him, but she humoured everyone; it was her nature and there was every reason she would forget him. But at other times, he looked at the telephone that had now been connected in his new Kensington house. It was still on the floor next to its coil of wire. He imagined it ringing and then hearing the breath of her voice soothing its way down the line with that laugh of hers that sometimes gushed in a little whisper. But because she didn't have his phone number, he was tempted again and again to phone her instead, his hand hovering towards the receiver, but each time he jolted it back again, wincing at the idea of her fury. He felt compelled to give her his telephone number, just in case she wanted it. But then his thoughts would revert again – why an earth would she want his number if she had forgotten him?

Eventually he found the perfect excuse to write to her again. He would apologise for failing to answer her question in the café about why he and Helena had broken off, which after all had been the reason for their meeting in the first place.

He thought for a day about the tone of letter that would please her. She liked things to be logical and concise, but warm and generous at the same time. He had already taken up the same manner – only yesterday the man in the newsagent's had short-changed him for his newspaper, and instead of being annoyed he did exactly as Elizabeth would have done, holding out the change in the palm of his hand and saying, very gently, 'Excuse me, I may have made a mistake, but is this the right change for a ten-shilling note?'

Finding exactly the right tone, he started to write very fluently, thanking her for paying for the coffees and for introducing him to Stubbs, who he had now looked up with great interest in the Kensington library. Did she know that Stubbs had spent eighteen months dissecting horses by way of anatomical research for the painting? Then he mentioned that his failure to explain the situation with Helena had been weighing on his mind, but he appreciated the opportunity was now lost. However, if she did happen to be in London again with some time to spare, he would be delighted to make everything clear. He told her of the thought he had given to her views about how to turn a house into a home, but he felt quite helpless – and hopeless! – about all the decisions she mentioned: the furniture, the lighting, the colours of the walls. And, of course, if she was ever in the Kensington area, he would be delighted to receive a visit from her, just in case she was minded to cast her expert eye over the challenges he was so obviously facing. But he appreciated that she was always busy, and should they not meet again, he wished her family all the very best for the future.

He put down his pen. Yes, of course he had overdone it. Yet he was pleased with the levity he had struck; it seemed to weigh with just the right level of ambiguity. The letter could be taken at face value, or not.

In a casual postscript, he informed her that he now had a telephone installed in his house as she could see from the number that he had written below his address.

His final touch was to send the letter in a brown envelope with a typed address to save her the embarrassment of explaining to Helena or Magnus at the breakfast table why on earth that boy with the spidery handwriting had written a second letter of thanks.

It took him several attempts to get the envelope exactly right. Sometimes he hit the wrong key on the old Remington he had been given, jabbing the letters of her address heavily, one finger at a time. Then he had problems controlling the shift key, lining up the envelope horizontally in the roller, and positioning the ribbon correctly.

But eventually he had an envelope with everything perfectly spelt and perfectly level. The ribbon he had fitted had plenty of ink and the words were clear and strong. He wanted nothing to be faint or faint-hearted.

10

Putting her face to bed, Elizabeth called it. It was one of those quaint family expressions that stick and is used forever. Helena, when she was very young, had been unable to sleep and came into the bedroom and asked Elizabeth why she was rubbing her face in front of the mirror. Over the years, putting her face to bed had become a prolonged ritual, even though she wore very little make-up. It was comforting to wash her face in the bathroom with her Bronnley lemon soap and then relax at her antique dressing table with its gilded trifold mirror, reflecting on her day and what the next day might bring. It settled her for sleep.

For three nights after her meeting in London with Adam, she had performed her dressing table ritual innocently enough. She had enjoyed talking to him about how to make a home. Most people these days seemed to think that interior design was purely a matter of fashion, rather than taste. Even Helena, who agreed with her on nearly everything, would listen only half-heartedly whenever Elizabeth described one of her favourite houses – its colour schemes, the choice of fabrics, the furniture, or the fine detailing of some decorative ironwork. But Adam had listened attentively. He had wanted to learn.

When she had put her face to bed the previous evening, Elizabeth had decided that everything with Adam was concluded. True, they hadn't discussed what had happened between him and Helena, nor had he apologised for his disaster on the station platform, both of which were the stated pretexts for their meeting in London. But she had put all that aside; they had shaken hands cordially in the National Gallery and would have no need to meet or speak again. She had placed him in the far distance, in one of her compartments, the one for former acquaintances.

But this morning she had received another letter. At first it irked her, because she believed that once something was laid to rest it should be left to lie. The letter perplexed her because it asked for nothing. It only suggested meeting again and it lay in her gift to ignore it. She was bemused by the typed efficiency of the envelope, which she picked up and scrutinised. Then she realised, placing it gently on the desk, that he was being considerate, taking the trouble to spare her potential embarrassment at the breakfast table.

She took her earrings out and placed them in her jewellery box, where she saw his letter and read it again before folding it and slowly returning it to the box, thudding the lid.

It wasn't the first time that matters with Adam had been closed and then had revived themselves. She remembered flicking over the pagoda of cards the morning after the party when she had first seen him across the room. The cards had scattered on the floor, but she had knelt and gathered them up neatly into the pack, which she had placed in the games drawer in the drawing room, next to the mahjong and the score cards that were used for bezique. Good order was restored, everything was in its proper place, in the right compartment.

She took up a jar of cream and started applying it carefully, looking in the mirror to her left while trying to fathom why it was proving so difficult to ignore his letter. At times he seemed very mature, but at others he was not worldly-wise at all and she felt an innate desire to protect him. When that battleaxe of a waitress in the café had scowled at him, she had wanted to confront the woman and ask her not to be so impatient – he was just making up his mind about which piece of cake to have.

He was respectful and merely seeking advice. It was all too evident that he needed her guidance; it was her duty. He seemed stranded without his parents to help him; it was irresponsible of them to buy him a house and not set it up properly. Care was what was needed, not money.

She had behaved impeccably in London. She had not encouraged him to write a second letter. True, it was impulsive to have suggested the visit to the gallery, but she would have behaved exactly the same with Helena had she been as ignorant of Stubbs; it was something that had to be put right immediately. But if her suggestion to see *Whistlejacket* seemed over-familiar, she had compensated perfectly. She was curt and distant afterwards, and they had said goodbye with formality – indeed with finality, she assumed.

In fairness to Adam, he had behaved impeccably too. There seemed to be no danger of him repeating his aberration at their previous farewell, so perhaps she should consider meeting him again to find out what truly happened between him and Helena. It was worrying that the moment they had finally got round to discussing the subject he clammed up completely.

But meeting him again might not be appropriate. How the women stared at her when she came into the café! Staring as they do, without being seen to stare at all. It was the same sometimes when she performed her hostess duties at home for one of Magnus's parties – her head held high crossing a room, her eyes fixed on the far distance, avoiding everyone staring – but you could feel the stares, the wandering eyes and the wondering thoughts, everyone willing you to slip up, just for once, to prove you were ordinary, someone like everyone else, someone fallible. Everyone would crow over the loss of her sanctimoniousness, the mighty fallen.

She couldn't deny her frisson of pride as she sensed the women watching her crossing the floor of the café, calculating whether she was a mother or an aunt or whether she might be something else altogether, their eyes narrowing with suspicion as she approached the impressive young man sitting in the corner.

These thoughts crept in like light under a door or the smell of a bonfire through a closed window. She wanted to seal up the door and the window, but the little doubts stalked her, trying to trip her up, daring her to err.

Sliding the jar across the kidney glass with a squeak that made her grimace, she turned her head to the right-hand mirror and started on the other side of her face.

What did he see when he glanced sheepishly at the *Rokeby Venus*? She admired the painting because of its shimmering colour and its naturalism, but what did everyone else see, treading their reverential steps in a famous gallery? Art critics and painters might press their eyes as close as possible to each canvas, squinting at the brushstrokes. Lesser mortals might step back from a painting and tilt their head, reminiscing: *That tree is like the one I fell out of when I was young*, or, *When we had that Easter picnic by the stream it was just like that*, or they might say, *Yes, I remember that harbour wall, I stood on it trying to net the little fish*. Yet others might stare in awe at the canvas, imagining themselves to be Stubbs himself in a paint-splattered coat, stabbing at the oils on the palette. But what did Adam see? She saw him look at the painting before turning his head away quickly, all in one motion as they continued walking. But then, in that casual way people do, he looked back again at the picture as if to say 'Look at me, I'm obviously not embarrassed because I'm continuing to look at the picture!' She knew what he had been thinking; he had been strangely coy and reticent as if quietly in thrall to Venus and the curves of her ivory skin, his imagination running riot.

She needed to be careful. In the garden this afternoon she had watched a wren darting about and its chatter kept making her smile. She thought she really shouldn't be smiling so warmly after reading his letter several times, so she dredged her memory for something else that would nullify the thoughts she shouldn't be having. She remembered Jackson, the officer who had sat her down to tell her the news that Ralph was dead, breaking the news stoically, without much detail other than when and where it had happened. 'Those are the facts,' Jackson had said, itching to get away quickly because her tears were starting to well. 'Sandy here has more of the information about the family situation, so I'll leave you with him.' Once Sandy had said his piece she vowed she would never weep again because it was too pitiful. She had almost succeeded.

She lifted the jar and took a swipe of cream and then thumped the jar down again on the kidney glass. But life was too short! There might be no harm in going to his terraced house, just to impart some advice on its furnishings and décor. He seemed to be in control of himself and had learnt from his mistake on the station platform. And she would also be in perfect control, she would make sure of that. There was no danger; there was no mystery; it was purely an interest of a maternal sort, the desire to protect. He had merely glanced at the painting, just as she had glanced across too. Besides, she had restored the situation perfectly – she had been short with him, he understood, and she had parted with a shake of the hand that was unequivocal.

Or perhaps it would not be wise to meet again after all. She really knew very little about him, yet there was a trust she did not understand, something disguised. She liked the way he didn't talk about the past very much, or the future. He was always occupied with the here and now, soaking up the present for what it was, looking at a picture, savouring the coffee, discussing the décor.

She looked ahead at the larger, middle mirror in front of her and drew the two table lamps on each side closer to throw more light, leaning her face into the glass. Were there lines? Maybe just at the corner of her eyes when she laughed. And she had laughed more than usual – in the café and in the gallery as well, which could do no harm at all.

She took up her hairbrush and put it down again, pressing its silver back with her palm so that the bristles bent against the top of the dresser. She would crush her madness out. What on earth was she thinking? It was merely the stream of whimsical thoughts that often tumbled through her head whenever she was ready for sleep. She yawned. There was no need to panic; she must stay calm and think it over, let it steep, let it all seep in. For now the matter was closed, closed as the lid on the jar of cream she had just twisted firmly shut.

11

It had worked! He hadn't intended to punch the air for joy and needed to sit down, because it was more like the air had been punched from him. Despite the crackly line, her voice had had its usual disarming effect, her precisely enunciated words tripping into his head, cutting him at the knees like the plants in her garden when she wielded her shears.

She had taken him by surprise, because after several days of waiting, he had given up any hope of her responding to his letter. He had calculated that if she did respond, it would be by letter rather than by telephone. Consequently, each morning since they had met in London he had snatched up the post from his doormat, searching for the flourishes of her handwriting on one of the envelopes. He had been careful not to raise his hopes too much, realising that if she did write, the letter might be a negative one, stating bluntly that a further meeting was both inappropriate and unnecessary.

When the phone rang, he hadn't rushed to answer it because apart from his parents, every call to his Kensington house had been from an electrician, a plumber or a roofer. The line was crackly because she had made her call from a telephone box. It was difficult to imagine Elizabeth grappling with grubby coins and forcing them into the slot, the line clicking and beeping. There was something delicious about her making the conscious decision not to make the call from her house, which had at least two telephones to his knowledge. Her voice had been a little breathless, he thought, but maybe that was the quality of the line, or the tiresome business of wrestling with her loose change. She said very little – merely informing him that the day after tomorrow she had a busy day in London but could spare half an hour to pop by and look over his house if he still wanted advice. It would be some time in the early afternoon, if that was convenient.

He had been a little breathless himself and replied that yes, any advice would be very much appreciated.

Leaning back on the sofa, he closed his eyes and dared to hope she wouldn't cancel the arrangement because of the weather or something like that. Otherwise, she would be here, in this very room, the day after tomorrow. In a flurry, he got up and darted around the room, first to the door, then to the window, and then sat down again, wondering what he could possibly do to make the house more welcoming. He could brush the steps, polish the brass on the front door, borrow some vases for the flowers he would surely have to place in every room – he would go to the florist that he had passed a few times walking towards the High Street. Thinking of flowers reminded him of their walk in her garden and the first time she had smiled at him properly. She had already told him about hostas, and when they walked past another clump later in the day, he said, 'And here we have some horsas again.' He must have been thinking about Hengist and Horsa from his history lessons at school. She didn't scoff, but pursed her mouth in amusement before correcting him very softly, raising her face so that under the brim of her straw hat he could see into the kindness of her eyes – blue mainly, but with grey and a trace of green glinting in the sun.

She had startled him so many times on that first day. Because of her neatness and poise, he had mistakenly assumed she would be fragile, but when she crouched down to take out some flowers that had died he was startled by her vigour, rolling up her sleeves to set about the task, her hands ripping away at the stems. He was struck by her sense of purpose – that having decided something was an obstacle, nothing would stand in her way. She was oblivious to him watching her; he was merely a visitor walking through her dominion. Another time that day he mentioned that a leaf had fallen into her hair, which she swept with her hands, revealing the back of her neck, and he looked away for fear of staring.

He jumped up, snapping out of his trance because he had more urgent tasks to attend to than thinking about flowers and gardens. If she was to be here the day after tomorrow, he had to make the house presentable. He didn't have much time. That evening he had agreed to have supper at his parents' house. They had summoned him, rather ominously, saying there was something very important they wished to discuss. He wondered whether he had said something out of place, or whether they were having second thoughts about setting him up with the house, or whether they wanted to speak to him about the bills he had been running up with all the house repairs. He was very fond of them, but they could be ponderous, taking ages to mention anything that played on their minds.

It was likely to be a long evening.

*　*　*

Adam had heard the story many times about how his parents had bought their Holland Park house soon after they married in 1936. It seemed that very little had changed since then. Constance and Arnold's world was an unchanging one of antimacassars, barley-twist tea trolleys and brown Windsor soup. Yet Adam was very grateful for his solid upbringing. Although comfortable, it had not been an exciting childhood – there had been few lavish entertainments, and he had never been abroad with his family because their summer holidays had always been taken in Broadstairs at an unprepossessing family hotel. Yet Adam had no regrets. They had been generous in his education, and although they often seemed remote, they had taken very good care of him.

They had made very little fuss about giving him the run of the Kensington house as if it were his in all but name. It was typical of their understated way of doing things. Without mentioning anything specific, they seemed to have concluded that he had reached an age when he could be released responsibly into the world, their duty done. There was nothing callous about it – callousness was an alien concept to them – they were just preparing him steadily for the future in their own steady way. His parents had clearly arrived at a time of life when they planned for it to be quieter, like twilight. His father seemed relieved now that Adam had promised to take on the family civil engineering business once he had graduated. An orderly transition was in place and Father could look forward to a peaceful retirement.

Adam's parents had started to talk about settling eventually in France. They had been over to Normandy several times over the last few years to visit his mother's family, who still lived in Caen, and Adam suspected some agreement had been reached – that in exchange for his mother's life in England for thirty years, his father might spend the last part of his in France. Their agreement wouldn't have been a formal one, more a tacit understanding, which was the way they seemed to navigate their comfortable marriage.

All three of them were getting used to the new arrangements now that Adam was spending much of his time at the Kensington house. Adam was still visiting Holland Park occasionally for a meal or dropping in for a coffee and a chat.

On this occasion, the supper conversation was as good-natured as ever, but Adam thought his mother and father were ill at ease. They discussed ideas for Adam's house, the weather, the woes of the Wilson government and the unacceptable queues in the self-service supermarket that had just opened down the road. But beneath the customary cheeriness, there was an air of foreboding.

But that was not the reason Adam was distracted. He kept thinking about Elizabeth. Usually, he was good at listening, but each topic of conversation linked back in his mind to her. When the weather was the chosen topic, his mind drifted away to their walk across Trafalgar Square to the National Gallery, when it had started to rain. And for the discussion on house décor, he reflected on her complicated views about the handling of colour.

'Now that you have a place of your own, it won't be long before you settle down,' his mother said. 'It's a pity things didn't work out with that friend of yours. What was her name? Helen, was it?'

'Yes, Helen*a*.'

'She sounded a nice girl, and her parents sounded very nice too, particularly the mother.'

She's called *El-iz-a-beth*, he wanted to say, the four syllables chiming in his head, reminding him of the time she gave him permission to use her name. He breathed in honeysuckle and could hear the sensuousness in her voice; it had a slight huskiness that was enough to make him swoon. To think how quickly her magisterial charm had reduced him to a botched kiss on a station platform. But there was hope: she would be with him, in his house, the day after tomorrow. He must not think that way; she was simply visiting to share some knowledge.

He jolted up in his chair. His father was speaking to him. 'Adam, are you listening to your mother? She's trying to tell you something.'

'I'm sorry, I was miles away, I haven't been sleeping well recently.'

At least that was true, even if his explanation omitted to mention Elizabeth as the cause.

The conversation halted and all that could be heard was the ticking of the grandfather clock and the sound of cutlery as they ate the fish pie.

He could feel it brooding – that his parents were on the brink of announcing whatever was on their minds – but he would have to wait, sliding his knife politely.

His father resumed on the subject of Helena's parents, this time enquiring about Magnus. 'He's in the advertising business, isn't he?'

There followed Arnold Matlock's assessment of the advertising profession, peddling its jingles and intruding into every walk of life. In fact, he wondered whether it was a profession at all ...

Adam's attention wandered off again; he thought about why Elizabeth had married Magnus in the first place when they were obviously so incompatible. Helena had told him that they had separate suites in the house, and he caught his breath, thinking about her closing her door at night.

'Still, there's money in advertising, that seems to be very evident,' his father said. 'Even if it is money for old rope. Commercial television was never a very good idea ... Oh! we seem to have lost you again, Adam. I was just saying, commercial television is rather ill-conceived. Anyway, I think it's time you and I retired to the sitting room while Connie does her clearing up.'

In the sitting room, his father seemed hesitant and confused, fussing around the room, pointing out the new sofas he and Adam's mother had chosen, checking the curtains were properly drawn, straightening the framed Madonna above the piano. He decided the electric fire wasn't needed and turned it off, the elements ticking as they contracted.

Adam sat patiently, waiting for whatever was to come. Yes, it could be second thoughts about the Kensington house. Or perhaps their money had run out, or was it illness? Or even divorce?

'That was a fine fish supper your mother cooked, was it not?' his father said, standing with his back to the mantelpiece, rocking on his feet with his hands behind his back.

'Ever since I first met Connie, she's been meticulous about the making of a fish pie, though it's helpful of course having that friend of hers who's involved with Billingsgate ... Would you like a whisky?'

Adam thought his father might have remembered that he did not care for whisky. 'Well, yes, if you're having one, I'll join you, thank you.'

His father clapped his hands and marched to the drinks trolley that stood in the corner under a standard lamp with yellow tassels. He faced away from Adam, pouring the whisky meticulously as if he wanted to pour it forever to an exact line on the glass that wasn't there.

After the burble of the whisky pouring, the grinding of the glass stopper and the thump of the decanter on the silver tray, his father handed him the glass and sat down on the sofa opposite Adam.

'Now where was I?' he said. 'Ah, yes, to the serious business, I suppose. I've been skirting around it, Adam, avoiding it, so to speak. I apologise for that.'

It was as if his father had been asked to recite a poem but was struggling to remember the words. He leant forward, sinking his face into his hands. When his attempt to settle himself failed, he looked up and said, 'I can't do this. It's problematic, you see ... I'd better get Connie.'

But before he stood up she came in and sat next to Adam's father.

'Connie, would you like a glass of whisky?' he said falteringly.

'You know I never drink whisky. You haven't told him yet, have you? And we promised. We promised to tell him, Arnold.'

'You will see why this is difficult, Adam,' his father said, pausing to swallow before finally gathering his composure. 'We have always loved you, and brought you up to the best of our ability. It was a very bad time, the war.'

He paused to take a sip of whisky. 'It was bad for everybody, of course, but especially for Connie and me. We bought this house before the war, hoping to raise a family. We lived here all through the war while I worked for the MOD on construction projects, but by the time 1945 came around we still hadn't been successful in raising a family. As the Allies pushed on into Europe, it became safe for Connie to go back to her family in Caen, where she was desperately needed after her father had been killed in the bombing. We made a fresh start, living with Connie's family, with me working in France to help with the reconstruction. Lord knows there was enough to do. It was a strange time because despite all the devastation, it was a time of great hope and renewal. We began to discuss whether to adopt a child for our new life. Connie started conversations with the state orphanage in Caen and took a shine to a baby boy. I took a shine to him as well. It was clear soon afterwards that I wouldn't be successful building a career in France. My French wasn't good enough and the MOD wanted me back again to work here. So that was it, we all came back to England.'

'What your father is trying to say, Adam, is that you're adopted. It breaks our hearts that we have never told you, but we have never thought of you as adopted. We have always loved you as our very own son. We've tried our best ...'

Adam stood up as his mother got up from the opposite sofa and came towards him. It was a clumsy embrace to hide her tears. His father got up as well, and then the three of them did something they had never done before. They stood together in a huddle, saying very little.

As they stood back, his mother wiped her eyes and said, 'Will you forgive us, Adam, for taking so long to tell you? There never seemed to be a right time. It's been eating away at us.'

'But of course. You mustn't worry. It doesn't matter to me at all really ... Sorry, what I mean is, it makes no difference. I have always thought of you as my parents, and always will. You've always been very kind.'

His parents seemed puzzled for a moment. Perhaps they had been expecting him to make some kind of scene.

'Well, I must say, you've taken it admirably,' Arnold said, looking relaxed for the first time that evening. 'I'm impressed. Now then, after all that, would you like another whisky?'

'Yes, I'll join you if you're having one.'

'And you, Connie? Of course I know you're not fond of whisky. But what can I get you?'

'I'll have a very small glass of sherry, please, now that everything is in the open.'

They sat with their drinks, and the conversation continued much less sombrely. Adam was tired, but listened as attentively as he could while his parents spoke at length about the circumstances leading up to his adoption and the adoption procedure itself. It was as if they were only able to find some form of closure about what had happened in 1945 by unburdening every detail about the orphanage in Caen, the havoc in the city after the Allied bombing and the bereavements in his mother's family.

His father described the complicated documentation that was required for adopting a child in France and bringing it to England during the general chaos at the end of the war.

Then he veered off into a series of historical reflections. 'It's quite fascinating, you know ... ever since the Ancien Régime, France has had a different approach to the rest of Europe on family matters, particularly regarding anonymous child adoption. It was Napoleon who first formalised the arrangements at the end of the eighteenth century ...'

How typical it was of his father, Adam thought, to find relief by immersing himself in the minutiae. He warmed to his theme, relating fact after fact and relishing the opportunity to emphasise the importance of due procedure and accurate documentation.

'Now the Pétain government in 1941 revised the law ...'

As his father's waves of commentary washed over him, Adam tried to concentrate, but his mind drifted away again to Elizabeth's visit and what he needed to do in the house.

'You seem to be glazing over, Adam. I was talking about *Accouchement Sous X*, which is a system of anonymous adoption unique to France—'

Fortunately, his mother interrupted. 'Perhaps it would be better, Arnold, if we left all the detail for another time. There's an awful lot to take in. The important thing, Adam, is that we've kept all the documents safe and sound, and we can go through them whenever you're ready.'

'Thank you. You're right, there's quite a lot to take in.'

'But overall, you're not shocked? This hasn't upset you?'

He was not surprised that she was seeking reassurance, because he had sat and listened impassively throughout their account while thinking about Elizabeth. The truth was that imparting the news about his adoption seemed of far greater significance to his parents than it did to him. He felt uncharitable for appearing indifferent, belittling their effort to find the courage to tell him about his origins.

Should he feel guilty for being unmoved? To him, it was a matter of logic. What happened so long ago didn't change who he was now or how he felt about himself. In and of itself the new knowledge didn't make him a different person. The war seemed to have visited far worse ghosts and tragedies on the world than a child being lost and found. He considered for a moment who could be uncaring enough to give up a child, but it was wrong to judge someone he would never know.

'No, I'm not upset at all,' he replied. 'I'm upset that you're upset, if you see what I mean – it must have been very worrying for you, wondering when would be the right time to tell me. It doesn't change anything for me because I'll always think of you as my parents. And I'm very grateful to you, as you know.'

'Let's leave it all there for now then,' she said, 'unless you have anything you wish to ask?'

'Well, there is one thing, I suppose. Do we know anything about my real ... my other ...'

'Do you mean your birth parents?'

'Yes, I suppose I do.'

'Arnold and I have been talking to someone who specialises in these things and gives advice. It's quite natural for you to ask about that, Adam, but we know nothing. In France you can give up a child anonymously. That was what your father was beginning to explain. We will never know who they were. But we can explain more about that another time, when you've had time to think it all over.'

Walking home, Adam felt ashamed that the moment he had left his parents' house, his mind was besieged again by what he needed to do in his house to prepare for Elizabeth's visit. His list of tomorrow's tasks was daunting: the trip to the florist, the cleaning of the house, and shopping for some special food in case she decided to stay for longer than thirty minutes ...

These things weighed on his mind far more than what his parents had just revealed to him. He wondered whether the way he was preoccupied with the here and now was normal. When Helena had made it clear there was no hope of them becoming more closely involved, he was able to put the past aside and accept his failure. Equally, what his parents had just told him about his past was already supplanted by the immediate urgency of preparing for Elizabeth's visit.

He decided that cleaning the house should be the main priority. She would forgive him if the house was not tidy because she would understand that he had only recently moved in and therefore the furniture would not be properly arranged, and there would be boxes scattered about the place. But grime was something she would abhor. He had noticed that the little office she used in her house was quite scruffy but meticulously clean.

Unless the weather was exceptionally hot, she would probably arrive in a coat, but would she mind if there were no coat hooks in the house? In fact, what would she be wearing? Prior to Elizabeth, clothes had been of little interest to him –

by definition they were superficial. It was more important to know who a person was than what they wore. Protocols were necessary, of course; he thoroughly approved of everyone in an orchestra wearing the same formal dress because any expression of individuality needed to shine through the music, not through appearances. But in the café he had noticed her blue suit and how its sharp tailoring lay across her shoulders, the cut of the wide lapels against the cream of her blouse, which dazzled him. No, he would not bother with coat hooks. If it was a warm day she would take off her jacket and he would lay it over the arms of a chair.

He dreaded the trip to the florist in the morning. He would ask about the flowers they had in stock, and they would ask what type of occasion it was. He would reply that it was a special one and he might even blush because he would mention the names of a few flowers he had learnt – then the woman in the shop would assume he was knowledgeable, but would soon find out that he wasn't.

It was ridiculous to think of going to the shops to buy some special food. He had to keep reminding himself that she was only dropping by for half an hour. And besides, how could he possibly prepare anything that would be fit for her consumption? But then she said it would be a busy day for her, so perhaps he could buy a flan, or some pastries or some cake, just in case she had no time for lunch. She would know immediately whether everything was fresh, so he would have to go to the bakery on the morning of her arrival.

He approached the steps of his house as she would be doing the day after tomorrow. Unlocking the front door, he urged himself to think sensibly. She might cancel her visit. If she didn't, she might stay for just a minute or two before rushing on to somewhere else. Why would she want to be with him for any length of time? She had been furious with him on the station platform. They had met only once since, a cup of coffee between acquaintances and their fleeting visit to the National Gallery.

Closing the door behind him, he tripped on the doormat while wiping his feet and dropped his keys. He was thinking about a painting, and it wasn't *Whistlejacket*.

12

Helena had largely kept to the strict revision schedule she had announced to Elizabeth at the breakfast table several weeks ago. The lapses had been when the weather was fine and she had gone for local walks around the hills and down by the river. And she had allowed herself two complete days off when her father had given her a lift to London and she had visited her friend Philippa in Chelsea who was having a shocking time. This morning, there was nothing to distract her because the rain was pelting the window in front of her bedroom desk, the water shimmering down the glass, obscuring the view of the garden. For her English literature revision, she was poring over *Troilus and Cressida*, not because she thought it was a good play but merely to impress. If everyone could quote freely from Shakespeare's more famous plays, it would be fun to pepper a conversation with something from a more obscure one. *Modest doubt is call'd the beacon of the wise*, she read. The iambic rhythm chimed melodically with the rain clattering on the window.

But was it true that wisdom depended on having at least a little doubt? It didn't seem to be the case with her father, for example. At many of his parties, people had told her how clever he was to have built his advertising empire – they hadn't used the term wisdom specifically, but they attributed his success to his tenacity and his renowned ability to judge which advertising jingles would persuade consumers to part with their money. It was wisdom of sorts, but he never shared a shred of doubt about anything as far as she could see.

The same was true of her mother. When people commented on the magnificence of the garden or the house or indeed her own magnificence, they invariably mentioned how wise she was in any social situation; she could hush a room when she entered yet simultaneously put everyone at ease. But she too never seemed to have doubts about anything. That was not to say there wasn't something changed in her mother recently. She'd been behaving rather oddly. Was it the committee meeting she attended in London? It seemed quite high powered, but that wouldn't be enough to rattle her, surely? She could hold her own with anyone. It could be the job, though, because recently she had come back from London, not flustered exactly, but evasive and clearly with something occupying her mind.

A gust of wind thudded another slew of rain against the window, making her duck as if a bucket of water had been thrown towards her.

And how about Miranda? How did wisdom and doubt weigh with her? She was an interesting case because she had a good amount of wisdom but also doubts about lots of things. She would sometimes start to say something, then have doubts about saying it. When Philippa was expelled from school the previous year, it was she who had encouraged Helena to stay in touch with her. But just the other day, Miranda had made her doubts about Philippa abundantly clear. They had been sitting in her kitchen having coffee. There had been the usual godmotherly advice about the importance of Helena keeping up her music practice and 'knuckling down' to her holiday revision without distractions.

'Elizabeth tells me you've been to see Philippa twice in the last fortnight?' Miranda said.

'Yes, she doesn't like her new school and she's being pestered by Quentin, a boy she knows. I'm the only one of her old friends from school who's kept in touch with her. We talk. She needs me, I think.'

'Well, that's very thoughtful of you. Just like Elizabeth. And her parents? Can't she talk to them?'

'They're away a lot.'

'Ah, yes, someone mentioned her parents are in the music business. Not your kind of music, as I understand it. Apparently, Magnus knows them through his work. They sound rather bohemian. A few things have been said.'

Helena had been about to ask what had been said, but she decided not to be drawn into a conversation where she might let something slip about Philippa and Quentin. It would shock Miranda, and if Miranda was shocked, Elizabeth would hear of it and be shocked as well. Presumably both of them privately accepted it was only normal for teenagers to acquire a little alcohol occasionally and that smoking was harmless if it was just for a bit of experimental fun. And they had both more or less advised, in their roundabout way, that a kiss and a cuddle could be affectionate and perfectly acceptable provided nothing went further than that. Phillipa and Quentin's experimentation was far beyond such cosy boundaries. Philippa had described everything in graphic detail – her alcohol consumption with Quentin seemed to match the excesses of Magnus's parties, the smoking was not wholly of tobacco, and the relationship was rather more than a kiss and a cuddle; it was the 'whole way', as the expression went, and then some, seemingly.

None of this shocked Helena. All her friends at school talked of little else. Anne, Susan and Virginia all thought her odd for not hankering after the same thrills, while Louise and Claudia always teased her for being a goody-goody because she preferred her cello and her studies to any fascination with boys. There had even been a conversation with her friend Isabelle who wanted to know whether Helena was more interested in girls. If she hadn't been considered so attractive, or had been weak in some way, she would have been bullied. Thankfully, she had found ways to earn respect. She had learnt to laugh with everyone else whenever she was the butt of jokes about being a bluestocking – and she was careful never to appear aloof when it came to lurid discussions about bodies or banned behaviours. Having served canapés at her father's parties since the age of four, she was used to the alcohol and the smoke and had certainly seen one or two things that a four-year-old should never see. Physical excesses in themselves no longer surprised her and seemed rather incidental. Being blasé about excess was her saving grace at school; instead of being regarded as naïve, her friends seemed to admire her for being so worldly-wise.

It was as if the world existed on two different levels. She could happily listen to Phillipa gossiping all day about her carnal escapades with Quentin, but they seemed trivial compared to things on a more important level entirely. She had asked Philippa what she really felt about Quentin. Of course there was pleasure in the physical side of things, but what of the deeper things that could make pleasure complete – the loyalty and trust, the imperishable respect – love, in fact? Philippa had looked a little blank, lying back in her bed rather decadently, propped up with several pillows and still in her nightie even though it was nearly noon. So Helena had explained what she truly believed – that the key in life was to experience and understand those deeper feelings before the more superficial ones could make proper sense.

'You've been reading too many books,' Philippa had joked. 'Or listening to your mother too much. I do understand all those things, but the world is full of Quentins – particularly at our age.' But then Philippa had confessed the full details of her anxiety about Quentin, who was pressuring her into things she didn't want to do.

'Then you mustn't do them,' Helena said.

'But then he'll leave. Oh, you're right, of course, but I can't help it.' Then Philippa had dropped her bombshell. 'I probably need someone like Adam, who you got rid of.'

The starkness of the phrase was like being hit. Even worse, Philippa listed Adam's qualities one by one – that he was rather reserved, yes, but decent and considerate, thoughtful, and quite as attractive as Quentin. She said the quiet ones were the best and lasted longer. And to compound it all, Philippa had ended by asking for Adam's address. Helena had almost reached for her bag to retrieve her address book containing the details for Adam's parents in Holland Park. Instead, she told Philippa she would try to find her address book when she got home.

Philippa had overstepped the mark in other ways too. The phrase 'listening to your mother too much' rankled. She always tried to mask the degree of need and worship she had for her mother in case people thought her immature – usually by being flippant or pretending not to care. But the worship would endure and the need remain hidden; it was like the devout praying in secret to avoid appearing too devoted.

The rainstorm was easing, the rivulets on the glass diminishing. She read the line from *Troilus and Cressida* again. It might not be wise to express doubts about whether she had treated Adam unfairly.

She could see the garden again as the sky brightened. What had her mother said? That it was best not to 'go round breaking hearts'. The wise thing would be to wait and see, to think carefully about whether she had erred.

13

Elizabeth ran an uncommonly extravagant bath. She was pleased with her decision to have a day to herself for once. It felt rather daring to be doing something just for fun. She would have a leisurely breakfast, then drive to Miranda's to drop off some plants before going on to the station to catch the train to Paddington and then the underground to Gloucester Road. From there, she would walk to Adam's house, which she would briefly survey and provide him with some ideas. That would take half an hour or so, she imagined, leaving her time later in the afternoon to visit the V&A and to explore Biba, the shop that Helena kept raving about.

She had strict rules for her bath. It should not be excessively deep, and once the bath was run, she never allowed herself the luxury of pouring more hot water in from the huge steel taps. It was a frugal habit she had adopted soon after the war and had kept up ever since. But this morning, having already languished in deep water for many minutes, she had indulged herself and leant forward to run more hot water before submerging herself again, her body supine beneath the foam, stretched in warmth like a cat. In the billowing steam she closed her eyes to take stock.

She thought about the telephone call she had made to

Adam the day before yesterday. By her standards, the decision to make the call was impetuous – a simple reaction to having had one of the vilest arguments to date with Magnus. But there were other reasons. She had concluded that generally she needed to get out more, to be less occupied with the running of the house and provide more space and time for herself. It was perfectly rational, she assured herself.

Miranda had become increasingly insistent during recent weeks that Elizabeth needed to change her outlook. 'You need more oxygen, Elizabeth – you need to breathe' was the strange expression Miranda had used on more than one occasion.

Elizabeth sank further into the bath's heat, the water covering her chin. Unfortunately the hot tap was dripping. It was a slow drip, the worst kind, because you had to wait longer for the next drip. She could sit up and lean forward to turn the tap, but that would chill her shoulders, so she attempted to turn the tap deftly with her toes, but they lacked the strength. She stayed still with her chin in the steamy water, thinking about Miranda's advice.

The many phrases Miranda had used poured into her mind with each drip of the tap. You need to live a little, Elizabeth! Be kind to yourself. Smile more and people will smile at you. It will make you feel good. Nothing sudden, mind, nothing to cause dismay. Oxygen! Perhaps you could move with the times a little. Make life a little more comfortable. You could wear tights, for example, rather than all that paraphernalia. Clean lines and comfort. *No*! not mutton dressed as lamb, Elizabeth! The wrong view, a man's view. On your own terms, always. Just a little comfort that's all. Not like Celia, not like Shirley, coquettish. To be free, not lax. For *you*! It'll be like putting a houseplant out in the sun.

The tap dripping. Which was the lesser of two evils, the drip-dripping or cold shoulders?

And where has it all led? she thought, leaning forward quickly to run more hot water before wrenching the tap closed and submerging herself once more.

It had led to her telephoning Adam. She had thought that if she was to experiment with the idea of going to London purely for leisure, she may as well tie the trip in with a visit to his house as he had requested. Or suggested, or whatever it was. It could do no harm.

She had been reluctant to telephone Adam from the house because she had heard a click on the line the previous week when she was making her hair appointment. She didn't think Magnus would stoop to spying on her calls, but she decided a call from a public telephone would be prudent. She couldn't very well make the call from the telephone box on the Holt because people noticed that sort of thing. Someone would have asked her at a party, accusingly, why she was in a telephone box. So when she was in the town, she went to the phone box by the parish church, with a scarf over her head and wearing sunglasses even though it was a cloudy day. There was no reply when she rang, so she went off to do her shopping before repeating the rigmarole of disguising herself and returning to the telephone box a second time, which was hateful because it reeked of tobacco. She hadn't said very much to Adam because she wasn't sure whether she had enough coins, and she had to remind herself that there was no need to be talkative. It was just a call to say that, as it so happened, she would be in London in two days' time and could visit briefly to provide some advice on his house if that was still required.

She had put the phone down very deliberately, blowing her cheeks out as she stared at the receiver in its cradle. She had been short and to the point. For days she had considered whether to make the call at all, on walks along the towpath by the river, and up on the chalk hills above it, but it was done now.

* * *

'Those look fabulous,' Miranda said as she took the plants from the boot of Elizabeth's car. 'And look at you! A new coat and you're wearing eyeshadow! Have you time for a coffee to tell me all about it before you go to the station?'

Normally Elizabeth would have followed Miranda through to the kitchen and they would have talked while making the coffee. But she stayed in the living room, looking out at the garden, concerned by Miranda's obvious approval of her appearance. She didn't want to stand out, to be gawped at. It felt wrong.

When Miranda came back in she put down the coffee and sat down on the sofa, patting the space next to her and nodding towards the coat draped over a chair. 'So, go on, tell me all about the coat then.'

'I saw it yesterday in the window of that new boutique that's opened next to the town hall. I liked the colour. I'm not overly fond of cobalt or powder blue, but this one was exactly right, halfway between the two. As for why I bought it, I've been thinking a great deal over the last few days.

'I had a terrible argument with Magnus on Sunday evening, the worst ever, I think. It started in the usual way. He was carping on about some trivial mistakes I'd made, the usual list of faults. There was a mix-up with the order from the wine merchants – he had specified six bottles of Noilly Prat and a dozen of Cinzano and I had accidentally reversed the numbers. When I said it was all vermouth at the end of the day and gets mixed in with gin and God knows what else, he became angry. Usually I stay calm, but it ended up with me mentioning the blonde hairs I found recently on his barathea suit, and the little missive signed by a Felicity, which I had found in an inner pocket when I was sorting the dry cleaning. It had lots of exclamation marks with those little circles people use nowadays instead of dots, or points or stops or whatever they're called. He wasn't defensive at all, and boomed out very huffily, "May I remind you of our arrangement ..." He proceeded with the usual tirade: he earns the money, I do the house. I nearly went the whole hog and said that from now on there would be a maximum of six parties a year and a dinner party every two months. But I didn't. I merely said that I would keep everything going as long as I could have some free time to myself occasionally. He had the gall to say that yes, that would be all right, as long as I didn't make a fool of myself. What's that supposed to mean?

'Anyway, that's what I've decided. I'm going to be myself more. I will go to the places I wish to visit. I will buy a new coat if I wish to. I'm sorry for being cross, Miranda – I'm not angry with *you*.'

'But you don't realise what marvellous news it is, Elizabeth. It's exactly what I've been trying to say. You deserve better and you must stick with it. So what are you going to do today?'

'I'll go to the V&A and idle my way around South Kensington. It will be nice just to stroll, to feel free to go for a coffee or a little lunch maybe. And visit some interesting shops – I certainly want to investigate Biba and find out what all the fuss is about.'

'It sounds delightful, and I wish I was coming with you. Perhaps next time. You'll need a chaperone looking ravishing like that. If I was that way inclined, I'd ravish you myself. Men want to undo you – I've heard them say it.'

'Oh, stop it!' Elizabeth said, smiling bashfully as she got up to refill their coffee cups.

'And the make-up, Elizabeth, tell me about that. It's very well done – wearing it without seeming to, if you see what I mean.'

'Looking in the mirror the other day I began to see lines, proper lines.'

'Don't be ridiculous. You don't look much older than Helena. Your skin's the same.'

Elizabeth fell silent at the mention of Helena, who she had turned away that morning when she had come bouncing along as usual for their early morning conversation. Locked in her bathroom of steam, Elizabeth had said they could talk at breakfast instead, and she heard Helena's feet padding away disconsolately along the corridor.

'Don't look sad, Elizabeth, it was meant to be a compliment.'

'I'm sorry – you made me think of Helena, who played some rather mournful pieces of Schubert after breakfast earlier. I wanted to thank you, by the way, for encouraging her with her cello. Yesterday morning she practised for nearly three hours without being asked. I could hear her very clearly because I was sitting in the drawing room reading the newspaper and the fugue she was playing flowed and filled around me, making me happy and sad at the same time, which always seems to be the way with Bach. I paid very little attention to the newspaper. My eyes were going through the motion of moving down the columns and along the lines of print, but I saw nothing. I remembered nothing of all the news and the things one's meant to read, the opinions and the dead thoughts. Instead I just let the Bach flood in. When Helena came out of the music room I said how much I'd enjoyed it. She was annoyed that I had been listening, and said that the notes were not all perfect, though they seemed so to me. In fact, she scolded me, and frowned at me for listening, and she mentioned your name. She said she was practising for Miranda – she respected her godmother and would practise as she was told. So it is you I have to thank.'

'Not at all. It's a pleasure to see her growing up. She's going to be formidable. She told me the other day that she had put Magnus in his place. Can you imagine that?'

'Yes, I can. She's not frightened of him in the slightest. She's the only person he ever listens to, but I've never turned it to my advantage. I could easily ask Helena to persuade him to behave differently, but it would be wrong. She mustn't take sides.'

'You're never going to leave him, are you?'

'No. You have to live with your choices, lie in your bed and all that. The mistake I made in life was before Magnus, before my clean slate, my vow to wipe it all away and start again. Life with Magnus was not so bad when we first met. I had Helena to replace the son I lost.'

'Do you ever wonder about him?'

'I try not to. Making a mistake doesn't mean it has to stalk you all the time. Best to keep things locked away. But yes, when I fail, I do think of him, want to find him. Can we talk about something else?'

Miranda clapped her hands and stood up. 'Yes, you need to be off to London,' she said, helping Elizabeth into her coat. 'London expects you in your new coat! You won't be alarmed if someone strikes up a conversation, will you? Not everyone's a cad. Some people just want to sit and talk. It's not a sin, you know. I hope you have a lovely time and I want to hear all about it when you get back.'

Miranda stood by the door watching Elizabeth walk to her car. 'Nice tights, by the way,' she shouted.

Miranda was incorrigible sometimes but meant no harm, Elizabeth thought as she drove to the station in her Triumph Herald, crunching the gears because she was still learning the intricacies of its synchromesh.

* * *

On the station platform, waiting for the train, Elizabeth found herself standing in the same spot that Adam had four weeks previously. She edged a few steps to her left.

There was a wasp. First it buzzed round her and thumped into her beret, which she had bought to match her coat. She thought that was the end of the wasp, but it soon returned and she tapped it away with the back of her hand. *It must be my lemon soap*, she thought.

It was like the other wasp, the unmentionable one she didn't want to think about, darting into her thoughts each time before she flicked it away.

The train arrived at last. It was not many years ago that she would have stood here surrounded by clouds of steam, the smell of soot and the screech of steel amid the whistles and the hissing. But now it was a shiny diesel that approached the platform with quiet mechanical efficiency. She should be grateful, she thought, for there being any train at all because the little branch line that joined the main line into Paddington had been spared in the Beeching cuts.

Soon she was hurtling towards London, sitting by the window and staring out at the smokestacks and cooling towers of Slough power station. She should have been delighted to have a day to herself, but it seemed irresponsible to be travelling to London for no particular purpose. Normally she would be sitting on the train, slightly nervous about one of her committee meetings. There was no such meeting today, yet her shoulders were tight and stiff. She sat back to relax them, trying to savour her new-found freedom and Miranda's cheerful words of encouragement.

It had been perfectly reasonable for Miranda to ask about the trip to London, but her reply had been dishonest. Just a stroll around South Kensington, taking in the V&A and Biba. There was no lie, no fib, but she omitted to mention a visit to a certain house. But that was all it was! Half an hour, perhaps, to look at the design of the place and what might be done to improve it, to help Adam, just as she would help

Helena whenever she came to have a place of her own. She bit her lip.

She was about to swat the air as if there was a wasp again, but the military-looking gentleman sitting next to her would think her strange.

Staring out of the window, she tried to focus on the houses and their back gardens ticking by, imagining the people who lived there, their joys and sorrows. Their little guilts too, the envy of a neighbour's new car, a forgotten birthday, insulting someone's choice of newspaper. For years her life had been different, avoiding all the little guilts, the everyday ones, in compensation for her one great guilt: abandoning her child all those years ago, which could have sapped all her energy if she had allowed it. That was why she always strived for harmony, never sinning or causing offence.

She didn't want to think of sinning. The houses and the back gardens continued to flash by, along with her misgivings: her quarrel with Magnus, the vanity of her new coat, refusing to tell Miranda the reason for going to London. Half an hour's advice, that was all.

The train juddered across a set of points and it made her lurch inside, a darker thought crossing her mind as she saw a building site with a man wielding a sledgehammer. Was Adam entirely sane if he could switch so rapidly from one mood to another, from a lunged kiss on a station platform one moment to a steady calmness at the next meeting as if nothing had happened? The control was perfect, like a studied letter. Yet she felt completely safe; her trust in him seemed innate.

As the train picked up speed, her thoughts gathered with

it, thinking about Adam and a bond she was unable to understand, this yearning to protect. She put the flat of her hand across her cheek, glaring out of the window again in case the colonel or the brigadier or whoever he was should see that she was hot and use it as a ploy to strike up a conversation. He would say the guard must have turned the heating up, and then all the usual questions would follow, whether she had a nice day planned in London and that it looked as if the train might be late.

Soon after arriving at Paddington, she was on the Circle line rocking from side to side on her way to Gloucester Road. She looked down the carriage through the fug of smoke, and then at the cigarette ends ground between the slats of the wooden floor. She should have taken a taxi because now she would smell of tobacco. Adam didn't smoke; he might disapprove. She would think of something else, the man behind his newspaper, the woman with her knitting, the vicar who had just taken out his pocket watch. Would she be late? But she couldn't be, because she hadn't given a precise time to arrive; it was not an appointment – or an assignation, she kept reminding herself.

With a sigh, she willed herself to be distracted by something else, so she glanced along the row of passengers again, wondering what all the fuss was about with the nineteen sixties, this new age that was meant to be fresh and exciting with its shiny newness and Wilson's white heat of technology. None of it was here in this carriage, that was certain. It was drab, with badly printed dresses, sturdy shoes, and shapeless cardigans. The contents of the Sunday colour supplements were fiction.

She didn't want to be seen wandering the streets looking lost when she got out at Gloucester Road, so she took out her street map to memorise again the walk she would take from the station to his house. What if she were seen by someone from the Holt, who happened to be in London for the day? Where were you going, Elizabeth? What were you doing? Would she say it was private, it was personal business and none of theirs? Or would she say she was visiting a friend to provide some advice, the colours of the carpets and the curtains, that sort of thing, just for half an hour?

The train rumbled out of Notting Hill Gate. She closed her eyes. Adam would merely offer her a cup of tea and share a sample book of Baker's fabric designs, or Liberty prints perhaps. They would sit together on a tea chest or whatever furniture he had managed to improvise, and leaf through the book of fabric samples cut with pinking shears, feeling the folds of the fabric, and he would say thank you and put the sample book away, discuss the weather perhaps, or the Tube journey, or her train timetable, and nothing else. And she would look at the sample book, compliment him on the tea and advise him to think again about his choice of furniture, temporary or otherwise.

She felt conspicuous marching the streets of Kensington and realised she was still wearing her beret. She stopped under a tree to fold up the felt carefully, swapping the hat for the headscarf she had in her bag. She walked on, her steps clipping out the rhythm of her recurring thoughts; she deserved some solace, a salve for herself for her own pleasure. *But it's only advice I am to bring, my wisdom offered freely. Stay calm!* Try pressing the air down with your splayed hands towards the pavement flags as you walk and take a gasp of breath. Keep walking steadily and straight or you'll be conspicuous, and someone will notice you. Imagine the shame! To slip up and be the subject of gossip; she would be at a party and people would *know*. There would be triumphant glances; she was not flawless after all and not the prude they thought – the same as us, we told you so, the mighty fallen at last from some pedestal, off her high horse. Whistlejacket again, shivering in the cold or sweating in the heat, his urge to race with his scared eyes, abandoned in galloping speed. Ridiculous! Keep walking, steadily please, merely a day in London, visiting a house, to go over it, the layout, the décor, the roof, the floors, the colours of the walls, and whatever should furnish the whole, the lie of the land, the riddling of a fire perhaps.

She found herself walking in the middle of the paving slabs, trying to avoid the lines between them with her feet, a silly habit she had drummed out of Helena years ago. Surely it was doubtful he would slip up again. No, there would be no menace, no attic, no cold damp cellar. A friend only, needing only advice. But then the wasp returned, the thought thrilling her bones, the shiver of heat, the illicit deliciousness of it, daring her and making her mouth dry as if it were stuttering and uttering unspeakable sighs, with an arched back, quailing with a hushed rush of breath and subsiding afterwards in silence.

She was two streets away from the house and needed to stop to compose herself, to draw breath against the fluttering inside her. She stood in front of a wall opposite some houses that showed no signs of life. It was a quiet spot where nobody would see her pausing to take out her compact case, checking her eyes in the mirror and applying a dab of powder.

She struck a bargain with herself then, took a vow, that the moment she snapped the case shut the sound of it would banish all the ludicrous thoughts. The wasp would be tapped away and gone.

When she arrived two minutes later in front of the black gloss door, she was completely composed, ready for her fleeting visit, to offer some plain advice in the plain light of day.

She rapped the brass dolphin twice; very businesslike it was, the second rap louder than the first.

14

There was nothing more he could do now, Adam thought, collapsing into an armchair. Elizabeth had said she would arrive in the early afternoon and he set about thinking about what time that meant. It was now noon, so she could arrive in the next few minutes, theoretically. When did an afternoon end? Perhaps at five? Say six, so the midpoint is three o'clock. Therefore, she would arrive some time over the next three hours unless there was some delay, in which case she would have to find a telephone box. He got up to walk over to the telephone, to make sure the receiver was properly in place; it wouldn't do for her to find the engaged tone. It would annoy her.

He certainly wasn't going to sit down and wait for three whole hours, but it was a relief to rest just for a few moments. Throughout the morning and the whole of the previous day he had been rushing around the house, cleaning the rooms, arranging the furniture and running various errands.

If she completely forgot about her visit or phoned to cancel it, his work would not be wasted. He would derive some satisfaction from having made the place more respectable. He had been very methodical with his list of tasks, the length of which had alarmed him initially. But it was like most things that are daunting; it was sensible to break them down into their component parts and attack them one by one. Sometimes a music score could be daunting when you first saw it, with its complicated notation, the clefs and the quavers, the sharps and the flats, the trills and the octaves strewn across the page, but working at it bit by bit meant the whole could always be strung together eventually. It was the same with maths or physics – solving the problems and finding the proofs was hard work sometimes, but if you analysed each element one at a time you could find the right result. It was a question of exploring all the boundaries and letting logic prevail.

But Elizabeth was different. He couldn't explain her away or understand why he was sapped of energy, unable to think properly or make simple decisions. One moment he would be darting around, completing his tasks, only to become listless the next, wondering what to do.

The vase of flowers was not positioned centrally on the side table, so he got up to slide it across a little, admiring the flowers again, which he had arranged in the way the woman in the shop had advised. He wanted to see the surprise on Elizabeth's face when she saw the flowers – that he had learnt from her about colour and how flowers should stand in a vase that was of a complementary shape. Even if the arrangement was not quite right, she wouldn't criticise; she would merely suggest how it could be improved, whispering her wisdom.

He missed her and had become preoccupied with calculating a series of losses and gains. The greatest gain would be to earn her trust to such a degree that they could share a bliss he could only imagine because he had no experience of it.

When the dream took hold it felt pure and nothing could sully it, not the difference in age nor the practicalities of her marriage, nor the fact that he may have already nullified his chances because of that kiss. But the dream was unrealisable without some risk of loss – it could never be achieved without declaring his hand to some extent and he knew that could mean losing everything. Which was better? To perpetuate their friendship by not giving a hint of his true feelings, or risk losing her forever because of the offence he might cause by laying his cards on the table again.

He had chosen the former. The prospect of never seeing her again was a far more powerful force than the ridiculous fantasies that occasionally carried him away. If he behaved innocuously, there was a chance he could at least earn her friendship or even her affection. But if he relapsed, that would be the end of it, he would never have the chance to be by her side, hear her speak and see her smile.

It was simpler that way, merely to cherish her. It had clarity and meant he could avoid those other thoughts of burying his face in her hair or the crook of her neck. Such thoughts were an insult to her, given his belief that she was incapable of sin. It was unreasonable of Magnus to take her for granted, but her vows would be sacrosanct, he was certain of that.

He would settle for her mere presence and wouldn't collapse. He would be the picture of innocence, the welcoming host, taking a leaf out of her book, composed and beyond reproach. It would be enough to have her walking around the house, looking at its walls, breathing its air. He would suffocate if he imagined any more than that – the thought that it was warm today and that she would take off her coat, or loosen the top button of her blouse, kick off her shoes even. But that would not be wise; the floorboards had nails.

He got up and went to the kitchen to pour himself a glass of water. He put the glass down on the wooden draining board and stared at the Belfast sink still gleaming after his efforts with the baking soda the previous evening.

He went to the front door to rehearse how he would greet her, shaking her hand and taking her coat if she had one. One of his errands had been to the ironmonger's to buy a brass hook on which to hang it, next to his. Walking back to the sitting room, he looked at the rug in the passageway. What would she think of that? It covered a broken tile, but which would she find worse, a cracked tile or an unpleasant piece of carpet? It was hard to tell.

One moment he would despair because everything seemed wrong, the pictures, the doors, the very rooms themselves, none of it fit for her arrival. Then the next he would remember her kindness and that she was bound to understand.

As for the net curtains – what would she think of those? They had come with the house and he hadn't known whether to remove them. They were hanging on a wire across the divide in the sash windows.

He had just started to unhook the wire at one end when he saw her approaching along the path to the door.

The apparition paralysed him for an instant and then he hastily re-hooked the curtain. It wouldn't do for her to think he had been looking out for her, besotted.

For two days he had imagined the exact moment of her arrival but was unprepared for the bold rap-rap of the brass dolphin and the customary squeak of the hinge as he swung the door open for her.

Hopefully she hadn't noticed his little catch of breath. She looked purer than ever, but rather guarded in her headscarf, which she slid off and handed to him with her coat after they had shaken hands and exchanged pleasantries about her journey in the sunshine.

He didn't stare at her hair springing over her shoulders when she slipped off the headscarf, which lay warm in his hands. It was thrilling, the utter delight of her presence, the relief of standing next to her, talking and smiling. It settled him immediately and made it easy to be cheerfully polite.

'Come on into my humble abode,' he said. 'It's not much, and you'll see there's much to do. You'll already be busy with ideas, I'm sure.'

At the entrance to the living room he stepped back and ushered her in like an accomplished estate agent.

'But it's delightful!' Elizabeth said. 'What a well-proportioned room, and the floorboards are superb. You could renovate those and then you wouldn't need that Persian rug. Rugs like that can look homely when they're slightly worn, but let's face it, that one's past its best.'

Elizabeth walked around the room, tapping some of the walls and peering into a large cupboard in the corner, commenting on which should be his immediate priorities and which could wait. 'One should never be in a hurry to do everything at once,' she said. 'These shutters, for example, are in a terrible state. Lots of people just rip them out, but they're original and will look wonderful when they've been properly restored. They're perfectly serviceable for now, and you can sort them out after the more urgent tasks such as the rug.'

Elizabeth walked into the tiny dining room next to the main living room. 'Now here you have a big decision,' she said. 'You need to get a surveyor in to check, but I think you could knock this wall down and have one spacious room rather than two small ones. It would work very well – the mouldings in both rooms are the same and in very good condition.'

They walked into the kitchen.

'Oh!' Elizabeth said. 'This isn't a difficult decision. I think you'll have to rip the whole thing out and start again. It smells a little musty. Those cupboards are not very well made and certainly not original. The recess is lovely, you could fit a little Aga in there. And you would get more light into the place by making that window bigger. It could be a very cosy kitchen in the evenings once the strip lights have been taken out. You could settle for tall lamps with big shades – nothing too elaborate, mind you, because it's a practical room at the end of the day. How much cooking will you be doing?'

'Not much, I suppose, I've never really learnt much about cooking.'

'No cooking?'

Elizabeth seemed to check her expression, which changed quickly from one of initial shock to something much more considered, something sympathetic rather than disapproving. He could read her thoughts: she was thinking he shouldn't be owning a kitchen if no one had taught him to cook; it was a shame.

She became subdued, so he led them out of the kitchen and tried to lighten the conversation, looking first at the little scullery at the back of the house. 'Not even you will have many ideas about this little room. And I can't imagine me doing much in the way of laundry.'

As they walked to the foot of the stairs, he said, 'I realise the whole place is probably rather compact by your standards, and not very grand, but you've given me some excellent ideas. Thank you.'

'Nonsense, it's a lovely house! You could make it into a real home if you want to. But you need to be practical, Adam. It's always important to be practical.'

'Anyway, that's all there is downstairs,' he said.

Then the momentousness of the imminent walk up the stairs struck him. The staircase was small, but to him it suddenly appeared cavernous. The steep steps seemed to narrow upwards into the shadowiness. He could hear a scaffolding team working outside in the street, clanking the poles onto a lorry, the shouts and metallic thuds seeming very loud.

During the two days before Elizabeth's visit, he hadn't allowed himself to dwell on the moment they might climb the stairs. He had locked it out of his mind because she would merely be taking a tour of the house; it was a fact.

He prayed that she might interrupt the awkward stillness, but she had fallen silent too.

Recovering his estate agent's demeanour, he stretched out his hand and said, 'After you.' He had no idea of the etiquette. Perhaps for climbing stairs he should have led, because now she was ascending gently and was on the fifth stair, his eyes level with her ankles.

He swallowed, unable to move his feet, but then gathered himself to follow her up, and said, 'Of course there's not much I can do about the steepness of the stairs. You need to tread carefully – there's the banister if you need it.'

She did not need the banister, but continued her measured ascent and said, 'Yes, they are somewhat steep, but there's nothing that can be done about that.'

They arrived at the small landing at the top of the stairs, where she gathered her breath, brushed the side of her dress down and slid her hand over her hair as if recomposing herself.

'Lead on,' she said, with what seemed to be a forced smile, something she didn't mean to say. So he led, first to the bathroom, which she did not enter but stood on the threshold and looked in. She said nothing other than it needed to be ripped out like the kitchen and that she was not particularly fond of linoleum.

There were three other rooms upstairs – the main bedroom overlooking the street and two much smaller ones described in the estate agent's details as second and third bedrooms. Adam stood back while Elizabeth peered into them.

'Well, they're very compact.' she said as if struggling for words.

It was only a few steps further to the front bedroom, and neither spoke above what seemed to be the deafening noise of Elizabeth's heels on the floorboards and the thud of his brogues.

When they came to the narrow doorway, they stood side

by side, peering into the bedroom. He wondered what she was thinking. Was she about to march towards the window to ask whether there was a nice view onto the street? Or should he walk in first, remarking indifferently that there was not much to see in there before marching promptly out again? He couldn't find the words to squeeze past her into the room. She seemed transfixed as well and the only sound was their breathing. Then, just as he leant forward to enter the room, she did too and they spun into each other. They stood absolutely still and entwined, Elizabeth's face buried in his shirt and his head resting on hers with its terrifying warmth.

* * *

When Elizabeth woke two hours later, she tried to sit up, but she was trapped by arms enfolding her that were not hers. She pressed the back of her head firmly into the pillow as the reality sank in. Still asleep, Adam lay motionless, other than one of his arms flopping away from her shoulder as she tried to free herself a little.

The shock came in steady waves: how she got there, what had happened, the rapture, whether she would be late getting home, and the surprise of having slept during the day. She never slept in the day – she had eight hours solid sleep every night; it kept her skin youthful and her conscience clear, which would now no longer be the case. She looked at the bentwood chair by the wall with her tights draped over the curve of its dark wood, her dress cast idly over the rattan seat, and her shoes and the rest of her clothes scattered across the floor. The untidiness was wild, yet she felt strangely complete.

Slowly, she extricated herself from Adam's other arm and leant on one elbow, collecting her thoughts as she looked down at him. The strange half smile he wore deep in sleep was the same as Ralph's, with the same neat chin. But the physical resemblance was not the reason she had succumbed; it had been the similarity to Ralph's temperament, a zest for life that was not brash, the rare modesty, the attentive consideration. It made her smile.

To wake him, she tapped the neat chin more firmly than she intended, so he awoke suddenly, starting up in surprise, just as she had, his eyes blinking brightly, and then they lay silently together in a tight embrace, in the knowledge that nothing needed to be explained just yet.

Eventually, Adam said, 'You aren't cross, are you? You have no regrets?'

'I'm surprised, but no, I have no regrets. Confused as to what it will all mean, certainly. I feel happy. And you?'

'The only regret I ever had was making you so upset that time at the station. I've tried so hard not to make everything obvious.'

They lay smiling again until Adam said, 'But now I'm going to make you some tea. I should have offered it when you arrived at the house, but my mind was occupied at the time. A very poor host.'

'Thank you,' she said as they laughed, then kissed.

When Adam returned with a tray, they continued in the same frivolous tone. It was as if they had decided to make light of the step they had taken, to savour its immediacy, pushing aside the worry of considering the consequences. She mocked him for bringing a tray with cups and saucers, saying she knew he usually used mugs because she had noticed them in the cupboards and on the draining board when she was in the kitchen. 'I noticed lots of things, actually. For instance, do you always have vases of flowers dotted about the house?'

'No, I bought them this morning to make you feel more at home, but I needed a little help. The lady in the flower shop is always very friendly when I pass her on the way to the station. I asked for her advice about which flowers would be the most fragrant to brighten the place up.'

'It seems to be a habit of yours, asking ladies, as you call them, for advice?'

'No, no, you don't understand me—'

'I was joking. I do understand you – perfectly as a matter of fact,' she said, kissing him on the forehead.

* * *

It was part of her mystery, Adam thought, the puzzle sometimes of whether she was being serious or flippant, this art that befuddled him with its laughless jests and barbless comment.

'Anyway,' Elizabeth said, 'your flower lady advised you very well, suggesting the gardenias. They're a favourite of mine and Helena's.'

Mentioning Helena's name seemed to remind her of something.

'Talking of my beloved daughter, why *did* you two break off? We never got round to discussing it.'

'Oh, it was nothing serious. We didn't have an argument really, we just drifted apart through a misunderstanding.'

'A misunderstanding?' And what was this *misunderstanding*?' she said with a low growl, smiling and tapping his chin.

Adam rolled onto his back with a sigh. He had no desire to talk about Helena, but at the same time he thought about the sequence of events: if he hadn't met Helena, he would never have met Elizabeth and therefore would not be lying next to her now, beyond all hope. It was something that often occupied his mind, the way life was a concatenation of events, a series of one thing following another, a chain of causality.

'It was a misunderstanding about my age,' he said. 'It was silly really. We hadn't got to know each other very well before I came to your house. All we ever talked about properly was our music. Nothing else seemed of great interest. If we had been friends for longer, we would have had more conversations about other things, and she would soon have discovered that I had worked for my father before university and was much older than her. But she took it personally, as if I had concealed something from her, been deceitful, or even lied to her. But you see, I didn't conceal anything—'

'I'm sorry to interrupt, but what *is* your age exactly?'

'I'm twenty-two.'

Elizabeth said, 'So you were born when? In 1945?'

'Yes.'

'When is your birthday?'

'January.'

'January the …?'

'Twenty-fifth.'

'But you were born in England, here, with your parents, in London?'

'No, it turns out I wasn't. My parents have told me recently that I was adopted.'

Elizabeth's questions rose in a frenzy. She sat up, panting, clutching the bedclothes tightly up in front of her, her face contorted. She drew her knees up and lowered her forehead onto them. When she spoke into the blanket it was a muffled, guttural whisper. 'Where? Where were you born?'

'Apparently it was in France, in the war.'

'Where in France?'

'I don't know where exactly. My parents said they adopted me from an orphanage in Normandy. When they told me, I didn't ask about where I was born. It didn't seem important. Why does it matter?'

She was trembling now, her hands wrapped tightly round her head, pressing her face harder into her knees.

Stunned, he moved closer to wrap his arms around her.

'*No! Don't!*' she said, pushing him away and then, much more softly, she shook her head and smiled flatly. 'Not like that, I mean.'

'What's happened? What have I done?'

She gasped and buried her face again, repeating 'No, no!' several times, retching the words into her hands. He felt helpless, looking on in confusion, clueless about what was wrong. All he wanted was to soothe her agony with no thought to her torrent of questions and their possible meaning.

She rocked herself to and fro as if waiting for a storm to subside.

Eventually, she sat up straight and looked at him calmly. She even smiled, but differently from how she had before; it was serene, a smile of profound care, the smile reserved for Helena.

She spoke very steadily. 'This is what we're going to do. I'll turn away while you get dressed and go downstairs. I'll have a bath and join you shortly. You mustn't be upset – you've done nothing wrong – it's not your fault. I'll explain everything when I come down. Now go!'

She turned onto her front and pressed her face into the pillow as Adam got up and dressed, too dumbfounded to speak.

Sitting at the kitchen table, he waited for her, numb and empty. The water pipes in the ceiling thumped above as the bath was run. A few hours ago, the idea of Elizabeth taking a bath in broad daylight in his own house would have made him swoon. The sight of her smiling at him when he woke was already a distant memory. The thudding pipes sounded an end to it all. She was clearly convinced of several facts, even if he hadn't been informed of them yet. It was easy now to guess what they might be as he recalled the rising desperation of her questions: where was he born? When was he born? No doubt she was preparing to tell him *why* he was born. He sat staring at the table, enfeebled by disappointment, too drained to feel anything else. She had decided some new truth and he would have to wait to hear what it was, his hopes torn away.

The water pipes ceased their hammering; she would be getting dressed. He continued staring vacantly at the table, waiting for her steps on the stairs, waiting for her to come through the door, to sit down and explain, tell him what was what. It would be like a history lesson.

When she entered, her transformation was complete.

Every trace of sensuality had disappeared. She wore no make-up; her hair was wet.

As she sat down opposite him preparing to speak, he got up and said, 'I'll make you some tea – in a mug this time, not a cup.'

She smiled patiently at his little quip and said, 'I'll wait if you like, until you're sitting down again.'

'No, please,' he said, 'please carry on. I can tell it's going to be difficult.'

He set about filling the kettle, putting spoons on the worktop, pouring milk into the mugs and then returning the milk bottle to the fridge. The door sounded loud when he closed it.

'Yes, but it will be easier, Adam, if we talked properly, here at the table.'

He returned to sit opposite her and she took a breath.

'During the war, I signed up as a volunteer and was posted to Dorset for my training, helping with the preparations for D-Day. I was only seventeen, and rather foolish I suppose. I met Ralph, an army officer. You're very like him. He was not much older than you are now. I had a child ... no, stay, Adam, please—'

But he couldn't bear to sit and listen, so he leapt up and went over to the sideboard, leaning on it with his elbows, the heels of his hands in his eyes, listening to the kettle coming to the boil. It would be impossible to sit opposite her, mesmerised by her plain beauty yet having to realise that she had been conjured into something else. He wouldn't be able to look at her. His thoughts would judder between recalling the stare of her eyes in the heat of the bedroom, and now this distance, its matter-of-factness, the cold explanation.

In the silence after the kettle had boiled, Elizabeth said, 'We have to finish the conversation. Nothing's your fault ... we weren't to know. I have to tell you about it.'

He sat down opposite her again, the chair scraping.

'Ralph was killed at Arnhem in September 1944. I loved him very much. I went to pieces. Our child was born on the twenty-fifth of January 1945. In my despair I gave him up in a Normandy hospital for anonymous adoption. It has preyed on my mind ever since. It isn't just the dates and the places adding up, Adam. Everything makes sense to me now. I know you're my son as only a mother can, the way you look, the way you are.'

She pressed her hand on top of his, smiling exactly as she always did with Helena. Then she snatched her hand away, her joy turning to disgust in an instant. 'What we have done today is detestable. Monstrous. Utterly vile. We must erase it. You can do that, Adam?'

'I don't know that I can. I'm sure Normandy was a busy place after D-Day with lots of people travelling through, lots of things happening. The chaos of war. I don't know precisely where I was born in France, it could have been a different hospital to where you were. I can see you're convinced, but I don't want it to be true. You've been yearning for a son for twenty years, but I haven't been looking for a mother. My feelings for you are different. I've been consumed by you for weeks. When we were upstairs, I—'

'Stop! Please, *stop!*' Elizabeth shouted, her arm thrust out, her fingers splayed as if to obscure him.

She was trembling, and said, very quietly, 'You must never,

ever think that way again. You are my son. Do you understand? All the facts fit. Your resemblance to Ralph, the year you were born, the exact date in January, that you were adopted and where you were adopted.'

'I'm sorry, but I can't adjust that quickly—'

'You have to! You must!' Everybody will need to adjust. Not just you, but Helena, Magnus and your ... parents.'

She stumbled over the word. It was as if she saw things from his point of view for the first time, accepting that his adjustment might be very fraught – that for him, he already had parents, already had a mother. Or maybe she had stumbled because she realised that informing his parents might prove even more complicated than informing Magnus and Helena.

Gradually she became more settled as she interrogated him, trying to understand why he didn't believe her. Each time he tried to explain that he was not convinced she was his mother and that his feelings for her were quite different, she dissolved into revulsion again.

There was no anger. That they could agree to disagree so amenably made him wonder whether they might be kindred spirits after all. Their discussion circled around matters of proof, of what was beyond reasonable doubt. Elizabeth remained adamant about her version of the truth, but reluctantly conceded that he might need some time to recognise it.

'One day the proof will be easy,' he said. But when he tried to explain the scientific advances being made in the science of genetics, she was impatient.

'I know the answer already, Adam – now – not in some theoretical future,' she said. 'You're not very practical sometimes.

If you insist on finding more proof, you're going to have to find out more about your birth and your adoption. You said that your p— that Constance and Arnold will have all the necessary details? You could find everything out?'

'Yes, I could. They said that whenever I was ready, they would tell me more about my adoption.'

'Well, that's encouraging,' she said, 'at least we have a plan now. Things will be a lot simpler when everything is out in the open and everyone knows. You need to find out all the details as soon as possible to confirm the facts, not just about the adoption, but the details of the birth as well. It's probably best you don't write to me or phone me at home. I'll phone you in a few days. I have one of my committee meetings next week, so we can meet then and go through everything you've been able to find out.'

Adam imagined her speaking in the same clipped, efficient manner when she was seventeen in the war, organising supplies, ordering stock, accounting for every detail.

'Now I really must go. I'm going to be horribly late home.'

'Do you want to use the phone to let Magnus and Helena know?'

'No, I'll use a public telephone at Paddington. Find out all you can,' she said, hugging him with the same casual affection reserved for Helena. As she drew away, he wanted to hold her for longer.

She stepped back and stamped her foot. 'Don't you understand, Adam? We must forget today. We must eliminate it. Do you promise?'

He stood blinking at what he had lost and couldn't find the words to promise.

Then she recovered immediately and smiled, patting her hand on his shoulder. 'You need time to adjust. That word again. I do understand,' she said. 'I'll see you next week.'

His house was empty; she was gone. She had arrived to fill its spaces with colour, vibrancy, joy, and life itself, but now it was like a cold and empty shell. He sat in the living room until he was lost in the dark, aghast at his loss.

15

Elizabeth sat on the train home, trying to appear composed, with her hands crossed over her lap. Then the fidgeting began again; it was difficult to stop her shoes from sliding to and fro on the floor of the railway carriage. She glanced down at her feet, forcing them to stay still, and then stared out of the window, wishing she had a book to read but knowing she would not be able to concentrate if she had one.

She sat on the side of the train that didn't have a view of Slough power station so that she wouldn't be reminded of the thoughts she'd had on the way to Adam's house. Similarly, when she had left his house, she zigzagged her way to Gloucester Road station via different streets from those she had trodden on her way there. None of it worked. She was proud of her ability to banish unwanted thoughts, but it had failed on this occasion. She uncrossed her hands and crossed them again, changing which hand was on top this time, keeping her knees tightly together, sliding her feet just a few inches before sitting with her back straight in the hope of sitting still.

A businessman sat opposite her, obscured by *The Evening News* held high in front of him like a shield, the top of his thinning head just visible above the newspaper. Occasionally, the pages would rustle, and each time she would stare fixedly out of the window because she sensed that with each page turn he glanced at her, bemused perhaps by her turmoil.

But for a moment her shoulders relaxed and she was completely still. She smiled, remembering something Adam had said when he came to stay. It was a dinner party with the Cartwrights and the new people at the bottom of the Holt, Paul and Serena. Magnus was voicing his disapproval of the government's socialist agenda and its plans to relax the criminal law. It resulted in a very uneasy silence around the table because Serena and Paul were clearly of a more liberal persuasion. The ensuing discussion became uncomfortably heated. Without appearing to interfere, Adam stepped in to smooth everything over, remarking that absolutes were a useful concept, but everything was relative at the end of the day. She couldn't remember exactly what he had said about the relative seriousness of different crimes, but it had restored harmony to the dinner table. Normally she felt comfortable with absolutes; they made life simpler, but she could appreciate the benefits of relativity. No, she thought, that was something different, Einstein in fact. If everything was relative, her betrayal of Magnus a few hours earlier at Adam's house was somehow less of a sin than the other unmentionable one, which made her sweat each time she thought of it. She pressed her hand to her forehead and could see out of the corner of her eye that the man with the newspaper was looking at her, so she stared even more intently out of the window, frowning with all the terms juggling in her head: relativity, relativism, relationships. And relatives: a daughter, a mother, a son. A son! She smiled again.

She stared at the houses darting by. Washing was hanging in a couple of the back gardens, and she quailed at the memory of her tights draped over the bentwood chair. The repugnance at her sin alternated with the enchantment of finding Adam. It was like a light flashing or a clock ticking. Of course he was her son. When they had sat at the kitchen table to discuss what to do, his calm rationality was identical to Ralph's, delivered with the same furrowed brow.

She could tell that her son wasn't perfect – nobody was – there were many things she would set about improving once all the dust had settled. The ideas she had given him for sorting out his house were a minor matter. Much more important would be certain things to do with himself, such as his rather scruffy appearance at times and his posture – the way he slumped in a chair for instance. And he needed to walk and stand with less of a stoop; it was a common fault taller people acquired from having to duck through small doorways or avoid the low beams of a cottage roof. And she was not convinced that an engineering career was right for him at all. He would make a very good barrister – and studying law was far more appealing than a science degree. He had a good command of language and an understated forcefulness when required. It was admirable. Yes, a barrister would do nicely. All these things could be addressed in due course and fortunately the important things were largely in place: his morals, his manners and his sound temperament. She and Ralph could claim the credit for the temperament, surely? But his excellent morals and manners were a different matter – the credit for those must be due ... elsewhere. Her thoughts stalled and she swallowed a little. It was silly not to accept Constance and Arnold as his 'parents' if that was what Adam called them. She wouldn't begrudge them for looking after him so well. It would be a difficult conversation when the time came, but she would be profusely grateful. In fact, she would grow to know them and like them because they were part of his life and therefore would become part of hers.

Very soon he would be talking to Constance and Arnold about his adoption – a tricky business, sitting them down and demanding the details, the places, the exact dates, and the paperwork to prove it. How would he go about it? Would he set about trying to disprove her? Despite what they had agreed, would he still be infatuated?

She leant forward, sinking her face into her hands.

The businessman's newspaper rustled as if it had been crumpled down completely. She was sure the man was staring at her, but she didn't move.

Eventually he said, with a little cough, 'Excuse me, madam. I couldn't help noticing. Are you all right?'

She sat up, brushing her dress straight over her knees. 'Oh yes, I'm absolutely fine, thank you, just rather tired, that's all. It's kind of you to ask though.'

She forced an appreciative smile before looking out of the window again, wondering what the man would have said next. She decided he had been about to say *I hope your day in London has not been too onerous?* or some such device to start a conversation. He must have thought her impolite because the newspaper rustled upwards again as if to say he was only trying to help.

She wanted to be home and longed for comforting sleep.

She had phoned from a call box at Paddington to say she had missed her train and would be late. Helena had answered and asked if she had had an interesting day. It was too tiring to think about how Helena would react to discovering that she had a half-brother. And besides, there was no immediate need to consider it because it would be best to wait until Adam had spoken to his parents and confirmed all the facts.

As she drove the Triumph home from the station, she tried to harbour only positive thoughts of finding her son, that everything would be settled and happy, everything in the open – with Helena, with Magnus, Constance and Arnold, and Adam himself. It made her smile in the dusk of her gruelling day. Then in the headlights she saw a dead fox by the side of the road, breaking her train of thought as she imagined the impact, the writhing and the reek there would be after a few days of the corpse lying in the hot sun, causing people to pass by on the other side.

Before arriving home she decided to compose herself, drawing into a lay-by, the same one with the bus shelter that she had stopped at after she had driven Adam to the station that time. His kiss on the platform seemed so innocent now, but the memory of it started another churning cycle: her guilt, her impulsiveness, her risible attempt to set herself free with her day in London, the shame of wilful self-abandonment. What would Celia and Shirley say now, if they saw her bedraggled and spent, or had witnessed her clothes scattered across the floor?

But then she remembered her despair in 1945 and how she had fought her way back. She would do it again. She started the car; her mind was clear and positive. He was innocent, she was innocent, they could be forgiven and exonerated in the court of the Holt's opinion and anyone else's.

It was nearly nine o'clock when she arrived home. Helena welcomed her in the hall, taking the blue coat and hanging it on the row of hooks. 'But you look utterly exhausted. What's happened? And how come you look so plain? You were beautiful this morning.'

'I'm too tired to talk about it, Helena. I ended up wandering aimlessly around the streets of Kensington. I was confused and lost. I miscalculated. I didn't even manage to visit Biba to buy you a present. I think I'll go straight to bed.'

'Oh, that's a pity because I wanted to talk to you about something. But I can see it's not the right time. I'll see you in the morning.'

'Yes, let's talk then. You and Magnus have had supper?'

'We have. He was not pleased about you missing your train and has gone to his study.'

In her bedroom, she didn't have to sit at her dressing table for very long, looking into the three panels of her mirror to put her face to bed, because she had wiped her make-up off in the bathroom of Adam's house. She had wiped it off frantically, like tearing away at a mask. She remembered the moment when she had instructed him to go downstairs, before she ran into the bathroom to sluice and purge her horror away. She was drained and empty, barely able to pick up her hairbrush to tidy her hair in the mirror. Her hand fell away and the brush clattered onto the dressing table glass as she lowered her head, summoning the strength to walk to her bed.

After turning the lights out, lying on her back in the safety of the dark where no one would see, only then did the tears spring in warm streams from the corners of her eyes, tapping onto the pillow like a gutter overflowing. Alone at last, she could be released; all the paradoxes that bound her could unravel; the strands could uncoil: the abhorrence and the joy, the shame and the love, the guilt and the pride. They were like burns that freeze and ice that scalds.

Eventually she lay still. Her breath was quiet and even, the tautness gone. She would regain control, perfecting her power to forget. It would be like destroying a letter in a fire when the flames fail to consume the words still legible on the frail grey gossamer of the burnt paper, the filaments raked over into the hot embers, collapsing them to illegible ash. Such would be her thoroughness to expunge the moment of her defilement and fix solely on her son who was lost and is found. She too would be found; she would find herself again in the morning.

16

In the few seconds of waking up, Elizabeth heard a drumming noise that seemed to grow louder as she became conscious. She sat up, blinking briefly in the darkness, emerging from the shifting dreams that had troubled her sleep. Her memories of the previous day flooded in, but they didn't register fully because the drumming noise was becoming more urgent. It was Helena, of course, playing the little game with her fingernails on the bedroom door, the sound of a galloping horse. It was a habit she had acquired when she was about eight, practising her trills on the piano before she gave it up for the cello. Usually, Elizabeth was fully awake when the little taps came on the door, and she would smile and listen to them before telling Helena she could enter. 'Come in,' she said sleepily.

Helena skipped across the room to open the curtains, then leapt onto Elizabeth's bed, sitting with her legs folded under her like a foal. 'Tell me about your day in London. Why didn't you make it to Biba? I was drumming for ages, but I'm not surprised you slept in. You looked very tired last night.'

'Yes, I was, and rather negative I'm afraid. I wasn't as aimless as I made out. I was just having a day to myself for once. It was very strange to be ambling about with no particular plan. I got a little lost. You know how bad I am with maps. So you and I will have to go up to Biba together some time and we can go to the V&A, which you haven't been to for years.'

Helena said she didn't want to hear about the V&A, or the ambling, or even Biba for that matter. 'It sounds like you made the best of it,' she said. 'Now what I wanted to talk to you about was Adam. I've been thinking about him. I'm wondering whether I treated him rather shabbily and whether I should try and see him again, to apologise.'

'Apologise for what?'

'I think I may have been unfair. Have you ever liked someone at first, then gone off them? Then, worse still, change your mind back again? Is that normal?'

'I see ... it depends on the reasons, I suppose. It may be acceptable to change your mind if there's a good reason, but allowing whims to come and go is not good at all. It's best not to be capricious.'

'Well, I hope I'm not like *that*, although I've actually forgotten what it means.'

'It means being given to sudden changes of opinion and changing your mood for no apparent reason. Why have you changed your mind?'

'I don't know. It's crept up on me. I think it started soon after I palmed him off onto you, which made me feel guilty. It was very kind of you to take him under your wing like that. And you were very patient about the way he was so obviously flirting with you. Surely you noticed?'

'No, I didn't.'

'There's no need to look shy! It was very sweet of you to

look after him. And I'm proud that you've managed to still look so young. Anyway, I think I made a mistake and I need to put it right, as you always say. So I'm going to try and see him again.'

'I really don't think you should. It would be unwise, going back on yourself.'

Helena traced her fingers wistfully on the paisley pattern of the silk bedspread. 'Have you never changed your mind about anyone?'

'I'm sure I've made my fair share of mistakes over time, but you have to live with them sometimes. You mustn't let them get on top of you.'

'Why don't you think I should try again with him?'

'I have my reservations. I learnt a lot about him when we met, and I don't think he would be suitable.'

'What reservations? Why isn't he suitable?'

'Helena, I'm going to ask you to trust me on this occasion. You can be very impulsive sometimes. My instincts tell me it wouldn't be a good idea to meet him. In fact, I'm going to forbid it, at least until you've had some time to think about it properly. Now I really must be getting up. There's an awful lot we need to do for Magnus's garden party on Saturday. Today, I'm going to arrange things in the garden and the house, ready for the marquee that's being put up tomorrow. Then on Saturday you and I need to supervise the caterers together. How does that fit with your revision schedule?'

'I can spare a few hours tomorrow afternoon and then help you with the party on Saturday.'

'Thank you. You're an angel.'

'I know,' Helena said as she leapt off the bed and went out.

* * *

One of Adam's rules was not to allow things to fester. If an unpleasant task needed to be done, it was pointless not to complete it at once, otherwise, in addition to the bother of actually completing the task, you had the unpleasantness of it hanging over your head and the risk that the procrastination itself could cause additional hardship. It was a piece of simple logic that applied even to the most mundane things. The other day he noticed the tap was dripping in his bathroom. Of course it would be a tedious business finding a plumber or attempting to change the washer himself, but delaying would have three additional negative consequences: putting up with the annoying drips for longer, worrying about it getting worse, and the possible consequences if the washer broke, causing a flood most likely.

It was the same with Elizabeth's insistence that he should find out all he could about his adoption. True, it was a much thornier problem than the tap washer, but the principles were the same. He dreaded the idea of another awkward discussion with his parents. But Elizabeth would be crestfallen if she rang in a few days to find that he had done nothing.

He had been crestfallen himself ever since Elizabeth had left the house the previous evening. Throughout the morning, he had felt sad and listless and unable to come to terms with his sense of loss. His emptiness had continued all afternoon as he tried to find the courage to pick up the phone to his parents. But now, finally, he had forced himself to dial the number.

His mother answered the phone. 'You want to know more

about it so soon?' You're not worried about it are you, Adam?'

'No, but I've been thinking about it a lot.'

'Well, come tomorrow evening. We'll have a light supper, so we can lay out the documents and explain them while we eat. It will be better for your father that way, keeping things light and relaxed. You're not disappointed, are you? In us, I mean?'

There was a sorrowfulness in her question that caught Adam by surprise. But he collected himself straight away, reassuring her profusely that he was not disappointed at all. She mustn't think that way, he loved them both. And yes, that would be best, a light supper to keep things light.

He put the phone down. The unpleasant task was done; it wouldn't fester. His rule was a very good one and he felt much better.

* * *

The following evening, Adam was eating a bacon omelette with his parents. His father had just tipped out the contents of a manila envelope onto the table. 'It's a job to know where to start, Adam. Let's see ... ah, yes, here we have the French adoption paperwork from the orphanage in Caen. It's quite simple, really – it just includes the name of the orphanage, the dates of your birth and adoption and all the relevant names – the registrar's, Constance's name and mine as the adoptive parents, and the names that were given to you at birth: Raoul Pierre Philippe. Rather grand, I think.'

'But the names are not the French equivalents of mine.'

'No, of course not. That's because your birth mother gave

you those names before you were handed over to the orphanage in Caen. It's what I was explaining the other night. You remember – France's anonymous adoption procedure, *Accouchement Sous X?* You look blank, Adam.'

His mother said, 'Yes, dear, that's probably because when you went through it all the other day, Adam must have been a little shell-shocked. After breaking the news to him about his adoption, it would have been difficult to take in all the details of the French system.

'Does that mean I've got to go through it all again?'

'Well, yes, I suppose so, but perhaps just the shorter version this time?'

Adam's father puffed his cheeks. 'When I was talking about the Ancien Régime and all that, I was trying to explain that France has a long history of infants being abandoned at birth, usually for reasons of shame relating to illegitimate births and that sort of thing. Napoleon enshrined in law a system of anonymous births to solve the problem. The general idea was that if the mother could be guaranteed complete anonymity and the infant taken into state care, there would be fewer abandoned babies left at church doors and on the streets. The law was updated during the war, when the Pétain government formalised the system further. You were born under what is called *Accouchement Sous X* – "*accouchement*" being the French term for childbirth and "*Sous X*" referring to how the birth is recorded. In the ledgers where the birth details are written down, there is a box where the name of the child's father is recorded and another box for the name of the mother. But for an anonymous birth, the boxes are filled in with a simple "X" to denote that there is no name of the father or mother included in the birth register.'

'But I still don't understand about my French names,' Adam said.

'Those would have been given to you when you were born, as French law permits. Under *Accouchement Sous X*, the mother has certain legal rights. She can choose to give the child three names, which by law have to be written in the birth records by the civil registrations officer, or *officier d'état civil* as he is known. The mother is legally entitled to demand that her admission into a maternity home or hospital be kept completely secret with no traceable record of her having given birth to the child. But in exchange, she has to surrender her child to the state for care or adoption. It must be harrowing for the mother because the moment the child is born it's covered over with a blanket and taken away before she ever sees it. But any given names for the child are written down in the birth records. When we decided to bring you up in England, we thought it would be better for you to have English names. We had to do a vetting interview with London County Council before applying for the adoption order, and they were far more concerned about whether we were suitable people to adopt than where you actually came from, so we were able to choose your names quite easily. Both of us had always liked the name Adam, so we chose that for your first name. We thought it would be nice to honour your given names in some way, so that's why your second name is Peter for Pierre. We ignored Philippe because we've always thought having three given names rather pretentious.'

After his father had been through some of the other documents and correspondence, Adam said, 'Thank you. You've been very thorough about keeping everything, but where was I actually born? There must be a birth certificate somewhere.'

'*Somewhere* is exactly the right word,' his father said. 'Actually they don't have birth certificates in France as we do here. All births, deaths and marriages are written down in ledgers kept at the local town hall, or *mairie* as the French call it. If people need a document, they go to the *mairie* for an official copy of whatever record is kept there. With *Accouchement Sous X*, the place of birth is not given to the parents, who adopt the child from the state orphanage, so you could have been born anywhere in France. However, the *commune* where you were born will have an entry in its register with the date of birth and your given names, but no details of the parents' names, which would be marked simply with an "X"'.

Adam said, 'And how many *communes* are there in France?'

'Oh, thousands,' Connie said. 'Calvados is just one of the three *départements* in Lower Normandy and that has over five hundred *communes*.'

'And each one of them keeps their own records?'

'I think so. It's a long time since I lived there, but I imagine everything is still the same. All the records for each *commune* are kept in a civil register at the *mairie*. But why do you want to know, Adam? Why do you want to know about your birth mother? You do think of us as your parents, don't you? We have always tried our best.'

'Yes. Yes, of course. But I just want to know the place. Everyone wants to know where they were born. It's a part of them. I'm intrigued. I suppose it's like most things – you learn a little about something and then you realise you want to learn a little more, and before you know it, you want to string the whole thing together.'

'Well, some things are best not strung together,' his mother said dolefully. 'How anyone could possibly have given you up has always baffled me. Even Arnold was utterly enchanted when he first saw you at the orphanage in Caen. It's very sad to think of someone giving up a child.'

'But the mother might have been in great distress. She might have been suicidal and didn't want her child to die as well. It's difficult for us to judge if we don't know the facts.'

'I suppose you're right, Adam,' she said, gathering up the documents and sliding them into the manila envelope. 'That's very generous of you to think that way. It's how we've tried to bring you up. Now, I think that's quite enough for one evening. Look after this envelope and we can talk about it again when you've had time to think.'

Constance walked over to the sideboard as he got up to leave. 'There are a couple of letters here that arrived yesterday. Oh, and while I remember, that girl phoned yesterday afternoon, the one you were seeing that we never met.'

'Helena, do you mean?'

'Yes, she asked to speak to you, but I said you were out. I wasn't sure whether to give her your new telephone number. I asked whether I could take her number so that you could phone back, but she said you already have it and was most insistent that you shouldn't phone her. She said she'd phone again. What should I say if she does?'

'Oh ... I need to think about that,' Adam said.

As he walked back to his house he thought about it a great deal. Why did Helena want to speak to him? Perhaps he had left something behind at the house when he went to stay and she wanted to post it back. Or she might be wanting him to post back some of the music scores she had given him a while ago. Had Elizabeth already spoken to Helena about her certainty that the three of them were related – and if so, how much had Elizabeth said about making the discovery in his house? Also, there was the mystery of why Helena didn't want him to phone her at home.

***

The next morning Adam phoned his parents to say that yes, it would be fine for Helena to phone him. It would do no harm, he said.

She did phone – that very afternoon – saying she was coming to London to visit him. At first it was difficult to make out what she was saying above the jazz music playing in the background.

'Hang on. I'll close the window,' she said and explained that she was on duty at Magnus's garden party but had managed to escape. 'I can't talk for long, but I'm coming to London tomorrow. In the morning, I'm seeing my friend Philippa who lives in Chelsea and then after lunch I'm going to come and see you in Kensington. You will be in, won't you?'

'Yes … but why, Helena? What's the reason for your visit?'

'Good lord, Adam, you're starting to sound like my mother! The *reason* I'm coming to visit is that I want to see you. I want to see how you're getting on in your new house. To be honest, I'm insanely jealous that your parents have set you up with a place of your own … but then again, I suppose you are *five* years older than me.' Laughing, she asked him to confirm the address and said she would see him tomorrow.

He didn't rush around the house preparing for Helena's visit in the way he had for Elizabeth. The circumstances were different. For Elizabeth's arrival, he had been lost in a fever of hope, but for Helena he was ambivalent, not knowing why she wanted to visit. He was still far too preoccupied with the loss of Elizabeth's sensuousness to be thinking about anything to do with Helena.

He remembered looking out of his net curtains when he was expecting Elizabeth. He lived in a street full of net curtains that twitched. He had met three families in the street and they had been charming, but having two uncommonly attractive women calling on him within a few days of each other might cause an uncommon amount of curtain agitation.

Helena arrived with two sharp raps of the brass dolphin on his front door, the second louder than the first. 'Hello, Adam. How nice to see you,' she said, kissing him on the cheek, which was something she had never done before.

'You found your way all right?'

'Oh yes, I sort of zigzagged through the streets from Gloucester Road. It was quite easy really. What a lovely place! You must show me round.'

'All right, but it's not really fixed up yet.'

He showed her the living room. 'It's quite a well-proportioned room. The floorboards are sound, but they need a bit of renovating. And the rug will have to go of course, but I'm in no hurry to do everything at once. The shutters are original, I think, and perfectly serviceable, but they will need restoring eventually.'

'Goodness, Adam, you seem to have become quite the expert in interior design. I thought I might be able to advise you because I've learnt a lot about old houses from Mother. But maybe there's no need.'

Standing in the little dining room, he told her of his plan to knock down the wall next to the living room to make one large space, commenting on the fact that the mouldings in the two rooms were the same.

'Yes, that's a good idea. I'm impressed! Lead on,' she said, guiding him forward with her hand on his shoulder.

She agreed that the kitchen needed to be ripped out entirely and that the recess was ideal for an Aga … and that the room would look fine at night with tall lamps and big shades.

They came to the foot of the stairs, where Helena smiled at him and said, 'It's a lovely little house, and will make a very nice home. What's upstairs?'

'Oh, there's not much to see up there, just a bathroom that needs ripping out like the kitchen, but you can go up if you like. I'll stay here.'

'Nonsense!' she said, her ankles already on the fifth stair, leading them up.

They looked at the bathroom and the two small bedrooms before taking the few steps to the front bedroom, which Helena entered, leaving Adam at the door.

Helena sat on the bed looking out at the street. 'You need some decent curtains for that window, but you must be careful not to block any of the light in the daytime. Here, come and see what I mean.' She patted the eiderdown and he sat beside her, looking straight ahead at the window, unable to look at her.

'You've been very shy ever since I got here, Adam. There's no need to be. I know I was abrupt when you came to stay, but we can put that behind us. We can be friends, can't we?'

He looked at her quickly and turned away again because it was as if a younger Elizabeth was staring at him. It took his breath away. 'Yes of course … if your mother allows it.'

'What on earth do you mean by that? We're adults, aren't we? We can decide for ourselves. You're not going to object, are you? Please don't be wooden.'

Adam certainly felt wooden, fixing his stare at the window.

Gently, she took his chin and turned it towards her.

'Don't look so alarmed,' she said, kissing him softly on the mouth. 'There, that wasn't too painful, was it? We don't have to rush into anything. We can take things very slowly if you like. There's no hurry. Let's go downstairs. You can make me some tea and I'll tell you about the cello pieces I've been playing.'

When they sat in the kitchen, they talked just as they had when they were going to concerts and study weekends together. She asked him about how often he had been practising his music and seemed appalled to hear that he had almost given up. His explanation was partly true – that practising a trombone in a street of terraced houses was unfair on the neighbours. It was a different situation from the music practice he had always done at his parents' house, filling the place with the instrument's sonorous power. It was an instrument to be played fully or not at all, in his view. He could hardly explain to Helena that the main reason for the lapse in his music was his preoccupation with Elizabeth, which for several weeks had been an obsession of an entirely different kind.

Helena urged him not to become disillusioned and said that if he didn't practise he'd lose everything. He should soundproof one of the rooms in the house, or find the discipline to put aside some fixed hours each week to practise at his parents' house, or find some rooms in a local music school. She was full of ideas. It was like listening to Elizabeth, reeling off her suggestions in a gathering stream.

He said he would think about her ideas and asked her about what she had been practising recently on the cello. She described very excitedly how she was giving Bach a rest and experimenting with Elgar and Dvořák. She spoke in gushes and waved her hands, making him realise how much he had missed her zest for music. He remembered the first time he had met her when they attended the same study weekend at Cheltenham. She was performing in a string quartet, completely absorbed, writhing with the cello in what seemed like anger, oblivious to her hair falling away and sticking to her face. At the end of the weekend, all the students had a few minutes each with the course tutor from Vienna, who told him in her broken English that technically he played the trombone very well, but which was more important, technical brilliance or something with more élan? She left the question hanging and then described the passionate way Helena Fortescue played the cello, attacking it from the heart, not from the head.

Eventually Helena said it was time for her to go. 'Maybe next time we meet I could bring my cello and we could practise together. That would create some noise in the street! And you will think about everything, won't you? You mustn't phone me – I'll phone you in a couple of days.'

'But does Elizabeth know you have come to see me?'

'No. It would be complicated if she knew we were seeing each other again.'

'But we haven't decided whether we *are* seeing each other again,' Adam said.

'Of course we have.'

She gathered up her bag and coat and kissed him very fully. 'Just think, Adam. Just *think*. You're very good at that!'

After she left, Adam sat at the foot of the stairs, groaning and pressing the side of his head, the warmth of her kiss still shimmering. There was something deliciously illicit about it, and he imagined Elizabeth looking on in furious disapproval. He got up to turn on the ancient ceiling fan above him. Even though it was on a slow setting, it would cool him and be easier to breathe if the air was moving. He wanted to run after Helena and explain why he'd been ungrateful and wooden, as she termed it. She had assumed him to be shy, not realising that he had been disarmed by the change in her. When she kissed him, he had closed his eyes in confusion, wondering whether it was her or Elizabeth. It was difficult to separate their images in his mind as the fan flicked its blades slowly above him. Elizabeth and Helena seemed to alternate, first one then the other until they fused together as one and the same, with the same composure and the same lie of silk on the shoulder.

He breathed out, looking down at the floor, listening to the fan's blades rotating slowly – this time modulating the differences rather than the similarities between Helena and Elizabeth, the impetuous and the imperious, the innocence and the wisdom. But it was a false choice, he reminded himself. He could feel Elizabeth glaring at him in fury for not resisting Helena's attention. Would he ever be able to adjust, reformulating his feelings into something that was purely filial, or into something akin to sibling respect? It was like sliding on ice, not knowing which way he would fall. He had seen Elizabeth once sliding her index finger along the mantelpiece in her drawing room, looking for dust. It reminded him of her sliding her finger along his collarbone. Helena had also slid, sliding her hand around his chin to turn it towards her. All it would take was a little slip.

He knew he should get up and turn the fan off to staunch his thoughts. He knew that he should snap himself out of these fantasies like a fish breaking out of water, but he sat for a long time listening to the blades turning and churning and making him numb.

17

Magnus held his garden party each year on the second Saturday of August. Everyone on the Holt was invited, along with some of his London friends and work colleagues from his advertising agency. In the same way that people might write Ascot, Henley or Wimbledon in their diaries, they wrote *Magnus's Garden Party*, even though Elizabeth organised it. She bore no resentment; it was part of their arrangement.

She had perfected the art of throwing the garden party after learning from various glitches that had occurred over the years. Once, the farmer who owned the field that was used for car parking had ploughed it in the spring, and the grass was too thin to prevent a quagmire caused by a summer deluge. Another time, the caterers had done a very poor job with the oysters and people were very ill. But a farmer could be persuaded to keep a field of permanent grass – which could be rolled as well if needed – provided Magnus was suitably effusive in thanking the farmer during his speech. As for the caterers, it was a simple matter of finding a reliable firm with permanent staff. Luigi had been her caterer of choice for years now, and she always made sure that he too was thanked effusively in Magnus's speech.

Even though it was only the day after Elizabeth had 'paid a visit to Adam's house' – a euphemism already firmly embedded in her thoughts – she had found strategies to deflect the memory of it. The recurrent image of her scattered clothes and her tights draped over the bentwood chair haunted her, forcing her to bow her head and wipe beads of sweat across her forehead. Each time this spectre appeared, she absorbed herself in the party preparations to avoid being consumed by guilt. Another strategy she used was to focus on positive thoughts for the future, which even made her smile. She wanted everything to be out in the open as soon as possible, informing the world at large that she had lost a son, but he had been found. Everything would fall into place: Adam would come to realise quickly that he was her son; Helena would be joyous at being an only child no longer; Magnus would just have to accept the new reality. And Constance and Arnold would be informed of the facts – a delicate matter, but she trusted herself when it came to matters of delicacy. It buoyed her up to think everything would be resolved. She would look forward, not back.

The annual garden party was one of the most onerous in Magnus's endless succession of entertainments, but she used the air of expectancy to buoy up her positive thoughts. Each time she thought of Adam she threw back her head and nearly laughed with delight, wanting to pick up the phone and talk to her son, to make sure that he was well and ask whether he had spoken to his parents yet about the details of his birth. But she would have to wait. She calculated that Adam would require at least a day to collect himself. Understandably, he had been visibly shocked by the turn of events and would need time to settle. But he would be methodical and think everything through, and then, being solid and steady, sound and sensible, he would find the courage to phone his parents, and surely they would then present irrefutable evidence for the truth about his birth and adoption. The facts would disabuse him of any other thoughts he still harboured, the ones that made her shudder with disgust if she allowed herself to think of them.

At first, she had considered phoning him as soon as Sunday morning, when everyone would be sleeping the party off, but she decided it would be too risky phoning from the house and far too conspicuous to be driving into town to find a telephone box. People would ask why on earth she was in the town on a Sunday when all the shops were closed. So she would wait until Monday to phone him and fill the time by immersing herself in the garden party preparations. And besides, it was only reasonable to allow Adam a few days to find a suitable opportunity to clarify everything with his parents.

Today, her task was to ensure the garden was looking its best before the marquee arrived tomorrow afternoon. She wanted to check that everything on the gardening list she had given to Mr Roberts at the beginning of the week had been completed to her satisfaction. Poor old Roberts was becoming unreliable. When she took him on fifteen years ago he was a sprightly fifty-five-year-old, but his bones had started to ache, he said, and his eyesight was definitely not what it was. If an urn was moved, it was often not put back straight, and the lawn edges were not as sinuously curved as they used to be. She didn't have the heart to take him aside one day and whisper gently that he was no longer needed. So she had hired a young assistant gardener, but the experiment was not working well. The two men were of different eras and of different opinions when it came to interpreting Elizabeth's instructions. It baffled her because she took great pains to ensure that everything was wonderfully clear.

And sometimes old Roberts and his assistant did things that were not part of her instructions – as she could see now. The hebes! She stood back, aghast, slumping her shoulders and pointing her trowel to the ground. What an earth would possess anyone to do that? She had mentioned several times previously that the hebes should only be pruned once they had flowered and here were a couple of them butchered. She knew what the logic was – clearly Roberts or his assistant had taken it upon themselves to even things up by making all the hebes the same size, which was completely unnecessary. She liked good order, but nature needed to be allowed to run its course sometimes, to find its level – or its shape in this case. She liked the idea of a plant being left to express itself rather than putting one's own expression on the plant. It was why she was not overly fond of topiaries or bonsai; it was cruel to the plants. Nature shouldn't be tamed excessively. If there was a stray aquilegia, let it be! Although a Welsh poppy was a different matter, she thought, pulling one out.

There was nothing that could be done about the hebes, so she decided not to worry about them for now. She would have a word with Mr Roberts – that would be another delicate conversation.

She imagined Adam sitting in his house, planning how to approach his parents and how to find out everything about his birth and adoption. They sounded like stout-shoes sorts of people, or the sort to have a very traditional Sunday lunch. Maybe that would be when he would ask them about everything, at lunch on Sunday. He would be very respectful, and they would be very civilised, and all the truth would be plain to see. And then everyone would look forward and not back. It made her think of the story about the pillar of salt, but immediately she thought about the garden instead. Despite the hebes, the garden was in good shape, and she would make sure it was even more spectacular by the end of the day once she had watered a few of the plants, tied up the rose that had fallen down, and used her besom broom on the lawn to sweep some gravel back onto the path. Everything would be fresh and new and straightened out.

* * *

Elizabeth spent Friday morning in her office confirming all the final arrangements for the party. She phoned the taxi company to make sure they would have sufficient drivers on duty when the party ended because there were always one or two people who decided not to drive themselves home. She phoned Luigi to run through the catering arrangements once again and ensure he had understood them exactly. In the past he had added certain culinary flourishes to the menu of which she hadn't approved.

For the music, she phoned Stanley, the leader of the six-piece jazz band that she adored. 'Yes please, Stanley, if you could arrive at noon that would be marvellous – in good time for the party which starts at two. I've given you and the band your usual room at the back of the house, the one with the little patio. The caterers will supply a bite of lunch for you there. Yes, that's right, you need to be playing just before two o'clock when guests will start to arrive. Do take a break about halfway through as usual, won't you? It'll end around six o'clock, when Magnus will do his speech and invite people to have a last dance. Then, after your grand finale people will want to clap you, of course, but please remember, no encores, and if you pack up your instruments straight away it'll remind people to disperse. And, Stanley, please may I remind you? It's to be traditional New Orleans and standards, not some of your improvised experiments. There is a time and a place, you know.'

She phoned Vivian, the florist, to adjust the order. Elizabeth always phoned her on the Monday before the garden party with a provisional order and then phoned her again just before the party, having reviewed the condition of her own flowers in the garden. It seemed senseless to buy dahlias at great expense if her own were copious and in perfect bloom. 'Mine have come on tremendously this week, Vivian, so can we replace them with something else? Let's stick to the price we agreed, but I'll let you choose. No yellows, please. Nor oranges for that matter. You can surprise me if you like.'

When she put the phone down she thought of Miranda, who actually liked oranges and yellows, but then she liked gypsophila as well. It was a source of constant amusement between them: they agreed on everything apart from flowers. She had neglected Miranda, having not spoken to her since visiting Adam in London. The last time she had seen Miranda, she was standing by her front door waving her off to London, complimenting her on her fashionable tights. Elizabeth screwed up her face to force the memory out, to look forward, not back, the pillar of salt.

She would see Miranda at the party and would apologise for ignoring her. Of course Miranda would understand about the need to prepare for the party, but she was bound to ask about how the day in London had gone. That was something else to think about.

* * *

On Saturday morning, Elizabeth supervised the catering arrangements.

It was happening again – Helena's new assertiveness. This time it was with Luigi. It had shocked her the previous afternoon when Elizabeth had been passing the marquee that had just been put up. She had said Helena could oversee the interior decoration of the tent and she heard her talking inside it to Mr Saunders, who could be prickly sometimes. Elizabeth had walked by very slowly outside the marquee, not wishing to pry and listen in on Helena's conversation. Asking Mr Saunders whether the swagging could be neater seemed a very risky business because he didn't take kindly to criticism; there might have been an unseemly scene. But Helena had handled it supremely, complimenting Mr Saunders on his wonderful tent and adding how it might look even more like something out of *Vogue* if the swagging was twisted a little and more evenly looped, sharing a little humour, a little lightness, presumably with that smile of hers that could cajole the curtest curmudgeon. Elizabeth had been unable to resist peeping through a tent flap to see Helena standing on a chair, pointing out how the swagging should be done as if orchestrating it with the sweep of her arms, standing like the Statue of Liberty while Mr Saunders and his men looked on in wonder. As soon as Helena had got down from the chair, Elizabeth walked on quickly, hearing the murmurs of approval fading behind her. 'Very well, Miss Helena, we'll see to that right away,' Mr Saunders had said very humbly.

It would never have happened a couple of years ago. Helena had been too strident then, a slip of a girl in too much of a hurry to be a woman. But Elizabeth had noticed over the last year how often Helena would stand next to her at a party, listening intently, observing the handling of a conversation, learning how to agree to disagree, or put someone right without putting them down, the art of gentle strength. Before, Helena always sought to get her way by being obstreperous. It had been the only approach in her armoury. But she was unidimensional no more, having mastered a repertoire of strategies to suit any occasion.

Helena's assertiveness with Mr Saunders yesterday was now happening with Luigi, who was no longer under any illusions that Helena was an adult in her own right. For years Elizabeth and Luigi had worked together on the morning of the garden party, setting everything up while Helena pestered them pleasantly, a young child chattering away, getting under her mother's feet. The bear-like Luigi would humour the child, throwing her up in the air and catching her, then sending her away squealing in delight before busying himself again with the catering staff.

Even the worldly-wise Luigi had been wrong-footed

during the last two garden parties, when he had clearly failed to reshape his perception of Helena as she herself had reshaped. Last year, Helena had been self-conscious when greeting Luigi, but this morning they had met comfortably as equals with a perfunctory kiss to each cheek – another little skill Helena had acquired effortlessly from her mother as if by osmosis, proffering one cheek then the other at just the right interval, not too fast, not too slow, perfecting the demeanour as well, neither too demonstrative nor too dismissive. Helena had accomplished her transition, detaching any particular significance from the etiquette, appreciating it as a greeting, not a kiss, a bond of respect rather than anything ambiguously carnal.

Elizabeth admired Luigi's bravura, but occasionally it strayed into something else, a flirtatious glance or an innuendo. It seemed to be an instinctive game that Luigi found impossible to avoid, but Elizabeth found it could be quickly scotched with a certain look. She had never consciously thought about this look before, but now she saw it for the first time because Helena had just made it dazzle. It was impossible to define the reprimand. It was too fleeting to be a glare, too subtle to be a flicker of muscle that might signal resentment. But whatever it was, it had the desired effect. Helena had put Luigi right immediately – demolishing his flirtatious advance with that undefinable expression. He seemed to acknowledge her victory before continuing with the party preparations, clapping his hands and loudly encouraging his team of assistants, his *bella figura* intact.

These changes in Helena made Elizabeth happy and sad at the same time. Happy because she wanted to wrap her arms around Helena there and then for mastering such brilliance while still so young, but sad because it meant Helena was ready to be lost to the world beyond. Hopefully she would always love her mother, but she seemed fully fledged and independent now. Perhaps, occasionally at first, she might fly too close to the sun before learning to glide effortlessly wherever she wished. Surely Adam would be a steadying influence. They would learn so much from each other. Adam's natural reserve might curb Helena's flightier swoops, and in return she would be able to inform Adam of the point at which caution and modesty become an unwelcome diffidence that could do with shaking out. They were different but their values were sound; they would become kindred spirits and learn to love one another.

She returned to the task of checking that all the salt cellars were full before putting them out on the tables, sliding them into position. Everything would be in the open and everything settled. She could see it now as a photograph, the three of them sitting on the little bench up in the arbour at the very top of the garden. She would be in the middle with her arm around her daughter and her son, and they would be grinning back at the sunlight in their new-found comfort, strong and magnificent, caught in a moment that would be everlasting.

* * *

The party went just as Elizabeth had planned it. Magnus stood up to give his speech, thanking everyone for coming, for bringing the good weather with them, and for being such excellent company, his dear friends all. There were cheers in return and clamours for *Magnus! Magnus!*

'And now, before we close proceedings with the musical finale, let us join in thanking everyone who has made this lovely afternoon possible.' Magnus called out the names one by one to rounds of applause. 'To Stanley and his wonderful band! To Luigi for the finesse of his cuisine! To Mr Saunders for his palatial tent! And finally, to Elizabeth and Helena, who do so much of the organisation.'

Elizabeth and Helena stood arm in arm, taking in the applause appreciatively. It was just Magnus being Magnus, Elizabeth thought. He could have said *all* of the organisation, but everyone would know the truth. It was going to be an interesting conversation when the time came, informing Magnus that at last she had produced a son. It didn't alarm her at all. When the facts were all laid out, nobody would be able to argue; it was like the facts of life.

Stanley struck up a rousing finale, an improvised interpretation of 'We'll Meet Again'. Elizabeth knew Stanley was being mischievous because he grinned in her direction as she narrowed her eyes in mock severity. For a terrible moment Elizabeth feared some of the tipsier guests might start to sing along. Certainly Henry the architect and his noisy clique had started swaying to the tune, but in the end they only mimed the final words, *some sunny day ...*

People were beginning to disperse. She and Helena stood together laughing and shaking hands with everyone as they departed. After the last guests had filed out of the marquee, Luigi and his team started to clear up.

'There was something I forgot to mention earlier,' Helena said.

'Oh?'

'I'm going to London tomorrow, to Chelsea, to see Philippa. She's having a terrible time. I was on the phone to her earlier. She's having a crisis with her revision and being bothered by a boy. She needs my help and I need to calm her down.'

'But how will you get there?'

'Father said he would drive me to the station in the morning. You'll be able to have a well-deserved lie-in.'

'Well, check the Sunday timetable, because there aren't many trains on a Sunday. And I'm not sure he should be driving in the morning after all the wine that's been consumed.'

'But the new alcohol laws haven't come in yet! It'll be fine.'

'Must we always have laws to tell us about what is wrong and what is right?'

'You're always right about what's wrong and right. I sometimes wonder what would happen if you ever did anything wicked. But you never would, of course.'

'I should hope not ... Now I really must go over and have a word with Luigi. He needs to be thanked properly. Magnus was far too flippant in his speech.'

As she walked away, Elizabeth wondered whether Helena was also becoming too flippant. It seemed to be another of Helena's experiments, exploring the boundaries of flippancy as well as the boundaries of assertiveness. A year ago Helena would have asked permission to go to London on her own, and now she merely declared her intention. It was certainly an impressive combination, exuding both the beauty and the power to command, but it would have to be watched. There was no immediate need to confront it – a subtle remark to Helena at the right time would be quite sufficient. It would be good for Helena to see Philippa. Being wrapped up in her studies and her cello meant she might become too detached. She would never become introverted, but she needed to mix more with people of similar age. Adam would help her with that, surely. Being so affable, he seemed to have lots of university friends. They would go to parties as brother and sister and Helena would meet new people and mix a little more.

18

It was a relief when Monday morning arrived. Magnus was at work, Helena was spending the day studying, and practising her cello, and Mr Roberts and his team were taking down the marquee. At last, Elizabeth was able to don her scarf and sunglasses and drive down the hill into the town, where the first thing she would do was find a telephone box to phone Adam.

Her last call to him had been from the telephone box by the church to arrange her visit to his house. She didn't want to be reminded of it, so she parked her car in a different part of town and walked to the telephone kiosk on the street corner, checking that there was nobody about that she knew. She hated the subterfuge and the skulking; the sooner everything was in the open with Magnus and Helena the better.

She pressed the coins into the slot, smiled on hearing his voice, and started to ask a host of questions about how he was and whether he had sorted the roof leak that had stained the bathroom wall. He hadn't got round to it yet, he said.

'But you really should,' she said. 'You must get a roofer in to look at it. It may be just a loose tile, but it will only get worse and store up trouble. And have you been eating properly? I've been thinking about that and have cut out some simple recipes I need to give you.'

She was about to ask whether he had had his hair cut, but checked herself; it was best not to nag. 'Now tell me how you've been getting on. What have you been able to find out?'

'I had a long conversation with my parents. They've given me an envelope full of documents, which mainly relate to when I was brought to England.'

'But the details of your birth – what did they say about that?'

'They didn't have anything to say about it because it was anonymous, but the French adoption certificate does have my date of birth as the twenty-fifth of January 1945 …'

'And were there any names?'

For several days she had been thinking about what Adam might discover, forcing her to remember what she had spent over twenty years trying to forget. It amazed her how vividly she was still able to recall what happened in 1945. Walking up the steps to the hospital door, she had hardly been able to lift her feet such was her state of mind. The nun walking with her from the convent to the hospital led her by the elbow one step at a time, a kindly woman in a white wimple, whispering comfort as her wooden cross swung against her black habit. And as if it were yesterday, Elizabeth remembered the hospital administrator explaining to her the procedure for giving up her child anonymously. He gave her an old dip pen and a pot of ink to write a letter. He said it would make her feel better, setting it all down. So she sat weeping, scratching the words out on the thick paper, and sealed the letter, writing Raoul Pierre Philippe on the envelope – Ralph's names, translated into French. Setting it all down didn't make her better at all. Writing the three names devastated her, signing him away forever, handing the letter to the administrator before the child was taken away, never to be seen again. So she thought! And here he was, reciting his names down the line, Raoul, Pierre, Philippe – falteringly because his French was clearly not good. She felt a flood of joy warming through her as each name was pronounced, the final confirmation that she had found her son.

'I'm afraid that's all I've been able to find out,' Adam said. 'It does seem that I was born in France and was adopted and later brought to England, so that points to the possibility that we're related.'

'What do you mean, the *possibility*? Don't tell me you're not certain about it.'

'I … it's difficult. You see, I don't want it to be true. We could be as we were—'

'That's enough!' She hissed the words. Then, collecting herself, she said, 'Please, never speak of that again.'

Her words reverberated in the silence of the telephone box, and she looked out briefly at the street to check nobody was passing by.

Adam said, 'Unfortunately, there's an additional complication. Helena has been to see me.'

'What …?'

'She came to my house yesterday after visiting her friend in Chelsea.'

'What on earth for?'

'Well, she seemed keen to think we might carry on where we left off.'

'Keen?'

'I tried to discourage her because I knew you would disapprove.'

'But you put her off?'

'Yes, of course.'

'Does she know that you and I were having conversations before she came to your house?'

'No, I didn't mention it.'

'So she knows nothing about the three of us being related? But she must be told about it at once. We can't go behind her back, even if she seems to have gone behind mine in meeting you. Everything needs to be in the open, Adam. At once.'

'Everything?'

'No!' she shouted, stamping her foot and looking out at the street again.

Wiping her eye and taking a deep breath, she said, 'Now, I want you to listen. Helena will need to be handled very carefully because once she gets an idea in her head, it will be impossible to dislodge. She won't believe that you're related to her unless the facts are unassailable. So I need to check through all the documents you have and be fully prepared before sitting her down and telling her the relevant information. In the meantime you must ignore her if she tries to contact you. Here's what we have to do. I have a meeting on Wednesday morning and will meet you in the St Martin's café at two o'clock. You will bring all the documents that your parents gave you. Once I've looked through everything, I'll be able to decide how to approach Helena. She must be told everything as soon as possible.'

***

Adam was going to be late for his meeting with Elizabeth. The platform of the Circle and District line at South Kensington was very crowded, and people were grumbling because the trains were delayed. The man and the woman standing next to him had been arguing loudly about whether it would be better to take the Piccadilly line instead. They decided that it would be and turned to walk down the stairs, followed by other people nearby who had been listening to them. He wondered whether to do the same, but then the moment he was trapped in the rush down the stairs, the delayed train might arrive.

He had dithered similarly when he left the house. He had stepped out of the door and marched down the street for a few yards carrying the large manila envelope for his discussion with Elizabeth, but the envelope was bulky and somewhat tatty. So he had gone back into the house and taken out the relevant documents, which he folded and put into his jacket pocket.

He kept thinking about Elizabeth and Helena, who spiralled in his mind amid the babble of voices surrounding him and the people jostling around in circles on the platform, wondering which train to catch.

His worship of Elizabeth was that of a dutiful son one moment and something quite different the next. Equally, his thoughts about Helena were caught up in a struggle between being a sensible brother and someone else.

At last the train arrived and he managed to squeeze his way into the carriage. The doors closed and everyone was quiet now as if the breath was squeezed from them. Catching a glimpse of the station clock through the sea of faces, he realised he would be at least twenty minutes late for Elizabeth. She would be disappointed, but at least he had done as she had asked and had found out as much as he could from his parents. He wanted to pat his jacket to check the documents were still there, but the crush of people standing was too great.

He entered the café out of breath and saw her at the corner table. She didn't get up to greet him. When he had sat opposite her, she placed her hand on his, tapping it quite matter-of-factly, and said, 'It's very bad form, you know, to be half an hour late, and you're looking rather dishevelled. But it's nice to see you.'

In that instant, with that mother's studied smile, he knew he had to abandon all hope of them ever being as they were. He realised that she was utterly convinced of the facts as she saw them, and nothing would ever persuade her otherwise. When she patted his hand, it was equivalent to a mother ruffling a son's hair, packing him off to school or straightening his school cap. He tried to think of how they had been when she visited his house, but the memory was fading rapidly now that she had extinguished its vividness with her maternal demeanour, the new reality.

While they waited for the coffee to arrive they exchanged pleasantries about what he had been doing with the house, and she shared some anecdotes from her garden party.

'Well, this is all very nice, Adam, but we need to get down to business. I want to hear all the details about what your parents told you. But before that I want you to tell me about

Helena's visit.'

He described how he had shown Helena around the house and that they had then spent a long time in the kitchen discussing music. 'She suggested she could bring her cello one day so that we could practise together, but I said I was worried about the neighbours and the noise. She said I needed to consider soundproofing one of the rooms.'

'And was it all as innocent as that?'

'Yes. Yes, it was innocent.'

'You look rather flustered.'

'Nothing ... happened.'

'But she kissed you? You need to tell the truth.'

'Yes ...'

'Was it just a kiss to each cheek, like a greeting or a goodbye?'

Adam swallowed for a moment and said, 'It wasn't quite like that. It was friendly ... we were sitting down ... but I didn't kiss her, knowing what I do. But she can't be blamed if she has no knowledge of the situation.'

'I get the impression it was very intimate. How did you leave things with her?'

'She said she would be in touch in a couple of days.'

'I'm not cross with you, Adam, although it sounds as if you might have done more to discourage her. I'm very displeased with Helena, firstly for meeting you against my wishes and secondly for being so forward – it's outrageous. But it does underline the urgency of speaking to her, to give her the knowledge, as you put it. Now, I want you to run through the exact details of everything your parents have told you.'

Elizabeth sat patiently as he took his time telling the story, of how his parents had tried to have children and then had considered settling in France with their adopted child but had changed their mind and brought him to England. He laid out the adoption documents on the table and talked her through each of them one by one, avoiding his father's historical embellishments about Napoleon and the Ancien Régime.

When he had finished, Elizabeth said, 'You've done very well, Adam. I think this proves everything conclusively, quite apart from my instincts. Firstly, there will be very few people like you who were born in France in January 1945 and who have spent their whole life being brought up in Britain. Add the fact that you are adopted, when the vast majority of people are not. But in addition to all that, the date when I gave birth is exactly the same as your recorded date of birth. Even the location in France makes sense – it's understandable that France's anonymous birth system requires a child to be offered for adoption in a different place to where it was born, otherwise it might be easier to trace, but the authorities, particularly in wartime, are hardly going to transport children to the other end of the country. You were offered for adoption in Caen, which was far away enough from Bayeux. And above all, there are the names – the French names are exactly the ones I gave you. All I've got to do now is sit Helena down and tell her the facts. She'll be acutely embarrassed for making a fool of herself with you. It must be done very sensitively.'

She sipped her coffee and smiled, placing her hand on his again. 'You mustn't worry. Everything will be fine. It certainly won't be easy for me – in fact I'm dreading it because I've never told Helena much about my life before Magnus. She knows nothing of Ralph. It will appal her, my having had a child out of wedlock.'

'What will you tell her about us? She doesn't even know you and I met after she broke up with me.'

'That'll be very difficult too, but it has to be truthful. I'll tell her about your thank-you letter after you came to stay and your request to meet and explain why the two of you split up. And then I'll say that when we met I discovered your real age, your birthday and that you were adopted, and that I was in shock for days trying to come to terms with it all. As soon as I get home later, I'll say that you and I met today to be absolutely sure of the facts before telling her that you're her half-brother. It's the truth.'

'The whole truth? The meeting at my house?'

'No! It must never be mentioned. That vileness, that evil, must be forgotten. Crushed out. You must promise.'

As she shuddered out the words, Adam knew any hope he had was finally obliterated.

'You do agree to that, don't you? I want you to promise me, to swear it.' Glaring at him, she repeated, 'I want you to promise. I want to hear you say the words.'

'Of course ... I promise,' he said.

She settled back into her chair, her shoulders relaxing, looking around at the nearby tables as if checking nobody had been listening to their tense discussion.

She smiled and said brightly, 'When it's all settled it will be wonderful. I'm dreading the conversation with Helena, and I haven't a clue yet about what I'm going to say to Magnus, but in the end you, Helena and I will be very happy.'

'And I'm to ignore Helena?'

'She'll know everything as soon as I get home, so you'll be quite safe from her – I can assure you of that. She'll feel loathsome about her behaviour with you. But as you say, it's not her fault. In time, she'll even find the whole turn of events amusing. And then you two will need to spend lots of time getting to know each other. It'll be fun! But it needs to be taken steadily.'

19

When Elizabeth got back from London, Helena greeted her and announced very excitedly that the fishmonger's van had been that afternoon and she had bought all kinds of fish. She wanted to prepare a bouillabaisse but had forgotten the precise rules of her mother's recipe. Elizabeth explained them: that it was a heresy to use white wine, that the croutons should be generously rubbed with garlic and that the dish should not include langouste and mussels, which was an abominable variation found only in Paris, the city being too far from the sea to have supplies of the correct fish for an authentic bouillabaisse.

Amid the furious boiling and the saffroned steam, Elizabeth didn't think the time was right for her delicate tête-à-tête with Helena. Stirring the large saucepan, she said, 'I think the weather will be fine tomorrow. I have a few jobs to do in the garden if you would like to help me.'

'Must I? Let's see what the weather's like in the morning,' Helena said.

'Good. I think this is nearly ready,' Elizabeth said, tasting the bouillabaisse off the edge of a wooden spoon. 'You can lay the table if you like and call Magnus in while I pour this into the tureen and season it and let it stand. Remember, a bouillabaisse must always stand and steep a little before it's served.'

The family meal passed by in much the same way as usual, with Magnus relating some of the nonsenses from his office, Elizabeth talking about her landscaping and Helena listening intently, asking questions and offering her fixed opinions.

Over the apple crumble, Magnus said, 'Tell me, Helena, what happened in the end to that chap who came to visit?'

'Adam, do you mean?'

'Yes, that's the fellow.'

'What about him?'

'He seemed quite sensible. A little earnest, perhaps, but quite sound, I think. I just wondered whether we were going to see anything more of him.'

'I think I misjudged him. Mother doesn't approve of me meeting him again, so it's rather difficult.'

'I see. Well, no matter, I suppose. She usually knows best. Now I must get back to my study. If you're bringing coffee, Elizabeth, we could catch up on a few things if you don't mind?'

* * *

Wearily, Elizabeth went to the other end of the house bearing a coffee tray, wondering what Magnus's next tirade would be about. Once they were seated with their coffees, he wasted no time.

'What's going on?' he said. 'When I mentioned Adam at the dinner table, I watched you very carefully. I know you well enough – I could see you were disturbed by the mention of his name. You did that quizzical tilt of the head, that tiny nod you do when you're nervous. Oh, don't worry – nobody else notices it, I'm sure. I used to think it quite endearing. And why am I saying all this? Because I'm flummoxed.

'The reason I'm flummoxed is that this afternoon I was walking back from my lunch in St James's with a client, and I passed the little café near St Martin's I occasionally visit when I want a quiet moment. And guess who I should see sitting in the corner? I could have popped in to say hello to my lovely wife, but I didn't want to interrupt her. She seemed *very* absorbed. I saw she had her hand on this chap Adam's hand – it looked very intense, very charged, the way you were drilling closely into his eyes – you who are not usually given to such strong shows of emotion—'

'Magnus, please stop! There's a perfectly simple explanation. *You* were the one wondering about why the two of them had broken off. *You* suggested there might be something wrong with Helena. I got the distinct impression that you thought that as her mother I should have known why they had broken off. Helena wouldn't tell me why. But Adam wrote to me and said he wanted to explain why he and Helena had parted and I offered to meet him. He's not what he seems. He's a perfectly innocent boy ... but somewhat lost.'

'So there's nothing wrong with him?'

'No!'

'Then why do you disapprove of him seeing Helena again? Might it be, by any chance, because you are jealous of Helena taking an interest in him too? It all seems to fit. You had the opportunity to spend a lot of time with him while he was here at the house. Anyway, I'm glad you've been proved fallible at last. But if you're going to carry on like everyone else, I would prefer you to be more discreet. What made it so obvious was that you looked distinctly dowdy. You can still be rather beautiful when you make the effort, but one has to know someone very well to be that plain when out and about – to know them so well that there's no need for effort. I do wonder about him if he carries on with a woman twice his age. Maybe he's not right for Helena after all. Or maybe you and Helena could share him – I'm sure he'd adore that – it would be like carrying on with two sisters. Two for the price of one.'

The words rained down on her like the blows of a heavy stave, and she leant forward and glared at him. 'Stop it, Magnus. Stop it at once. How dare you! I can assure you my plain appearance was for precisely the opposite reasons you suggest. There is no desire of that kind. You disgust me.'

She would not give Magnus the satisfaction of seeing her eyes fill. She left the room without taking the coffee tray, biting her lip and clenching her fists as she marched. She would have it out with Magnus when the time was right, but that would only be when Helena and Adam were fully settled, the three of them together, a new-found family.

She would go straight to bed. She needed sleep now so that she was refreshed in the morning, fully prepared to tell Helena the whole story. It would not be easy; she could be unpredictable at times.

* * *

Helena had not come bouncing into Elizabeth's bedroom that morning, but was reading in the kitchen when Elizabeth came down for breakfast.

'I thought I'd leave you to sleep in,' Helena said. I heard

all the shouting last night. It sounded like quite a row, even from the other end of the house.'

'And did you hear what it was about?'

'No, not at all. I turned the television on. All parents row from time to time. It's got nothing to do with me.'

When they had finished breakfast Elizabeth said, 'It's lovely and sunny, I think I'll start in the garden. Are you coming out to join me? It's just moving a few plants around and you can help me tie up the wisteria that has blown down, and the espalier needs repairing.'

'I can tell there's something on your mind. You know I find gardening tedious. What's the matter?'

'It's a beautiful day and I just thought it would be nice to be outside together. We could talk.'

'But we talk all the time. It's obvious there's something you want to talk about, something to discuss. We could do it now.'

'Oh, it doesn't matter! I'll just have to work in the garden on my own. Don't worry about it. You're obviously busy with too many things to do.'

After an hour, Helena came onto the terrace where Elizabeth was standing on a stepladder, wearing her kidskin gloves, hammering vine eyes into the tall brick wall. Helena carried a tray with a jug of iced lemon pressé and two tumblers, which she set down on a metal table that needed new green paint. She sat down carefully on one of the two metal chairs either side of the table. 'I'm sorry, I didn't mean to snap at you. But the situation with Adam is niggling me. Why won't you let me see him, or even talk to him?'

Elizabeth stepped down from the ladder very carefully and joined Helena at the table. 'This is going to be very difficult,

Helena. It's going to be a shock. Neither of us is to blame, but both of us could have handled things slightly better. I have had some conversations with Adam recently, so I know that you've met him, against my wishes, it has to be said.'

'Adam never mentioned he had been in touch with you. What have you been talking about?'

'You may remember that when you broke off with him I asked you several times what had happened between the two of you and you were evasive. Magnus expressed surprise that as your mother I didn't know the reason. Fortunately, Adam himself felt an explanation was required and offered to meet me, which I did when I was up in London. Because you had finished with him so emphatically, I didn't think I was going behind your back in any way in meeting him. Magnus made it quite clear that he thought it was my duty to find out what the problem was.'

'And did Adam tell you?'

'Yes, he said that you had fallen out over a misunderstanding about his age, that he was five years older than you. I also learnt from him that he was adopted.'

'Adopted? He never told me that. But it's probably not very important.'

'Oh, but it is, you see. It's *very* important.'

Elizabeth got up from the table and went to the flower border to pull out a stray aquilegia, which she placed in a trug of weeds that lay on the gravel path. She smoothed her dress carefully as she sat down again and took a sip from her tumbler. 'The reason it's important, Helena, is that Adam is your half-brother. But I wanted to be absolutely certain before I told you.'

Elizabeth took the story slowly, telling it as a distant

memory so that she wouldn't upset herself. She could relive the sweep of her history and remain calm if she related it dispassionately, pausing occasionally for a sip of her pressé. It took twenty minutes at least to describe how naïve she'd been at seventeen, how she had met Ralph, his death in France, and how she had abandoned her child, racked with guilt and grief before returning to England after the war to start a new life with Magnus. She told Helena about the conversations she had had with Adam, that his birthday was the exact date when Elizabeth had given up her child in Normandy and that all the paperwork given to Adam by Constance and Arnold confirmed the facts that Adam was her abandoned son.

When Elizabeth finished, she thought how typical it was of Helena to have sat silently throughout with that quiet frown she always adopted when absorbing detail, sitting rapt and sipping her pressé.

'What was Ralph like?' Helena said.

'Rather like Adam, which is no surprise.'

'What, in appearance or manner?'

'In every way.'

'It's not like you to give up. Giving up a child sounds rather cruel.'

'I was seventeen, Helena. I was exactly like you are now.'

'But I would never do such a thing.'

'We'll never know the answer to that, I hope. Can't you imagine how it has haunted and eaten away at me for years?'

'All you've told me is the facts. Yes, you talked about your grief and your guilt in that matter-of-fact way you have, but I don't know how you felt. How you really *felt*.'

'But do you need to know that?'

Helena's answer was to stare back very calmly, without a flicker of the eyes, the fixed expression clear in its answer that of course she needed to know that. But Elizabeth didn't want to be sucked into an explanation of how she felt in Bayeux; dredging it up would be too pitiful. She was completely mystified by the turn of conversation, having expected Helena to be elated at the discovery of a half-brother, or, if not elated, at least deeply intrigued. She watched Helena still staring back at her, now with a bemused tilt of the head, demanding an explanation of feelings from more than twenty years ago. Or was Helena in shock, perhaps? Was she so taken aback at the revelation about Adam that she was reacting in this strange way, still waiting for Elizabeth to confess how she felt lest the charge of cruelty should stand.

'They were very different times then, Helena …'

Elizabeth stopped, unable to say any more. She couldn't bring herself to talk about Bayeux. If she stuck to just reciting the facts, as she had with Miranda, then with Adam and now with Helena, she could just about maintain her composure. But it was impossible to put into words how she felt in Bayeux. It would make her collapse. 'I was utterly distraught, Helena. It will make us miserable if I describe it, whereas I want the three of us to be happy. The first step is essential, which is for you and Adam to acclimatise gradually and spend some time together as brother and sister. You can have as much time as you like, and as soon as you're both comfortable with that, I'll inform Magnus – and Adam will have to inform his parents. Then everything will be calm and we can all settle down. I'll let Adam know that you and I have spoken and then you two can arrange to meet up. We must take things very gradually, one step at a time.'

20

Adam was waiting in his sitting room for Helena to arrive. When Elizabeth had phoned the previous day, she sounded very relaxed, which at first Adam assumed was because she was using her home telephone rather than wrestling covertly with coins in a public telephone box. But it was soon apparent that her euphoria was the relief she felt now that everything was in the open with Helena. Telling the whole story had been a very difficult business, Elizabeth had said, and it was a great weight off her shoulders. She said Helena was to be congratulated for taking it all in very calmly and sensibly and that Helena would be telephoning him shortly to make arrangements about meeting him. And sure enough, within an hour, Helena had phoned. She had said it was very important that they should 'acclimatise', which was not a word he had ever heard Helena use before, but it seemed exactly right for what she had in mind. Rather than the three of them spending time together straight away, Helena suggested it would be far better if she and Adam met alone and adapted gradually. They could go on a few excursions together, although she hadn't thought yet about what they might be.

Waiting for the squeak of the gate and Helena's steps along

the path, he weighed the words from the two telephone conversations. Both Elizabeth and Helena had spoken with the same breathy reassurance, which he could listen to all day, the smooth tones shimmering over him like soft music.

Even though he had been expecting them, the two sharp raps of the brass dolphin on his front door seemed very loud.

When he opened the door, Helena stepped in, smiled, and kissed him on the lips. 'I can see I've taken you by surprise! You were obviously expecting something more *sisterly*,' she joked before walking along the little corridor to the kitchen, already talking about her conversation the previous morning with Elizabeth. It was as if she lived in his house, the way she picked up the kettle and filled it while she talked, and then sat opposite him at the little table with the gingham tablecloth, kicking off her flat shoes, waiting for the kettle to boil. 'I have a bone to pick with you, by the way,' she said. 'I think it's most unfair that you two set about investigating this wartime story of hers without involving me.'

'I'm sorry, but I don't think we had any choice,' he said. 'Perhaps it's best to see it from Elizabeth's point of view. She's clearly deeply ashamed about what happened all that time ago and she's obviously spent years trying to conceal it – even from you. Elizabeth and I were not deliberately excluding you from the conversation about her wartime experience. When I met her to discuss why you and I had broken up, we weren't to know that the subject of my adoption would crop up and that all the dates fitted together. She didn't want to go through the ordeal of telling you about her past until she was absolutely sure about all the facts. Think of her embarrassment and shame in confessing everything to you, dragging up her past and reliving what she has tried so hard to forget. When you told her that you wanted to start meeting me again she was in a panic, telling me urgently to find out all the details from my parents. She only became certain of the truth a couple of days ago when I met her with all the documents my parents had kept. Then she told you everything as soon as possible afterwards. She acted as quickly as she could.'

'And you believe every bit of her story, about being in such despair that she would give up a child?'

'Yes ... It's not easy for me to imagine how she felt. I get the impression it was more harrowing than she's letting on.'

'And do you want it to be true, Adam? What do you think about it all?'

'I don't know what to think. I honestly don't. You're both so certain about everything.'

She laughed and stood up, and hauled him up too, saying she wanted to look round the house again to see if he had made any progress with all his planned improvements.

As Helena walked him around his own house, Adam was still trying to get used to her assuredness. She had stopped in the doorway of the little dining room to rest her hand on his shoulder while they were looking in, and in the scullery she had seen a piece of dust on his collar and brushed it away with a smile that seemed far too generous for something so trivial. He feared for the moment when it would be time for her to leave, imagining the sensuousness of her farewell. He could sense Elizabeth watching over him, frowning disapprovingly at his tacit acceptance of Helena's brashness.

He thought how cruel it was to have suffered this reversal. Just as he was denying Helena now, she had denied him before. He remembered the first time he had become captivated, watching her perform the andante of Schubert's second piano trio. She started playing her cello slowly, buttoned up in her severe green velvet dress with the white collar, lost in concentration, sweeping the bow gently to the stately rhythm. She gradually became more and more immersed in the piece, increasingly distant until she subsumed herself into the furious crescendo, her forehead creased as if in pain, driving her bow across the strings with a vigour that belied her taut frame. At the beginning of the piece, her hair was in a loose bun, held together with a hinged tortoiseshell comb, but as the crescendo gathered pace a ringlet of her dark hair came free, flicking to the angry rhythm, her head juddering from side to side as she attacked the strings, making them screech, tearing the air, the ringlet of hair stuck to her cheek. She was lost inside the music for herself, not for the violinist, not for the pianist and certainly not for him. When he tried to compliment her afterwards for the intensity of her playing, she thanked him politely, but looked aghast at the idea that a performance could be anything else. He changed the subject and asked her whether she was ever nervous before a performance and then listened to one of her opinions, which was delivered in exactly the same manner as one of Elizabeth's – forthrightly, with effortless charm. Nerves were fine up to a point, Helena said. They keep you on your mettle, but you must never let them take over, or they will do you no good at all. You have to keep them just there, just in check, or you'll be overwhelmed. They need to be tamed, kept hot, but just below the boil at that critical point where you control the nerves and they don't control you. That's when you can break free and be lost in performance. When Helena had finished her pronouncement she thanked him again for his kind words and walked away. And every time they had met afterwards she seemed to be walking away, ignoring his clumsy overtures, his lame attempts to show affection. Without a word she could make it quite clear that their connection was purely a musical one and that any ideas of that sort were unthinkable.

* * *

When it was time for Helena to leave, she led him to the front door, where she turned towards him and said, 'There's one thing that's absolutely right about what my mother has said. We must get to know each other. In every sense. I want you to take me out for a picnic. We could go to Richmond where they have boats for hire, punting for example. It will be fun. You don't object, do you?'

'No, not at all, but—'

'Good. I'll phone you with the arrangements. I've had a lovely time, thank you.'

For her unsisterly kiss, she reached her arms up round his neck and drew his face down towards hers.

She smiled and was gone.

As soon as he had closed the door he stood in the passageway, looking down at the floor, rubbing his neck. He should have found it comical – that in resisting her, he had cricked it. But he was unable to laugh at his confusion; one moment he wondered why he had resisted Helena at all, and the next he imagined Elizabeth's fury at his weakness. She would be clipped and precise, with that slight huskiness in her voice that seemed like a whisper. Helena's voice whispered similarly but was pitched more softly.

For the rest of the day he imagined Helena arriving home and sitting down with Elizabeth. Where would it be? Would it be in one of the arbours in the garden, or in the drawing room, or the following morning when Helena was in the habit of visiting her mother's room? Elizabeth, sitting in all her poise, would ask Helena how her meeting with him had gone and whether she had had a nice time. Could it be possible that Helena would voice doubts about complying with Elizabeth's request to grow 'acclimatised'? They revered each other too much for there to be an argument, but the thought of them having an animated discussion about him was thrilling. The two voices were voices of reason, one calm, the other more insistent. But in the end he decided that Helena would say she had enjoyed herself and that Elizabeth was quite right about the need to get to know Adam at her own pace.

* * *

'A picnic on the Thames sounds delightful, Helena. I can't think of a nicer way to get to know somebody properly. But you need to be aware that there's no punting to be had at Richmond. The river's far too deep there. If you want to go to Richmond, it will have to be a skiff. Punting is for shallower water, the Isis and the Cam of course, and more locally why not try the River Loddon? Wargrave has some lovely punts, I seem to recall. But are you sure Adam is able to punt?

I would certainly never want to venture out in a punt unless the person doing the punting was quite proficient. You know what men are like – they get carried away as if they were gondoliers in Venice. It can be quite dangerous if you fall in. But if Adam is sufficiently skilled, the three of us could go punting together, a nice family outing—'

At that point Helena raised her hand and swept out of the room, shaking her head as if to say she had heard quite enough about punting, thank you very much, and there was no need for all this fuss. She would get to know Adam in her own good time, she said.

Elizabeth thought Helena had been in a strange mood ever since she had collected her from the station earlier that evening and driven her home. It had been difficult to get any information out of her about what she and Adam had discussed. Helena had the habit occasionally of avoiding a conversation by simply walking away from it. It had been far worse when she was in her early teens, when she would sometimes storm out of a room after a disagreement, even slamming a door as she went. It was a phase that lasted about eighteen months or so and Elizabeth had been careful not to overreact, always finding a quieter moment to advise Helena about alternative approaches. Helena had long since mastered the skill of sweeping out of a room with impressive grace. The next stage would be to advise her never to quit the scene at all, because it was always best to remain calm and stand one's ground, to parry blows and win arguments there and then.

The following morning Helena came into Elizabeth's room and placed a tray on her bedside table. 'I've brought you some jasmine tea,' she said before hopping onto the eiderdown.

Pouring the tea, Elizabeth noticed her favourite lacquered tray and that the cups and saucers were neatly arranged on a lace cloth. One of Helena's special efforts.

'You look tired, Helena. Did you not have a proper sleep?'

'No, I couldn't get to sleep for ages.'

'Is it something you want to discuss? You're not ill or anything?'

'I don't think so, I'm just a little unsettled about this Adam business at the moment.'

'It's bound to be like that. It's very unsettling for both of us. I'm keen to tell Magnus about it all as soon as possible, but it wouldn't be right to do so until I'm completely confident that you and Adam are comfortable with the situation. Once it's all out in the open, I'm absolutely certain everything will be very much better. In fact, it will be marvellous!'

21

Helena was making slow progress with her Kodály sonata. Usually she enjoyed practising a piece for hours, anticipating the reward of being able to play it well. But neither the practice nor the end result were remotely enjoyable if one failed. It was like wanting something you can't have. Adam had clearly felt that way about her previously and now it was the other way round.

She remembered the time when he had first plucked up the courage to come and speak to her at the end of a music rehearsal. Afterwards, they started spending time together, attending the same music weekends, and the conversations became more animated. She knew what he wanted, but she'd been very clear that he should forget about anything of that sort. She said they would get along very well provided the connection was a purely musical one. He had grown to accept it, apart from the occasional lapses when she caught him off guard, glancing at her, or the little incidents when he came to stay, such as his reaction when he was told that his room was at the other end of the house from hers, or when he tried to peer into the untidiness of her bedroom, or when he lay next to her up at the tennis court. The rest of the time he had always behaved perfectly, but his studied saintliness had irritated her at times, the way he put on a brave face.

Now that the situation was reversed, she realised that all the advice that had been heaped on her for years had made her too pious. She had been permanently aloof with Adam up until the time he came to stay. Adam was rejecting her now because he was confused by her change of mood. But if she persisted, she would break down his resistance, surely? It would only be a matter of time before he responded to her new enthusiasm. Well, it was more than that!

It was Miranda and her mother who had made her pious. When she was fourteen, they had told her everything they thought she needed to know about boys – thankfully her school friends had filled in all the gaps. Miranda had been a trusting confidante on several very sensitive matters, but her godmotherly concern had perhaps been a little too puritanical, insisting that the interest boys were starting to show must be ignored and that the absolute priorities were her studies and her music. 'There'll be plenty of time for everything else,' Miranda had said. 'You'll be a very beautiful and intelligent woman and being pestered is to be expected, I'm afraid.'

Her mother's advice had been much the same, but she too hadn't really moved with the times by recognising the new reality that at seventeen one was a fully grown adult. With the older generation there was always a long delay between something happening in the world and people realising it. She had experienced this delayed effect herself at Magnus's parties. For years, she'd been allowed to stay up until nine o'clock, offering plates of canapés to the guests. They would stoop down to take a tartlet or a cheese puff, making a great fuss over Elizabeth's precocious daughter who always behaved so impeccably with her toothy little smile. But now that she was fully grown the same guests seemed puzzled taking the canapés, no longer having to stoop now that she was of equal stature in every sense. Some of the guests still persisted in speaking to her in that cooing, sing-song tone as if she were still wearing pigtails. It was a lack of judgement.

She had always worshipped her mother's sense of judgement, but it had wavered recently. The story about Bayeux in 1944 and 1945 was very moving but hardly convincing. It seemed that she had started to believe things that were not proven, which was not her normal way at all. She had been behaving strangely, her mind seeming to be occupied with things that were not discussed, being clumsy occasionally, knocking over a pepper grinder, over-boiling an egg or forgetting the butcher's name. It might not be old age, exactly, but it was a concern that her mother was no longer infallible, making errors of judgement, latching on to evidence that was shaky.

It was ridiculous to think of Adam in a brotherly way. She had no desire for it. Her desires were of quite another sort.

She tried the opening bars of the sonata again, but while the bow swept, the music didn't flow. To her ears, it was stilted and turgid and of little use. The Kodály had defeated her, for now anyway. She sighed and placed the cello carefully on its stand and packed her bow away in its case. She would make some sandwiches and go for a walk.

In the kitchen, the bread bin was empty apart from the end of a loaf that had lost its softness. She was tempted to wrap the bread in a moist cloth and put it in the Aga for a moment. It was a trick of her mother's, but she decided against it and took an apple instead.

After walking a while, she came to the little Norman church where she used to go to Sunday school. She remembered the times they were allowed up onto the tower and she would feel the churning sensation inside her when she looked down over the parapet, wondering what it would be like to fall.

After walking further, she came to one of her favourite spots, a hill high above the Thames with views stretching away into the distance, the land looking rather parched from the summer sun. She stood still, thinking about the trip on the river with Adam in three days' time. Wouldn't it be easiest just to declare how she felt the moment they met and be done with it? She felt strong, and surely he was bound to succumb. She suspected that underneath it all he felt the same as her. He had certainly felt that way before, and it was only his strange obedience to Elizabeth that was holding him back. He was cautious, but would surely have the same itch or urge or need or whatever it was. Yes, she could rap at his door, march in and lose herself there and then. She gazed into the far distance before deciding against it. It would be the wrong approach. It would be better to make him reach his own conclusions and decide for himself. It would be a drawn-out process, but all the sweeter for that maybe. She would take it very steadily. She would have it all.

She would have to be very careful of course to avoid the obvious risks. She would have to ensure she didn't repeat her mother's mistake when *she* was seventeen. It was not the kind of thing she would be comfortable talking to Miranda about, let alone her mother. And she could hardly share such a sensitive matter with Dr Greenwood. She imagined making an appointment to see him and how the conversation would go. *Hello, Helena ... I haven't seen you for a long time ... How is everything? ... How are Magnus and Elizabeth?* Well, that's what I wanted to discuss with you first of all, Dr Greenwood. *Oh! Is one of them not well?* No, they're both very well thank you. It's just that you know my parents socially. You go to Magnus's parties and the matter is a delicate one you see. Very delicate. That's why I asked your receptionist whether I could see a different doctor, but she said you were the family doctor and therefore the only one I was allowed to see. *Helena, I can assure you that complete confidentiality is our duty ... personally, I think too much is made of the fact that it's a professional duty ... in my view it's above all a moral duty ... whatever you say will be just between the two of us ... although how old are you now?* I will be eighteen next month. *Well, the technical position is you're still a minor. But morally, of course, you're nearer eighteen than seventeen, so I can assure you of complete confidentiality. Not a word will be spoken, you have my word. Now what's the matter you wish to discuss?*

No, it was not a matter she could discuss with Dr Greenwood. She would find another way. She would visit Philippa before she met Adam for the boating trip. It was clear that Philippa was well advanced in these matters. And besides, Adam was obsessively precautious and always prepared for every eventuality.

22

Adam was sitting in Terence's leather-backed chair as he often had, ever since he was a small boy.

'I thought you'd gone for good. I haven't seen you for eight weeks at least, I reckon. Mind you, it shows. Very tatty,' Terence said.

Terence had set up his barber's shop just after the war on a little shopping parade near the Matlocks' Holland Park house, and it had changed little since. Adam had often thought of finding a new barber's, somewhere less rundown. An alternative wouldn't have to be particularly fashionable, but somewhere without harsh strip lighting, the smell of ancient brilliantine and capes of lurid green nylon would be preferable. But he hadn't the heart to leave Terence behind; it would be like losing a kind-hearted uncle, one who had always chattered away with the snip of his scissors, always addressing him like an adult, even when he was five and having to sit on a plank across the arms of the chair because he was so small. On this occasion, Adam was finding Terence's prattle tiresome because he wanted to think about Helena's boating trip arrangements and the conversation he had had with Elizabeth earlier that morning.

'I had a young lad in here the other day and his hair was

even stragglier than yours. I know people like to wear it longer nowadays, but you still have to cut it to make it longer, if you see what I mean ...'

If it were possible for someone to wag a finger at you down the phone, then Elizabeth had done it. He was getting used to her maternal behaviour, the way she enquired about whether he was eating properly, and sighing when he told her that he still hadn't had a haircut, which was something she had mentioned when they were last in the café. His hair was scruffy, she said. That was why he was sitting now in a lime-green cape on a battered leather chair. During the conversation, he had unintentionally mentioned Elizabeth's visit to his house, and she had been very stern, reminding him to obliterate any memory of their evil, disastrous error. She had said it with such fierce conviction that he had come to believe her – that the irredeemable sin was best forgotten. But it was not easy to forget the reality of that afternoon, his memory of her lying next to him, the warmth and the softness, the thump of her heart, their faces touching.

'At first I thought all this wearing hair a bit longer was going to put me out of business, you see ... I thought I'd have to hang up my scissors for good, but it's only a fashion. It'll still need to get cut ...'

Elizabeth had insisted on Adam being patient with Helena; she often took a long time adapting to new situations. It might take her a week or two to recalibrate and become fully reconciled to the change in family circumstances, but once Helena was comfortable she would fall in with it very solidly and the truth would be cast in stone.

'Lax, I call it. Everything's becoming too lax. I'm all for

things loosening up a little. But all this do what you want, whenever you want, it can't be right. It'll all end in tears one day ...'

And as for Helena's picnic, what was he to make of that? She obviously had some grand design, ringing him up to check which sandwiches he preferred. She shared Elizabeth's precision about everything being done correctly. Right now she would be making cucumber sandwiches very purposefully, her pursed lips fixed on the task of perfectly cut triangles; it would be done with the same tilt of the head as Elizabeth's when things had to be just so. They even wore the same kind of long muslin dress when the weather was hot, and a wide-brimmed straw hat too.

'And I said to the missus, what do you want to go and live in Clacton for? The grass isn't always greener, you know. Anyway, I still love her to bits after all these years. You found yourself a nice girl yet?'

Whenever Terence had asked this question on previous occasions, it had always made Adam uneasy, having to reply that he had not. Terence would either bite his lip and say nothing as he snipped away, or say something about there being plenty of fish in the sea, and that there was no need to worry.

Unlike his friends at school, and more recently at Durham, he had not been able to boast an impressive series of girlfriends. In fact, Helena had been his first proper experience of what might be called 'going out' with someone – if the term could be applied to a common interest in music. He liked to think his reserve was the result of being less superficial than his friends, and that he didn't need a string of conquests to prove himself, pandering to the idea that virility was somehow proportional to the amount of success. But at the same time he recognised that his reflective nature might make him a less exciting prospect than his friends. It was the reason he had wanted to grow his hair – he wanted to fit in with everyone else.

The last time Terence had asked him whether he had met anyone was before he had met Helena. The thought of being able to answer Terence's question in the affirmative for once made him smile. He would choose his words carefully because he had a habit of picking up Terence's expressions and manner of speaking. What would be a Terence-like reply? Certainly something very blunt – that, yes, he had found someone very nice, an older woman, who had slung her hook, but he might take up with the daughter instead, if you see what I'm driving at, Terence, if you fill in the blanks.

'Yes, I think I have found someone,' Adam replied.

'Ah, that's good. What's she called then?'

'She's called Helena.'

'Been going on long, has it?'

'We met each other a few times before I was invited to stay at her parents' house, and then she broke off for a bit, but now she wants to meet up again.'

'And was it, you know, *serious*, as it were, before she broke off?'

'No, we were just getting to know each other.'

'Big house, was it?'

'Yes, quite large.'

'What, in town here?'

'No, a little place in Berkshire called the Holt.'

'Crikey, that's a famous place, that is! I could tell she was properly posh because of her name. Strange that, don't you think? How just adding an 'A' at the end of a name adds that bit of class, not that I've got anything against the name of Helen, that is, which is my sister-in-law's name as a matter of fact. So she wants to meet up again, does she? That's a good sign. A very good sign indeed. It's what happens with the classy ones – they don't rush at things like a bull in a china shop – well, not a bull, exactly. Sometimes they break off to have a little think about things. So she's invited you back to her house again, giving it another try, is she?'

'No, she wants us to go for a picnic on the river first. I'm meeting her this afternoon.'

'Ah, so that explains the haircut! Always best to look smart, always best to make the effort. And she's making the picnic, is she?'

'Yes, she probably knows I wouldn't be very good at that.'

'Well, that all sounds very promising, I must say. A picnic! I'm jealous!'

Terence hummed a tune brightly while completing the final snips before putting his scissors down and holding up a mirror behind Adam's head. 'There we are, that's a bit better now, isn't it? Not too long, and not too short, just as you said.'

Terence unfastened the lime-green cape and flourished it away like a matador, giving it a good shake. Adam crossed the brown lino floor to stand by the cash box where Terence said, 'That'll be two-and-six please, Adam ... and if you need something for the weekend, as it were, that would be an extra one-and-six. Better to be safe than sorry, I always say.'

Adam wiped his neck with a tissue and discarded it into

Terence's wastepaper basket. He paid Terence with two half-crowns, thanking him and saying he could keep the change. As he walked out of the door into the street he rubbed his neck again.

* * *

'The reason I look such a frump is because of a terrific argument I had with Mother this morning. I wanted to wear my Mary Quant skirt because the weather is going to be hot, but she absolutely insisted that something longer was required for sitting in a skiff.'

These were the first words Helena said to Adam after they met outside Richmond station. She had greeted him with a pecked kiss appropriate for meeting outside a station; it would have been a rule drummed into her by Elizabeth – to always conduct oneself decorously in public spaces.

Helena was wearing a wide-brimmed straw hat and a long white muslin dress, her dark brown hair rolling in waves against the white cloth, dazzling his eyes in the sun. 'Here, you'd better take this. I've been carting it around all morning and it's heavy,' she said, handing him the picnic basket. She linked with his left arm and they walked towards the river, Helena talking volubly about how she had just come from Philippa's and how nice it was to have escaped for a day out; she loved being at home, but it was even better being with him.

'I see you've had your hair cut,' she said.

'Yes, it was getting rather scruffy.'

'I think I prefer it longer, but never mind, I'm sure it will grow.'

At the river, while the man untied one of the skiffs to bring it alongside the landing stage, Adam said to her, 'Do you want to row or steer?'

'Goodness, I didn't think I'd be doing anything like that.'

'But you've been in a skiff before?'

'Yes, twice, when I was young. Father rowed, Mother steered, and I sat at the front, or the bows as they insisted on calling it. I know it's important to always step into the middle of the boat, but that's all I remember really.'

'Well, this should be interesting,' Adam said. 'Perhaps I'll row and you can steer. I'm sure it'll be fine.'

It was not what Adam had expected. When they arranged the trip, Helena had said, very confidently, that she had been to Henley and had been skiffing before. But now, after five minutes, it was abundantly clear that she'd never steered a rowing boat, because they had run into the riverbank twice and had looped out into the middle of the river several times, causing mayhem with the pleasure craft ploughing through the greenish water.

'Steering with a rudder can be a little strange,' Adam said. 'It's counter-intuitive, you might say. With a steering wheel, if you push up or forward with the left hand you turn to the right, but a rudder on a boat does the opposite – if you push forward on the rudder strings with the left hand the boat goes to the left. It's because in a boat you're steering the back round, whereas in a car you're steering the front wheels. See if that helps.'

It didn't help at all, so Adam suggested another idea: he would row along and get some speed up and then stop rowing so that Helena could stretch her arm down into the water and see how it made the boat turn in the same way that a rudder would. It would explain the principle, he said, the resistance of your arm in the water on one side of the boat would turn it exactly like a rudder. He watched her rolling her sleeve up methodically, right up to her shoulder, causing him to mistime a stroke because her upper arm was identical to the way he remembered Elizabeth's.

'It's expecting a lot to be brilliant at steering on your very first outing, Helena. Many people never get the hang of it even after trying dozens of times.'

At first, Helena frowned and was very quiet as she experimented with her arm in the water, first one side, then the other. Then she took hold of the rudder strings and told him to row faster. She wrenched on the rudder strings and nearly capsized the skiff. But having grasped the principles, she was soon steering the skiff along very happily.

'This is the life,' she said, leaning back in her cushioned seat and stretching out her legs in front of her, so that he had to row with his feet either side of her knees. When he was waiting for her at the station, he had feared she might find the river trip boring, but as he paddled the boat along she seemed very content, chatting away, pointing out the swans and the ducks and the ducklings, and enjoying the wash of passing motor cruisers which made the skiff rock from side to side. At first, each time it happened, she let out a little whoop, but she tired of it in the end and they glided along silently except for the oars dropping into the water like bell-notes, chiming alternately with the clunk of the rowlocks. Occasionally, she would watch him rowing and smile, her face close to his as he leant forward for each stroke. Each time their faces nearly touched he had to glance away at the river, or stare at the varnished mahogany, or count the number of copper rivets running in lines along the floor of the boat.

They had just rowed around a bend in the river and he could see her looking over his shoulder with an amused expression. He turned round to look and faced her again.

'You'll probably have to go outside that post ahead of us. There's not much room between it and the riverbank.'

'It's fine, Adam. Keep rowing. You can go faster if you like. There's enough room inside the post.'

He knew her well enough. There was no point arguing; she was too like Elizabeth. She narrowed her eyes, concentrating on the course ahead. He calculated that she would need to steer very accurately to avoid his oars hitting the post or running the boat into the reeds on the bank. She leant forward, her eyes fixed on the river, leaning slightly to one side to see round him. As she gazed intently at the water ahead, he couldn't resist staring at her pure form, startling him with its resemblance to Elizabeth's that time they lay close together. When he leant forward to row each stroke, she was close enough to kiss and when he leant back at the end of each stroke, he could see clearly the course she was steering by the perfect curve carved in the water behind them. The arc continued round and they passed the post with a matchbox's width between it and the end of his oar. On the other side of the skiff, there was not a flick of the oar against the reeds. The arc was complete and she steered straight ahead again. He said nothing and she said nothing. She made no trace of a smirk, but he could tell from the brightness of her eyes that she was pleased with her success. He smiled and she smiled back and neither of them spoke.

After a few minutes she said it was time for their picnic and would tell him when she had spotted a suitable spot. 'I want to find some shade, somewhere quiet where there aren't all these motor boats ploughing up and down.' After a while she said, 'That'll do, just there, under the trees.'

'There's not much headroom,' he said, 'and the tide is still rising for another hour or so, but let's give it a try.'

Once they had tied the boat to some overhanging branches, Helena insisted that he sit next to her on the cushioned seat. She opened the picnic basket and handed him a sandwich, which was indeed very neatly cut.

'What did you do with the crusts?' he said.

'Crusts! The crusts are for the birds. You can't eat *crusts*!'

'But I like them. My parents always told me the crusts were the best bit.'

'My mother says exactly the same. It must be the war.'

'These are very good,' he said. 'Usually I avoid cucumber sandwiches because they're often soggy.'

'The trick is to spread the butter thickly right to the edge of the bread. That's why you cut off the crusts. Then no vinegar gets into the bread. And you have to use proper vinegar – and milled pepper, of course, not that powdery stuff people use.'

'You learnt this at home?'

'Of course.'

He watched her biting softly into the bread, then saying nothing while she ate.

She continued, 'After lunch I think I'll do some rowing and you can lean back in this comfortable seat and have a nice rest. Is rowing even easier than steering?'

'Provided you follow some basic principles, it's quite straightforward.'

'And what are the principles? You're good at those.'

'The main thing is to keep the oars the same depth in the water and pull evenly, or you'll be going round in circles. It's best to keep your back straight and your head up, with wrists straight too, not gripping the oars too tightly or you'll get blisters …'

He imagined her rowing, puffing a little, frowning with concentration as her face floated towards his with each flick of the oars.

'You've stopped. Are those the only principles?'

'No, not all of them. But I don't want to bore you.'

'You're not boring me at all. Here …'

When she put her arm round his shoulder and kissed him on the neck he didn't dare to turn towards her.

'Tell me, Adam, what's the matter?'

'It doesn't seem right. Your mother wouldn't approve.'

'I sometimes wonder if you're in awe of her. I can assure you that if I thought her story was true, I wouldn't be sitting here under these trees with my arm around you. I love her very much, but on this occasion I think she's wrong, deluded even.'

'Why don't you believe her?'

'Oh, I *do* believe most of it. Her time in the war, being in France, her traumatic affair with Ralph. I've often asked her about her past, her life before Magnus, and she would always clam up or change the subject. So when I sat on the terrace and heard her open up about it freely the other day I nearly burst into tears, which she certainly wouldn't have approved of. I'm sure it's true she had a child and gave it up for adoption. But I don't think that child is you. I think I would know whether you're my half-brother. We just don't have enough facts. We can't rely on her distant memory of the exact date when her child was born. A child that could have been adopted by anyone in France seemingly. We're not related, Adam, so you needn't worry about it. I dote on her, she's taught me everything I know. I love her very much, but I really think she's confused herself unnecessarily. I've been thinking about it a lot. At first I thought she might have reached an age when memories start to play tricks on you. Can you imagine bottling up something like that for so long, letting the memories stalk you for your whole life and not sharing them with anyone, letting them fester and distort? But hiding it, letting it eat away for years, could affect your sense of judgement or even make you unbalanced in the end. It must mean that when some new information comes along that fits your story, you latch on to it so that everything slots neatly into place. It could be comforting. You do see that, don't you? I don't want to upset her by saying I disbelieve her, but it's clear to me that we're both completely free to do whatever we wish. Whatever we *want*, Adam. Now, I think it's time for pudding, don't you? I've made a very special chocolate mousse, except it's more of a tort than a mousse. And I've cut up some strawberries and added them in.'

He sat and watched her as she opened a cool box from the picnic basket, taking out two china bowls and a couple of long-handled spoons. Having served the mousse, she kicked off her shoes and lay lower in the seat with a sigh, indulging herself with the mousse. How natural it would be, he thought, to slide lower and be beside her as close as he was with Elizabeth, but instead he stayed upright in the seat, looking down at her turning the long spoon upside down in her mouth with each scoop from her bowl, which she held high towards her chin. Was she right to doubt Elizabeth's certainty? What if she was right about Elizabeth being wrong for once?

'You are enjoying this aren't you, Adam?'

'Yes, it's very rich. The puddings I normally eat are crumbles and pies and that sort of thing.'

'No, I meant us like this. You with me. Are you always going to be hesitant?'

'I'm thinking.'

'Tell me what you're *thinking* about,' she said as she jolted herself upright next to him. But as she did so the spoon full of chocolate fell down the front of her dress. 'Quick!' she shouted as she grabbed a bottle of ginger beer and poured it onto the chocolate, wiping it frantically with a napkin. 'Oh, it's making it worse! She'll be furious. She'll probably kill me!'

'Try dipping it in the river,' Adam said. 'I'll balance the boat by leaning out of this side of the boat while you lean out on that side.'

She knelt on the seat and arched over the side of the boat, splashing water up onto her dress and flicking away at it with the back of her nails. 'It's impossible! What should I do?'

He couldn't answer the question. He didn't want to think about it – helping her to wash the front of her dress. He certainly couldn't bring himself to make the most practical suggestion, which would be to remove it. He could promise to close his eyes and look away. And then she could brush the patch of chocolate in the river, rather than rubbing it in and making things worse. 'Can I help?' he asked.

'What a disaster,' she hissed, scrubbing the stain frantically with her handkerchief.

Finally, as she collapsed back into the seat, she said, 'It's hopeless. I suppose I could cover the stain up with my shawl to save me embarrassment on the train, but what will I say when I get home?'

'You'll just have to tell the truth.'

'Of course I'll tell the truth! But she'll be seething. She'll ask me how it happened, and I'll have to explain I was fooling around with my spoon, which will make her crosser still.'

He'd never seen her looking thoroughly miserable before. Annoyed, yes, aloof, or haughty even, but never sad and defeated. He couldn't just say nothing as she sat frowning with her arms crossed. 'We could cut short the rowing and get a cab to my house. You could wash your dress there. It looks like the sort of thing that would dry quickly on such a hot day.'

'Adam, that's a brilliant idea!' she said, starting to pack everything away neatly into the picnic basket. 'Mind you, I still want to row. I'll row us all the way to the boathouse with my head up, with a straight back and the oars the same depth in the water. I've remembered it all. You'll see.'

* * *

Helena sat on the landing stage eating an apple, while Adam walked up to the hut to pay for the hire of the skiff. The boatman said, 'Well she's a rare one, that's for sure. You need to hang on to her! When I saw you setting off earlier, I thought there's going to be trouble there. Going round in circles she was with her steering. But I've these binoculars, you see, to make sure all the boats are behaving, and I saw she was soon steering straight. And now she comes back rowing very neat. Done it much before, has she?'

'No, I don't believe she has,' Adam said.

'Well, that's a wonder, make no mistake! It's usually the prettiest ones who can't steer and can't row, but you've got the best of both worlds there if you don't mind me saying. That'll be nine shillings for the three hours, sir.'

After taking the money, the man winked and said, 'And I hope you have a very good evening.' Adam glared back at him. The man had no right to peer through his binoculars, or to pass comment on Helena, or to make such assumptions. He stared out of the window as the cab crossed Hammersmith Bridge, wondering whether the water flowing under it was the same water that had glided them along at Richmond. Thinking about the ebb and flow was like weighing Helena's and Elizabeth's opposing viewpoints, the one encouraging him and the other disapproving. He could hear Elizabeth scolding him – *Why on earth did you invite her back when you knew the situation perfectly well? It was utterly irresponsible.*' 'But I felt very sorry for her,' he would reply, 'she was distressed, sitting there with her ruined dress, knowing you would be enraged. I did act hastily, but I was trying to be practical, which is something you mentioned to me when you came to my house. You advised me to be more practical.'

As he unlocked his front door, Helena said, 'As soon as

we're inside, I'm going straight to that scullery of yours. Do you have soap and detergent and everything?'

'Yes, it's all in the cupboard under the stone sink. But how will we dry the dress afterwards?'

'I'm not going to wash the whole thing, just where the stain is, and then I'll sit in the bay window of the sitting room waiting for it to dry. It'll be boiling in there, facing the sun. But I have to get the stain out first.'

She marched to the scullery at the back of the house while Adam went to the sitting room to read.

After a good ten minutes, Helena came into the room. She was holding the ball of her wet dress out in front of her as if she were bearing a gift. 'I had to take it off in the end because the whole of the front got wet, but I think I've got the stains out. I'm hoping when it's dry that all the brushing hasn't ruined the fabric. I couldn't find a rack to dry it on. Do you have one?'

'Yes … I do,' he said, swallowing and fixing his eyes on the bundled dress to avoid being mesmerised by everything else. 'The rack's in the cupboard under the stairs. I'll go and get it. Then I'll go and find something for you to wear. You'll get cold. I've got a dressing gown upstairs.'

When he came back into the room, she was standing by a table near the window, holding her dress in her left hand while flicking through a National Geographic with the other. 'There's the rack,' he said, thrusting it down just inside the room and turning quickly to go upstairs.

He heard her shout, 'Thank you, Adam,' as he bounded up to the first floor. He opened his wardrobe, rattling the hangers along the rail one by one, looking for his dressing gown. It was hard to concentrate because he was seared by the image of her standing like an immaculate sculpture in the sun, offering her dress. He held his breath, dumbfounded by her exposure. Still clicking the hangers along, he told himself she was merely being practical. It wouldn't be pleasant to hold wet washing next to your skin, so you would have to hold it away from your body. It was wrong to be entranced, Elizabeth was telling him; he should have averted his eyes, should not have dared to look. He breathed out finally, shaking his head because the dressing gown had been hanging on the hook of the bedroom door all the time. He would take it down to her. How would he hand it over? Would he throw it into the living room and bolt out before she put it on, or would he open the dressing gown for her to step back into it, her head turning to smile at him while she arched her arms back into the sleeves?

She must have walked up the stairs quietly while he was rummaging in the wardrobe. 'I'm not wearing that scratchy old thing,' she said, standing in the doorway, nodding at the dressing gown. 'I've brought the rack and the dress up here because it will dry even more quickly. It's hotter here at the top of the house.'

He was stunned, watching as she put the rack up and fussed around it, arranging the dress to dry. 'But don't you want something ... to cover yourself, I mean?'

'No, it'll be fine. We can just sit here and talk while the dress dries. It'll be nice. Here, come and sit next to me,' she said as she sat on the side of the bed and patted it. She stretched her legs out towards the window and leant back on her hands, turning slightly towards him and talking casually about the trip in the skiff and how much she'd enjoyed it. 'It was very kind of you, Adam, to teach me to row and steer all in the same day. It *was* fun, wasn't it?' She leant forward and put her arm round his shoulder, kissing him on the neck. But all he could do was swallow speechlessly, trying to think of something else. She leant back on her hands again as he looked straight ahead at the window. He could sense her watching him, weighing his thoughts, wondering whether he was going to speak.

She got up and walked to the dress, which she picked up and turned over to dry on the other side, fanning it out in the hot sun streaming into the room. 'I don't think it's going to dry in time. I might have to telephone home and admit that I've had an accident with my dress – that it needs washing a couple of times at least and needs to dry before I can travel home. I'll say it'll be best if I stay here for the night and go back tomorrow. You wouldn't mind that, would you, Adam?'

She came back to sit next to him on the bed. He sank his face into his hands, closing his eyes and imagining opening them again next to her, in the morning, with the brightness of her skin in the sunlight and her hair lying in fronds across the pillow. He stared at his ancient walnut wardrobe. One of its doors was open; normally he jammed it shut with a piece of folded cardboard. He could see the drawer that reminded him of his haircut at Terence's. But it was as if Elizabeth was standing in the doorway, bitterly observing his conduct, reading his thoughts, making him ashamed to be thinking of the answer he could give to Helena's question. Very calmly, he could say no, he wouldn't mind her staying at all, and in the heat of the room he could breathe the smoothness, bury himself in the smile of her eyes, the fragrance, the whisper, the gasp, the glide.

He pressed his head even harder into his hands to break out of it. Finally, he walked across the room to close the wardrobe door. 'Oh, I don't think that would work at all,' he said. 'Can you imagine what Elizabeth would say? I can hear her words now, telling you to come home at once, and if you refused, she'd get in her car and come and fetch you. She'd be incensed. Staying the night is out of the question.'

'You've obviously been thinking about it. The thought of me staying *has* crossed your mind, hasn't it?'

'It's not something I can answer ... I'm sorry.'

'Tell me, Adam, do you dislike me?'

'Of course not! I adore you. There – I've said it!' He quickly gathered up the dressing gown into a ball, pushing it into her lap, and walked to the window, where he stared out, not wanting her to see his confusion. 'How could you ask if I dislike you!' He spat the words, then checked himself and said, 'I don't know what to like and what not to like anymore, or what is right or what is wrong. That's all I want to say. I don't want to discuss it further.'

'I've never seen you angry before.'

'I'm not angry. I'm just helpless and lost, that's all,' he said, almost in a whisper because he felt exhausted. He gripped the window frame and stared down into the street.

'So the only thing holding you back is Mother's story from the war and that we might be related?'

'I can't disbelieve her.'

'And if it were to be disproved, you'd change your mind about me?'

'It's a hypothetical question ...'

'But?'

'Yes …'

He looked over his shoulder to see that she had stood up and was putting on his dressing gown and tying its cord. 'This *is* a scratchy thing,' she said, coming over to stand next to him. They stared out of the window in silence for a moment.

She turned and went back to the rack to fan the dress out again. 'It's all right. I think it'll dry. Let's go downstairs. I think I understand perfectly now. There's only one difference between us and that is you believe my mother and I don't.'

In the kitchen, she sat opposite him with her elbows on the bleached pine table and her hands in a steeple with her chin resting on her fingertips.

He wanted to recant, to take back what he had said. He could say, gorgeously, that she could stay after all. He was about to utter the words when she started to talk calmly and clinically as if making a pronouncement. 'This is what we'll do. We'll establish the exact history and the exact circumstances. I'll find out everything from my mother, the exact details of what happened in Normandy and when. For your part, she seemed to think that you had got all the adoption paperwork from your parents. May I see it?'

'But do we want to go through all this now?'

'Yes, we must.'

He got up, went to the bureau in his sitting room and brought back the documents, handing her the envelope. She took it, saying nothing, and emptied out the papers onto the table, laying them out. He remembered previous occasions when her mood had changed in an instant. One of the exercises at the musical weekends they had attended was to be given the sheet music for a piece they had never played before. They were given a time limit to leaf through the score before playing it. With pursed lips Helena leant forward and burrowed her eyes into each page before turning to the next one with a frown. The whole room fell into hushed concentration, but hers was by far the most intense.

She asked him about the documents one by one. Anyone looking on would have thought her tone to be unnecessarily strict, but he knew well enough that this was merely Helena in her determined frame of mind, examining the sheets of paper, devouring the information, nodding her head when something registered, and tapping the air when something seemed particularly significant. She could have been conducting an orchestra. Elizabeth must have been the same running logistics operations in Normandy at seventeen; no officer would have dared to argue with the efficiency and the urgent sincerity. Nothing was left open to doubt or question; the sheer power anaesthetised any wish to argue. He wanted to interrupt her and say *enough*!

'Good,' she said, gathering up the papers very neatly and sliding them into the envelope. 'The adoption part of the puzzle seems clear. And you're sure, are you, that your parents have no information about the place of birth?'

'They were very clear about that – it's the way anonymous births work in France.'

'But it might be worth double-checking?'

'I could, but I don't want to upset them. They've been very good to me. It would make them very sad if I seemed determined to find my birth parents.'

'That's very understandable. You're quite right. And actually, the far bigger questions concern my mother and what happened in Normandy, where and when precisely. And why, too. I'll find out everything. I'll even ask what the weather was like, what she was wearing, the exact words she spoke in this hospital or convent or whatever it was. And there must be a birth record somewhere. We'll have to wait and see, Adam.'

She smiled and patted him on the shoulder before standing up and saying her dress would be dry and ready to put on. He watched her walk out of the room wearing his insufferable dressing gown.

When she came back down wearing her dress, she smoothed it out in front of her, smiling radiantly and saying it was dry and that it was time for her to go.

23

Elizabeth sat in her Triumph Herald as Helena came out of the station, tripping towards the car with her delicate steps, holding her hat in the breeze.

'Thanks for picking me up and I'm sorry it's so late,' she said, easing herself into the passenger seat.

'It's no problem at all,' Elizabeth said. 'When you phoned from Paddington to say you were going to be very late I was quite relieved. It gave me an excuse not to go to the Pilkingtons' for dinner this evening. I've been feeling rather tired, but that wouldn't have been an adequate excuse for Magnus. However, once you needed collecting from the station, he had to accept going to dinner on his own. Now I want to hear all about your boating. It's been glorious weather.'

Elizabeth had always found it endearing listening to Helena describe her day. There was rarely any chronological structure to her breathless accounts, no beginning, middle or end to the day as such. Instead, Helena would speak with a gush of words, flitting between the colourful events that had excited her most. She had learnt to row! – and explained the proper way to do it, with a straight back and straight wrists. There had nearly been an accident when a motor launch going far too fast had almost crashed into them while she was steering; the cucumber sandwiches were quite the best she had ever made, and she had shared the usual merriment with Philippa when she had gone to Chelsea in the morning.

Once Helena had described her day in London, Elizabeth suspected there was something on Helena's mind, something left unsaid. It could be tiredness because Helena's delicate arms were not trained for rowing. But then again, her arms were deceptively strong, and whatever was bothering her couldn't be fatigue because Helena always yawned far too demonstratively whenever she was weary; it was something Elizabeth had mentioned many times. Rather than weariness, it was *wariness*, more like – something tentative. The fact that Helena had hardly mentioned Adam at all meant that he must be the cause. She knew better than to ask 'And how was Adam?' She would wait until Helena was at home and had rested a while. Then whatever was on her mind would emerge, Elizabeth was certain. 'We're nearly home,' she said. 'I've made us a lovely salad with new potatoes.'

After they had sat down for their meal, Elizabeth said, 'You haven't talked much about Adam. How did the two of you get along?'

'We got along very well. In fact, we came to an understanding.'

'Yes? And what was that?'

'I want to talk to you about it, but I'm worried that you'll be cross.'

'Should I be cross?'

'No, you shouldn't be because nothing has happened that should make you cross. At least that's what I hope.'

'I'm sure it's best, Helena, to talk about whatever it is that's bothering you. And of course I'll try not to be cross.'

Had she been rash? All sorts of thoughts flashed through Elizabeth's mind, some of which would make her very cross indeed – for instance, if Helena had made any advances towards Adam, or worse still …

But to her relief it was nothing as bad as that. Helena unburdened all her concerns very methodically – she said she had been thinking endlessly about Elizabeth's wartime account, the trauma of Ralph's death, the birth in Bayeux, the adoption and how all the dates fitted together. She respected Adam's and Elizabeth's utter conviction about the truth, and she was bitterly disappointed in herself for wanting more certainty. 'I just want to be absolutely sure,' she said. 'It's a bit like religion, I suppose. Even the most fanatical believers have an occasional wobble. It's what makes them human. It isn't a sin to seek reassurance. It's not necessarily heretical, and certainly not hostile.'

Elizabeth had put down her knife and fork to listen to Helena's impassioned speech. She must have been preparing it all the way home from Paddington. It would explain her uneasy silences since they had got home. But the sincerity couldn't be ignored. 'But did you have this conversation with Adam?'

'Yes, we sat in his kitchen and discussed it for an hour.'

'In his *kitchen*? What were you doing there? You were meant to be on the river!'

'We *were* on the river. But I had an accident during the picnic. I spilt chocolate all down my front and I was in a panic because I knew you'd be furious, so we took a taxi to his house to wash my dress there. So that's what we did. It dried very quickly in the sun.'

'You took your dress off?'

'Yes, but he lent me his dressing gown.'

'And did he see you not wearing your dress?'

'Yes, but nothing happened.'

'That was most unwise, Helena.'

'Nothing would ever have happened, Mother, because Adam believes in you utterly. You should be proud of him. He's in awe of your opinion for some reason.'

'So what did you agree with him in the end?'

'Exactly the same as I've agreed with you. I'm asking you both to be patient with me while I try to find the certainty I need. I know it sounds ungrateful or unhelpful or whatever it is, and I don't want to upset you. I'm asking you not to be cross. It's a request.'

Elizabeth picked up her knife and fork again, wondering what to say. It would be pointless to argue with Helena. She had told the truth, that much was obvious, and she had clearly made a very firm decision.

'Very well then, Helena. But what form will your investigations take and how long will they take? I was hoping you would become settled with Adam quickly so we could tell Magnus, and Miranda and everyone else. I feel a fraud knowing what I do and nobody else knowing.'

'I don't know yet what form my research will take, but I'll do things as quickly as possible. Thank you for being so understanding.'

* * *

Adam was expecting Elizabeth to telephone. He had calculated that she would have collected Helena from the station at around nine o'clock the previous evening and that by the time they had finished their conversation it would be too late in the evening for her to phone him. For he was sure that she would want to speak to him once Helena had declared her need for more certainty.

He sat reading *The Times*, but he kept losing concentration, imagining what the conversation between Elizabeth and Helena would have been like. It was the same last night when he tried to concentrate on going to sleep. Helena had left his house in an almost fanatical mood, and it might have led to a great argument with Elizabeth. But every time he pictured them raising their voices, he remembered that was not the way they conducted themselves. Helena would have been very forceful, for certain, but Elizabeth would have listened patiently and realised that nothing would be resolved until Helena was satisfied, unearthing all the evidence she required. It was unsettling to think that they would have been discussing him in that way, but it was inevitable. He tried to think of what each of them would have said and how they would have said it, the phrases they would have used – the tone of the words, the little gasps, the breaths, the sighs.

Even though he was waiting for the telephone to ring, its loudness made him jump and he rustled the newspaper aside to the floor and stood up, straightening his shirt collar before picking up the receiver and waiting for the beeps to stop.

'Hello, I haven't woken you up, I hope? You weren't having a lie-in, perhaps?'

'Not at all, I've been up a long while, reading the newspaper.'

'I can well imagine you needing to put your feet up after yesterday. Helena has told me all about it, the boating trip ... and the unfortunate incident with her dress. Am I right to understand that you both agreed to go back to your house?'

'Yes, Helena was very upset that you would be angry, and I felt very sorry for her.'

'That's what I wanted to check – that it was simply a question of sympathy and that you don't share any of the doubts that Helena clearly has about the truth. She can be very affectionate sometimes. I suppose I'm seeking some reassurance that you're remaining completely aloof.'

'Yes, I am. I don't know what Helena's told you, but nothing happened yesterday. She merely wanted to wash her dress. Once she's confident of all the facts, there'll be no room for any ... misunderstanding.'

'Thank you, Adam. That's a comfort to know. I'm sorry to have stated the obvious, and I'm sure you'll be strong and resist any attempts to lead you up the garden path, as it were. Reluctantly, I've had to accept that this investigation Helena has latched on to will be her latest obsession. I've decided that we'll just have to let her get on with it and then everything will be fine in the end. In the meantime, while Helena is gallivanting around doing whatever research she's planning, there's no reason why you and I can't behave sensibly. My main reason for phoning is that I would like to take my son out to lunch ...'

Adam listened to Elizabeth explaining that it would be better to meet quietly in Windsor rather than in London, because if they were to be seen together, people might misinterpret the situation – that was what people were like, but soon everything would be settled much to her relief.

As she described a café she knew that served lunch, Adam thought about the strange way Helena and Elizabeth shifted around inside his mind. It was like going to the opticians for a sight test with that business of reading the letters that were blurred one moment and sharp the next. As Elizabeth was speaking now, she was sharp and crisp and *motherly*. But occasionally, in a blur, a memory would invade – of when they had first walked together, or the time they woke together. Fortunately nothing dissolved into a blur when Elizabeth was in her motherly mode as she was now.

'And Helena tells me you've had a haircut. That's very good.'

Helena caused him similar optical confusions. He was trying to keep her sharply in focus as a sister without the image softening into something else.

He was proud of the fact that he stayed focused most of the time, but there were embarrassing occasions when he drifted off into a trance, such as the other day when he was at the library and the woman was rather severe. 'I said, do you have a library card?' she barked, having to repeat herself and causing people to turn their heads. The same thing happened when he was in the watchmaker's, buying a new strap for his Timex. He hadn't been listening properly and the man was tut-tutting over the five-pound note. 'Let me ask again, please do you have something smaller, some coins perhaps?'

To keep himself on track, it was much easier to think of Elizabeth instructing her gardener than remembering her throwing her head back in laughter at a party. And with Helena, it was better to think of her as a cellist waiting impatiently for the room to hush than to remember her standing proudly in front of him, proffering her dress.

24

'Into the flower bed you go!' Miranda said. She was by far the better croquet player, and this was about the sixth time Miranda had won the right to hit Elizabeth's ball away from the direction of play.

'It serves you right, Elizabeth, for trying to hide things from me, but I knew something was up. You and Helena have been behaving very strangely recently. When she came to tea the other day, Helena let slip that she had been to the British Museum when she was in London. Now, I appreciate she takes her academic studies very seriously, but even her level of dedication hardly warrants a trip to the British Museum Library. And Helena's frequent trips to London made me very suspicious. I know she enjoys visiting Philippa occasionally, but three times in the space of a week! That was *very* suspicious, especially as her explanation was so thin. She said Philippa was having a very tough time and needed company.'

Wearily, Elizabeth retrieved her ball from the flower border and laid her mallet on the ground. Although there was no proper croquet court in Miranda's garden, she was very finicky about her house rules. She always insisted that a ball knocked into the flower bed had to be placed back on the lawn exactly a mallet's length from the edge of the lawn. She struck the ball with a loud *tock* and watched it roll back towards her hoop. It was a relief to have told Miranda almost everything. She had been forced to make her confession soon after arriving at Miranda's house. In a momentary lapse of concentration she had mentioned the planned trip to France. She had said, 'We're all going to take a little break in Normandy.'

'Oh, it's not like Magnus to join you.'

'Helena and I are going to Normandy.'

'No, Elizabeth, you said "*all* of us". I heard the word very distinctly.'

Elizabeth had been livid with herself. It was such a tiny word for such a big mistake and she had coloured a little while wondering what to do. She could have explained it away by saying she had been getting her words mixed up recently, which was true, but Miranda had looked very hurt, betrayed even, by Elizabeth trying to hide something from her; it was not the way their friendship worked.

But it was done now – she had told Miranda everything apart from her afternoon at Adam's. Once Helena had announced that a visit to the *mairie* in Bayeux was the only way of proving conclusively that Adam was Elizabeth's son, Elizabeth had made her decision. She, Adam and Helena would find an excuse to go to France, find the proof in Bayeux, and return to England ready to inform the world about the wonderful discovery of her long-lost son. It was complicated enough with just the three of them having to work their way towards the truth, which was why Elizabeth had decided not to confide in Miranda about the real reason for the French excursion. It was consoling to have told her, because concealing the details from Miranda had made Elizabeth feel very guilty. But there was a price, of course, because now Miranda had fully recovered from being excluded, she was in one of her garrulous moods, not only because she was winning at croquet, but because it seemed to amuse her that Elizabeth should have even attempted to keep anything hidden.

'I'll tell you a funny thing,' Miranda said. 'When you first told me that you had to give up a child – it was the day after that party when Adam came to stay with Helena – I very nearly mentioned that he could have been one and the same person. Obviously it was a wild hunch, but I didn't raise it because you would have dismissed it out of hand – pooh-poohed it, as you often do.'

Elizabeth was within three feet of getting through her next hoop. She would have to concentrate because missing it would cause Miranda yet more merriment. She thought about how different things would be had Miranda mentioned her hunch after the party. The ball hit the inside edge of the hoop and just managed to roll through.

Miranda stood leaning on the handle of her mallet and said, 'Now if you were ruthless, you would try and hit my ball away before I win the game with my next shot. But I know you won't. It's the same when you play Monopoly, Elizabeth. It's no good feeling sorry for your opponent. You think winning the game is unreasonable, like untidiness, blood sports or deceit. You're too *kind*.'

They shook hands when they finished the game, bowing to each other in mock formality before walking up to the steamer chairs by the swimming pool. Miranda made them one of her mint and cucumber juleps in a large jug and brought out two plates of sliced melon.

'I'll show you a little beauty tip I learnt from one of my magazines,' Miranda said, taking two slices of cucumber out of the jug and lying down before placing them over her eyes. 'You don't really need to do it, because you haven't any wrinkles, but it's very refreshing.'

With their cucumber slices in place, they lay side by side, their eyes staring sightlessly up to the sky.

'I can hear you trying not to laugh, Miranda.'

'I'm sorry, I know it's not a laughing matter, but I can't stop thinking about Helena grilling you for days with all those questions about where you were in Normandy, the name and address of the convent, and all the precise dates of what happened when. She would have had a huge list of all the things she wanted to find out. For Ralph, she would have ticked each item off as she checked the date and place of his death with the war graves people. She probably even asked you what you were wearing when you were told he had died and what time you had breakfast that day. And on her list of things to research she would have had a heading for "Blood Groups", not that that has proved anything conclusive by the sound of it. She and I had a discussion a while ago about career options and she said she might be a journalist one day. She'd be a very good one, I'm sure, very tenacious and persistent – possibly not always accurate, but that's the way it is these days. *Helena Fortescue*. It has a certain ring to it, the sort of journalist that would make you sit up and listen, or read on. I'm sure anyone being interrogated would melt when the thumbscrews were applied. You should be proud, Elizabeth – she gets it from you.

She's obviously sat Adam down and made some kind of deal about the need to find the facts. That's very impressive and practical for her age, to bury her emotions and immerse herself in pursuing the truth.'

Elizabeth said, 'I would call it wilful rather than impressive. When she latches on to something I have no choice but to let it run. I'm letting her unearth whatever needs to be unearthed. That way she'll discover the truth quickly and the three of us can be together like a proper family.'

'But what about Adam's parents? It sounds as if he's been brought up very well, faultlessly, in fact, so they might be hurt to learn Adam is seeking out his birth parents, don't you think?'

'Yes, it'll need to be handled very sensitively once Helena has completed all her sleuthing.'

Elizabeth removed her cucumber slices to eat her melon. She would eat it carefully because if she was clumsy and dropped some down her front she would never hear the end of it from Helena. She *had* thought about Adam's parents a great deal. She had imagined what it would be like if Helena had been adopted and had been brought up to adulthood before someone pressured her into tracing her birth parents. The thought was distasteful, like the cantaloupe, which she usually liked, but it tasted sickly and rather metallic. Perhaps it was the new stainless steel spoons Miranda had bought.

'And Magnus? What about him? He's hardly going to take kindly to you presenting a child from your past, is he?'

'That'll be a very big problem if Helena and I are at loggerheads, but I'm certain she'll come round to accepting the truth and we'll be able to present a united front. Even Magnus falls into line when both Helena and I strongly agree on something. Take last week, for example, when we both put our foot down about his idea of buying a speedboat to keep down at Lymington. A nice wooden yacht, perhaps, but not a speedboat! No, I'm confident Magnus will fall into line.'

'Yes, I can imagine,' Miranda said.

After they had lain back and sunned themselves for a few minutes, Miranda continued. 'I've been thinking. It's quite logical that Helena should be attracted to Adam, and vice versa I suspect. There seems to be quite a lot of psychological evidence that people seek out partners who resemble themselves to some degree. Although Helena and Adam have different temperaments, there are some obvious physical similarities. It's the same thing between mothers and sons, which was probably why Adam had his little crush on you.'

'Well, any misunderstandings on that front were sorted out long ago, thankfully. Here, you can finish this, it tastes funny,' Elizabeth said, handing over her plate.

'Fancy not wanting your melon – the ripeness is perfect, even though I say so myself. Now tell me about your trip. When are you off to France?'

'Thursday next week. It's the earliest booking we could get for the ferry.'

'And what exactly are you going to find out there?'

'Birth records. Things like that.'

'Are you being short with me, Elizabeth? Are you cross because of the croquet? The melon?'

'I'm sorry, I've been feeling tired recently and all that walking back and forth from the flower bed during the croquet hasn't helped.'

Miranda stretched out her hand and touched Elizabeth's. 'Don't worry, you needn't talk about France if you don't want to …'

They lay flat, silently sunning themselves.

After a while Miranda sat up and said, 'Still cross?'

'No, of course not.' Elizabeth laughed.

'Then tell me about France.'

'Helena has only been able to get so far, searching for the proof that she needs. She hasn't any doubts about my account of what happened in Bayeux, so she's been focusing on how the anonymous adoption system works in France. Adam learnt a little about it from his parents, but she of course wants to know about the whole thing from A to Z, hence the trip to the British Museum Library and the French Embassy, would you believe.'

'She can't go bothering people there!' Miranda said, covering her mouth in disbelief.

'That's exactly what I said to her, but she accused me of being old fashioned. Apparently the French Embassy gets enquiries about everything imaginable – people wanting to buy houses, how to import wines by the case and what to do about rabies. She wanted to know all about how birth records are kept in France and how one gets hold of them. She's got this fixation that there might have been more than one anonymous birth in Bayeux on the twenty-fifth of January 1945 – the day Adam was born. But she seems to accept that if there was only one, it would strengthen the argument that it was Adam. It would be pretty hard to argue with that. The man at the embassy told Helena that anonymous births are very rare. She asked him how to go about obtaining birth and adoption certificates and he said that in France they don't have birth certificates like we do, with the same piece of paper you keep for life. Instead, they keep records of everything – births, deaths, marriages and the rest – in ledgers at the town hall, and if you want an official document you have to contact them and they take the details from the ledger and issue a certified copy of the information.

'The man at the embassy gave Helena the telephone number for the *mairie* in Bayeux, which she rang without asking me – goodness knows what the phone bill will be like! But she hit the buffers there because the man spoke French far too fast for her, and in an accent that was quite different from the one she's learnt at school. So she bounced into my room the other morning demanding my help and I had to spend a long time talking to a Monsieur Denain. I've kept up my French quite well, I'm pleased to say. He was rather officious at first but was delightful once we had exchanged pleasantries and I had told him that I knew Bayeux and had been stationed there after D-Day. But the upshot is that because we are not French citizens we can't access the *mairie*'s records very easily. However, Monsieur Denain agreed that if we were to visit Bayeux with any documents proving a legitimate interest, then he would happily see us if we made an appointment.'

'And you're confident everything will be proved to Helena's satisfaction, Elizabeth?'

'Yes, I am. It's impossible to think there was more than one anonymous birth on the day Adam was born in Bayeux. And it sounds as if the French names I gave him will be written in the ledger. It's possible the hospital where he was born will also have something about those names, but you mustn't mention that to Helena. I honestly think I would break down if I had to go back to that place again. I could never face the memory of how terrible it was. My knees would give way.'

'Well, let's hope you find everything at the *mairie*. And if you do, are you certain Helena's feelings about Adam will change?'

'Yes, absolutely. When it's all settled, Helena will be very sisterly and appalled at the way she's behaved. She'll vehemently deny she ever had leanings of that sort. I have no doubt about that.'

Miranda got up and poured the last of the julep and then sat down again on her steamer chair, apparently deep in thought, sipping from her glass. Eventually, she said, 'I don't quite know how to put this. I do understand your argument, but what if, just by some miracle, Helena is right and you are wrong? I agree it seems impossible, but has the thought occurred to you? There, I've said it – as a friend. I don't expect an answer, but it's always best to at least consider all the possibilities, however remote.'

'Thank you, Miranda. I will of course try to think about that. But now it's time for me to go.'

Walking home across the common with the meadow grass brushing her shins, Elizabeth was annoyed to have been brusque with Miranda. But they often spoke very frankly, more frankly than with anyone else. Orange-tipped butterflies darted about. She bent down to watch one settle, but the fluttering unsettled her, so she watched a dandelion seed floating like a parachute instead, and then bent down to examine the dust of pollen on a bee's legs brushing an orchid.

The grass was scratchy, so she walked quickly towards the little lane that led back to the house, breathing the scents of the meadow grass, which was unusually pungent. What annoyed her most was that Miranda had exposed the possible thought of Helena being right. Elizabeth had refused to think about it because it was too outrageous to contemplate. She shut the thought out; it was too disturbing to be reminded of her afternoon with Adam, or to imagine Helena legitimately with Adam and having to vie with Helena for his attention. It made her feel nauseous, but that could have been the melon and the julep.

There! She had done as Miranda had asked. She had *considered* it, and now it was dismissed again; the possibility was far too remote. She stepped off the common onto the lane and flicked away the grass seeds sticking to her shins.

25

The fatigue was getting worse. In fact, Elizabeth hadn't had the energy to argue with Magnus when he suggested that after dinner it would be useful to have a little chat.

So she marched in procession behind Magnus through the rooms to the study, determined to hold her head high as she walked, following the sound of his bench-made soles creaking on the carpet, each step carefully paced and placed. He opened the study door and ushered her in. They sat opposite each other in the Parker Knoll chairs, one yellow, one green, his with a high back, hers not.

Magnus spread his hands in the air. 'I simply haven't a clue what's going on. I hope I'm not getting old or out of touch. First, I witness my daughter inviting some boy to come and stay with us for a week as if there was some serious wooing going on. Then she breaks off from him and I see you with the very same boy – oh, what shall we say? – *communing* very intimately, which you later professed to be entirely innocent. And now, you seem to be a happy family setting sail together for France, of all places. I'm not happy about it. Not at all. It's my job to move with the times – that's what my profession's all about, but it's a job to keep up with the three of you. And what am I to do for supper each night?'

'I'll leave you everything required,' Elizabeth said. 'All your favourites, a nice beef casserole with dumplings in a Denby dish, which you can just pop in the Aga. And for the second night, a shepherd's pie, your favourite, with carrots and crispy potato on top. And for your breakfast in the morning, I'll leave some kippers, which you can spread with butter and pop under the grill. And you know how to make the toast to go with it, I think. And if the percolator is too much, use the Nescafé for once. The world won't end just because I'm away for a couple of days. I'm sure you'll survive.'

After detailing some of the other arrangements, Magnus seemed resigned to the reality of her going away for a few days. In the end he flicked the air and said, 'Anyway, off you all go to France to have your happy holiday and I'll remain here with my dumpling stew. But one last thing. Please can you send Adam along. I would like to have a word with him too, if you don't mind.'

'What do you want to say to him?'

'Just a little word in his shell-like, that's all. Don't worry, it'll be perfectly civilised.'

* * *

Adam felt as if he was back at school, walking to Magnus's lair at the other end of the house. Elizabeth had been reassuring, telling him that Magnus was never rude to guests in any circumstances. It was one of his rules.

After a few pleasantries, Magnus said, 'I could ask you to explain what's going on between you and the ladies of my house. I haven't a clue whether you've been getting up to some serious mischief. You don't appear to be mischievous. Mysterious, more like, I suppose. God knows they're strong women, but they seem to have become even more forthright since you've been on the scene. It may not be your fault, but you seem to have upset the equilibrium of the place. Anyway, there's no point in me arguing about it – they've made up their minds, so there's nothing I can do, that's that. For my part, I've said Elizabeth can take the Jaguar to France. For your part, if you're to be accompanying them as the man of the party I hope you'll be looking after them. Have you enough money?'

The question took Adam by surprise. It was embarrassing that Magnus had no idea of the real reason for the trip to France, but Elizabeth had insisted on it. She had said it would be far better if Magnus was told it was a little holiday and was only informed of the new family situation once Helena was completely convinced that Adam was her half-brother.

'Look, I'm sorry to ask about money …' Magnus said. 'I don't want to pry, but my sole concern is that if you're in charge of the party, Elizabeth and Helena must be properly looked after. It's what they're accustomed to.'

He had expected Magnus to be more confrontational and it was almost touching to see him more preoccupied about Elizabeth's and Helena's welfare than his obvious suspicions about the three of them being together. 'They'll be properly looked after, I can assure you. We will all look after each other.'

Magnus blew out his cheeks in dismay and then shook his head from side to side, closing his eyes as if not wanting to contemplate the worst. Some people would have found the situation amusing, Adam thought, but the possibility of enraging Magnus was too frightening. Instead, Adam was sympathetic – it wasn't Magnus's fault that Elizabeth had chosen to tell him that they were going to Bayeux for a short break, to see the tapestry. The more laughable idea was that anyone other than Elizabeth could be in charge of the trip to France, although it had to be said that Helena seemed somewhat in charge of it as well. For his own part, he had never felt less in charge of anything in his life; it was ridiculous of Magnus to think that he had any control over Elizabeth and Helena. He didn't feel weak or embarrassed in the slightest; he merely admired Helena's and Elizabeth's assertiveness – that they were strong didn't mean that he was weak.

He acknowledged he might be weak in other ways, what with his occasional lapses. Most of the time, he was able to obey Elizabeth's insistence that he should ignore Helena's attentions. Elizabeth was so convinced that he was mostly convinced himself. But occasionally, something Helena did would trigger his doubts. She had clearly made a determined pact with herself to avoid making advances towards him until her case was proven. But even she had lapsed on a couple of occasions. The previous week she had smiled at him just as she had done when they sat together on his bed. And when he had met her for a coffee in Bloomsbury after one of her visits to the British Museum Library, her hand had lingered on his shoulder fractionally too long to be entirely innocent. Both times, something dared him to succumb. It was as if something in the background was whispering to him, provoking him to fail by doing the opposite of what Elizabeth demanded. It was thrilling to think of the unthinkable.

As for his thoughts about succumbing to Elizabeth, they had become non-existent – the ones that had previously consumed him. It was obvious that Elizabeth had erased their afternoon together from her mind, that her stomach would turn at the thought of it; she had blocked the memory out forever and the strength of her disgust meant he was able to do the same. He was cured of her. He recognised her as his mother – indeed revered her as such – the way she was in control of the sortie to France just as she was of everything else. Helena thought she was in control but actually Elizabeth was, deploying her art of being in control without appearing to be. It was as if Elizabeth was waiting patiently for a storm to pass. Evidently she had become resigned to Helena's obsessive fixations over the years and was confident this latest tempest would blow through once the truth was revealed and Helena's delusion quelled.

After the interview with Magnus, Adam walked back to the other end of the house. In the morning he would be travelling with Helena and Elizabeth to Southampton and over to France. The uncertainty about what they might discover there ate away inside him. It was exhausting and he just wanted it to be over one way or the other.

* * *

Usually Elizabeth fell asleep the moment she turned off the light.

She could pretend her restlessness was the thought of the early start in the morning for the ferry trip to France. The weather forecast wasn't good, but she was resilient at sea; she had good sea legs. Maybe she was not quite herself because Helena seemed to be wresting control, which was admirable in a way. This whole investigation of hers had shown Helena in a new light; some of her impetuosity had been tempered into a new, conscientious restlessness. The way she had announced that Adam was to come and stay before the trip to France was impressive. So too was the way she had sat Elizabeth and Adam down and told them about what the three of them needed to do in Bayeux. Helena had even booked the ferry tickets and written down an itinerary of all her arrangements in one of her old exercise books.

But Elizabeth knew her own restlessness was really about something else entirely. She didn't need the little cramps to tell her what was going on because she'd suspected it for some time – the realignment that was taking place, the tiny tugging sensations, things sliding into position like the shutters on a camera. All sorts of images kept entering her head: a caterpillar squirming on a leaf, a butterfly fluttering haphazardly, a fledgling cast from the nest.

It would take all her strength to keep the three terrors at bay that would overwhelm her if she let them. The births of Helena and Adam had been excruciating, and the prospect of experiencing that agony again was terrifying enough; but even that ordeal was as nothing to the twin tortures of experiencing an everlasting reminder of her sin with Adam and that its legacy might be a consanguineous abnormality holding her to account forever.

She mustn't panic just yet. Nature might take its course one way or the other long before the kicks came. From a practical point of view, nothing would show for ages. In the war she had worked in the supplies department well into her third trimester and nobody had noticed, although the baggy standard-issue clothes must have helped. It was the same when she'd been pregnant with Helena, when she had remained neat and compact nearly to the end.

She would find the determination to remain calm for now because the immediate priority was arriving at certainty with Adam and Helena. That would be her entire focus. It would be like Ralph in the war, according to the account she had been given, that he had been bent solely on completing his mission regardless of the hunger, the thirst and the fatal wounds. It was disappointing that Helena demanded her level of proof; it smacked of a lack of trust. But at least she could trust her own body; she respècted its wisdom. Her confidence surprised her and she felt sleepy at last.

26

Elizabeth, Helena and Adam sat at a table in the dining saloon of the Thoresen ferry *Viking II*, which was steaming out of Southampton harbour.

'Always best to have a hearty breakfast, isn't it?' the steward said, serving briskly from steel trays resting on the white linen cloth draped over his forearm. 'Yes, it's good to get something inside you while it's calm in here. I think it'll be a bit bumpy once we're out past the Isle of Wight. It's been building from the west for a couple of days now, so there'll be quite a swell all the way to Cherbourg, I think. Force seven or even eight they say.'

'Fortunately we're all good on the sea,' Helena said heartily. 'Otherwise we would have postponed our trip.'

'Are we going off on a little holiday then? A little break perhaps?' the steward asked.

'No, not really,' Helena said. 'We're off to Normandy to study some history, as a matter of fact.'

'Ah, history! That was my favourite subject at school. Mind you, that was more years ago than I care to remember. The Normans, is it? The tapestry?'

'No, actually, it's to do with the war.'

'Ah, yes, the war. There's a lot of history there,' he said, nodding his head sagely as he walked away.

After breakfast, Helena and Elizabeth seemed in no hurry to finish their coffee, so Adam left the table, saying he was keen to go up on deck before the sea became too rough. The truth was he needed some time to himself. Up on deck, he found a slatted wooden bench beside the funnel of the ship, where he sat catching the acrid smell from the billows of smoke and listening to the engines rumbling below. Everything seemed awkward and strained. When the three of them were getting into the car earlier to drive to Southampton, Helena had wanted him to sit next to her in the back, but Elizabeth had insisted that he sit next to her in the front. She had been quite subdued throughout the journey, whereas Helena had been full of lively conversation despite it being so early in the morning. She had taken charge, confirming again the details of their itinerary and listing what they were to do in Bayeux. She had planned everything with precision and efficiency, just as he imagined Elizabeth would have done in 1944, going confidently about her duties. He felt that in becoming so absorbed in her arrangements, Helena was forgetting what was at stake. She was focusing on the means and not the end. Surely she couldn't have lost sight of the implications of their visit? If she was right about them being unrelated, then the two of them would be free together, and if Elizabeth was right they would be brother and sister. Or perhaps Helena was only too aware of the stark contrast between the possibilities and was masking their momentousness by looking busy and keeping things light. It was impossible to tell.

He wrapped his scarf around his face and over his head so

that the only thing he could see through the guardrails were the large waves rolling towards him.

The improvised hood shielded him from the wind, but not from the beauty of the two faces that occupied his mind. Helena and Elizabeth appeared before him in a series of flashes, first one and then the other. They were like the waves he watched piling in from the west; in wide angle they were all the same, but in close reality each was entirely different.

The ship was running obliquely to the waves and, as it lurched slightly, Helena came to the forefront of his mind. He was ashamed that his thoughts were so base, but it was impossible to escape them. Haunting him was the recurrent image of Helena holding her dress out to him, offering it freely as he stood spellbound by the innocent exposure of her shape and her pure skin.

Thinking of waking with Helena in his arms made him dizzy. He leant forward and buried his face in his hands as the ship lurched again and he thought of Elizabeth instead. His adoration of her was in complete contrast. She had become a source of noble admiration rather than slavish attraction. He would never reach for her again, at least not like that, enfolded. She had detached herself completely and was gone.

Helena returned to his thoughts. This time, they were lying enthralled in each other's arms as she looked at him with that intent gaze of hers. He tried to think of something else, pressing his hands to his face, breathing in the salt blowing off the sea, which stung his eyes. He couldn't escape the possibility of Helena being proved right. If there was no conclusive proof that he was Elizabeth's son, would he have to choose between the two of them? Would Elizabeth's intimate desire return as suddenly as it had been withdrawn if the facts changed? Wilder, ridiculous fantasies enveloped him before he recovered his senses and concluded that Elizabeth would be proved right. The endings of the story kept changing.

Looking out to sea again, watching the line of foam from the wake of the ferry competing with the waves, Adam knew that however awkward life might become, he would never throw himself off the side of a ship. He was strong, he was sound, he was calm. But that didn't staunch the craving for the relief that would come from finding the answers in Bayeux – to break the endless cycle of Helena and Elizabeth alternating in his mind.

The ship lunged down again as he leant forward once more with his elbows on his knees, closing his eyes. He inhaled a gulp of the swirling wind and held his breath for a long time, his childhood habit.

After a minute he breathed out.

'Oh! I've made you jump,' Helena said, standing above him. 'That was a very big sigh. Are you all right? I thought I'd come and find you.' She smiled and sat down next to him. 'What are you doing wrapped up like that? Have you been *thinking*?'

'Yes, I've been thinking,' he said, attempting an innocent smile as he unwound the scarf from his head.

'What about?'

'Oh, this and that. How strange this whole thing is. It feels as if some kind of fate is waiting for us in Bayeux. I really hope we'll find out the truth. Either—'

'It's all right, Adam, I know exactly what you're going to say.' She held up the flat of her hand in a peaceful salute. 'You don't have to spell it out. You're thinking that either we'll be one thing or the other. We've just got to put up with it until we find out.'

'But how can you be so calm about it?'

The wind, billowing strongly around the funnel of the ship, blew another plume of diesel smoke around them and Helena waved it away, puffing her cheeks. 'Because there's nothing we can do until we get to Bayeux. We need to wait until then, when I hope everything will be settled. People worry too much. It's such a wasteful activity and serves no useful purpose. You should only worry about something when there's something you can do about it. Don't you see? Worrying about what we'll find out in Bayeux won't achieve anything because the answer is already there and worrying about it won't change the result. The worrying isn't just a waste of time. It's destructive because it makes you fret and the acid eats away inside you.'

'Something Elizabeth taught you, I suppose?'

'Yes, naturally. You guessed. It's logic – you're meant to be good at that.' She punched him gently on the shoulder, smiling.

They sat for a moment staring out at the writhing sea.

'Do you think I'm like her?' Helena said.

'Yes, in some ways, you're very like her.'

'You'll have to explain.'

'It's obvious you're mother and daughter. It's not just that you look alike, it's the things you think are important. You like things to be exactly right. Everything has to be clear and certain and if it isn't, you set about putting it right. At first I found it frightening, but I think I'm getting used to it.'

'Oh dear, you make us sound like ogres. And the differences?'

'Maybe there aren't any. It's difficult to tell whether you're a younger version of Elizabeth, or she's a slightly older version of you.'

'Do you think I'm immature? Does she seem old? Did you say *slightly*?'

'No, none of those things!' He hadn't intended to spit the words.

Helena crossed her arms and frowned out at the sea. 'You *did* say "slightly", by the way. Anyway, that's not the point. I think it's fair to say you like me. I think it's much more than that. I hope so. But logically, what you've said means you must find Mother attractive – which I can understand – most men do.'

'She might be my mother, Helena ... please.'

'I'm *not* your sister, Adam.'

'If you're so convinced, why are we going to Bayeux?'

'Out of respect for Mother. I could never act in a way she thought was evil. And I *know*, deep down, you have your doubts as well. You mustn't worry, Adam. Everything will soon be settled. Here ...'

She leant across and gave him an exaggerated kiss, cupping his face with both hands. 'There. Only joking, Adam! For now, at least.'

He had to smile at the way she could make light of the situation. They fell silent again, looking straight out to sea as if seeking answers.

Eventually, Adam said, 'I'm concerned about her. She's not well, you know. She hardly spoke on the journey down and she looked very pale at breakfast.'

'No, she's not herself at all. I noticed it when she was very quiet at supper last night.'

* * *

Elizabeth couldn't sit in the restaurant any longer as the ship rose and fell in the gathering sea. Some cups had crashed to the floor. A headache was starting to press behind her eyes. She looked away from the greasy plates that had still not been taken away. She craved fresh air on deck. It was not fair of Helena and Adam to be up there for so long while she looked after their coats and Helena's bag. They should have been wearing their coats anyway, out in that blustering wind. Putting her own coat on, she asked the people at the next table if they would look after their things. She had spoken to them earlier and had decided they were trustworthy. The couple smiled and said they would, and told her they weren't going anywhere with this storm still building. They advised her to be careful if she was going up on deck.

She was normally strong, but she could barely keep her grip on the rail as she pulled herself up the stairs step by step. Each time the ship pitched, she clung to the handrail and felt everything tightening inside her. She was almost at the top of the stairs when a great swirl of air rushed in above her. It was one of the ship's officers on deck hauling the door open.

'Oh, you're coming up,' he said. 'Are you sure you should be, madam? I really don't advise it. You don't look well, if I may say so, and it's quite slippery up there.'

'Thank you,' she gasped, 'but I know I'll be better off in

fresh air. The motion of this ship seems most unnatural.'

'Do you know, madam, I couldn't have put it better myself. *Unnatural* — that's what it is. It's the stabilisers, you see. They change the motion of the ship, not always for the better, in my opinion. Anyway, I can see you're determined to go up.' As he held the door open for her against the wind, he said, 'Unnatural! You're absolutely right there, madam.'

When she walked along the deck she saw Helena kissing Adam passionately. Elizabeth turned and ran back quickly through the door and almost toppled down the stairs. She seized the rail and closed her eyes, panting. For a moment her sickness disappeared while the shock of what she had seen sank in. She felt betrayed. For days, she and Helena had played along with the sensible idea that Bayeux would provide them with the certainty they needed before deciding how to behave. Such a sensuous embrace could only be that of two lovers, what with Adam accepting it so compliantly. Why were they traipsing over to France on this godforsaken voyage if Helena had already made up her mind? They had deceived her. If she hadn't felt so queasy, she would seethe with anger.

Her headache and sickness returned, along with a new pain lower down that chafed like pieces of grit whenever the ship heaved.

She winced and bowed her head. She couldn't face returning to the dining saloon because she knew she would be ill down there. She urgently needed fresh air but felt too weak to go up on deck again to confront Helena and Adam, so she stumbled down the stairs, crossed over to the other side of the ship and clawed her way up to the other deck. Halfway up, the ship swooped over a wave and Elizabeth almost lost her grip, her shoulders crashing twice into the side of the stairwell. At least the pain took her mind off the sickness. She didn't care that there would be bruises and that she wouldn't be able to wear her halter dress, the vermilion one with the sash.

Out on deck, she held on to the door, surveying the conditions. Here, on the port side of the ship, there was more shelter and the wind screeched less, and the motion of each vast wave seemed different. She didn't want to sit on a bench; it would compress whatever was cramping her. She waited for the right moment between two waves to let go of the door and shuffle across the deck with outstretched hands to the guard rail, which she grasped with relief when she reached it.

She would hang on here to keep the welling nausea at bay, fixing her eyes on the horizon and breathing deeply. Briefly, there was a flash of bronzed sun through the clouds heaped in the sky. If she could just hold on until they arrived in Cherbourg, but her eyes shifted to the foam on the waves, which made her think of boiling milk, and then other foods, her gorge rising as she remembered the egg at breakfast with the spot of blood on its yolk, the colour of raw liver. The ship slithered down a wave and churned up the other side. She would have to go below to find somewhere to stoop and retch, her deeper pain twisting now as if a heap of wires were tightening inside her.

But no, she would hang on, hang on to the rail, and she set her jaw to fix on the horizon again, trying to keep it straight as the ship plunged down another wave.

The wind buffeted her ears and if it blew much stronger

she would lose her scarf, so when the ship was level for an instant she snatched it off and thrust it into her pocket, her hair running free. But the fronds stuck to her forehead and her cheeks in the salt spray. She didn't care if she looked a fright, a bedraggled hag with grey-green skin most likely, fighting for air.

She had never felt so defeated – not since the war – yet she would never throw herself into the sea unless she fell down into it by gripping the rail so tightly that it broke. She looked down, watching the salt spray spitting on her shoes as the ship fell away again. Holding on with one hand, she placed the palm of the other hand on her belly.

Finally, she could bear it no more. She had to find somewhere completely dark and still where she could curl up. The ship started another of its surges, making her gag, and the headache pressed behind her eyes, which she closed in a cold sweat, her knees nearly giving way. Everything was cramping inside now and she made her descent into the ship.

The engines were grinding and the smell of diesel oil and disinfectant hung in the air as she found her way along a corridor where some passengers stood, pushing their hands against the walls to keep themselves steady, talking bravely as the ship rolled. But they made room to let her pass, and a woman in a black and white dogtooth jacket said, 'You do have our sympathies if you're thinking of going in there ...'

And sure enough, the air was fetid, trapped. Everything was tying up; she thought she might black out.

Several minutes later, she was blinking awake from her trauma; the gasping and the knife-like cramping had ceased.

She was purged; it was gone; she was free.

She shed no tears because it was for the best. She even smiled for a second in relief, imagining myriad molecules dispersing in the ocean like pink ink burgeoning in the water. We all came from the sea, she thought, the sea from whence we came. She had trusted her body; the spot on the yoke of the egg had gone, a skin sloughed off, a freak cast out.

She set about making herself look presentable again. She longed for the hotel in Cherbourg where she would have a long soak in a hot bath, but for now she washed her face and straightened her wet hair as best she could. There were no towels, so she took out her handkerchief, the one with the cherry motifs around the border that Helena had ironed the previous morning in that particular way Helena always insisted upon, first the square, then folded into a triangle, then yet again to an even smaller triangle. Staring into the mirror, Elizabeth could see some colour already returning to her face. She could stand up straight again, with her shoulders back and her head high. She even practised a smile to show that the worst had passed and she could be herself again. The motion of the ship seemed less wild. She could cope with it now; she was reconciled. She folded her handkerchief back into a small triangle and put it in her pocket, thinking about how she was going to confront Helena about that dreadful kiss.

When she came out into the corridor, the people were still there, pressing the walls for balance. They said they were glad that she looked better. People are kind, she thought; it's the kindnesses of the world that make life worth living. It made her want to be even kindlier herself, less fierce, perhaps, less demanding. As soon as she found Helena and Adam, who might be worrying about her, she would be kind. Maybe she should give them the benefit of the doubt, maybe in the cold sweat of her illness she'd been too quick to judge – what if that kiss had been largely innocent? And if it wasn't, it was too late and there was little point worrying about it – that was the rule she had drummed into Helena over the years, so she should abide by the rule herself. No, she wouldn't be cross. She would get to the root of things very calmly, and she made her way up to the dining saloon.

'We wondered where you were,' Helena said as Elizabeth sat down opposite her and Adam. 'Where have you been? Were you feeling unwell?'

'I was feeling a little off colour, yes. I spoke to a very nice man up on deck, the purser or an officer, I think he was. He explained that the stabilisers on this ship cause an unnatural motion and I quite agree with him on that.'

'But whatever it was has gone now?'

'Yes, it has gone now, whatever it was.'

'Well, you're looking a little better, thankfully. You looked like a ghost. You were grey,' Helena said before they were interrupted by a loud Tannoy message about landing cards in Cherbourg.

Elizabeth blocked out the noise of the announcement, made by a man in clipped English. How nice of Helena to say she was looking much better now, but she would have to be confronted about that kiss. It was galling to be going to Bayeux if Helena had already decided everything.

The man making the announcement cleared his throat and attempted to repeat it in very dubious French. At least she would be able to do better than that when they landed in

France, she thought, for she would be the one doing most of the talking when they got there. During the war, she was fluent. She used to ride on a heavy black bicycle with a basket each morning to the *boulangerie*, where they greeted her with open arms. Her French had been good enough to share jokes about De Gaulle and Churchill with Monsieur Chevalier, who owned the shop and was fond of sharing his thoughts about the finer points of making bread. There she had discovered her favourite bread of all, *ficelle*, which she would eat for lunch, the bread in one hand and a piece of cheese in the other.

She closed her eyes, thinking of the *boulangerie*, breathing in the freshness of the baguettes. Before Ralph was killed, she'd been happy in Bayeux, despite the chaos. She was barely out of school in a foreign country gripped in the havoc of war, yet her startling confidence carried her through.

The man finished his announcement. Yes, her French would be better than that – she knew it from the odd occasions when Magnus had invited colleagues over from his Paris office, impressing them with a wife who spoke perfect French.

She looked at Helena and Adam sitting next to each other. 'And what about you two? What have you been up to?'

'Talking, mainly,' Helena said.

Elizabeth breathed in deeply and said, 'I may as well tell you. When I went up on deck after breakfast to find you, I saw you kissing and it made me run away. It was very intimate—'

'No, no, you misunderstand,' Helena said, 'we were merely—'

At the same time, Adam said, 'It's not like that. It was

innocent, it was—'

'I was mistaken, then? I'm sorry to interrupt, Adam, but I think it would be best if Helena and I were left to discuss this alone.' She drew out her purse and offered him a ten-shilling note. 'Please, take this. There's a cafeteria towards the front of the ship.'

'How long will you be?'

'We'll come and find you when I've finished with Helena. I want to look at the cafeteria in any case to see if it would be more comfortable than this restaurant for the return journey.'

When Adam had gone, Elizabeth said, 'There's no point in me being angry with you, Helena, but I do want to know what's going on. It was no ordinary kiss. We expressly agreed that you would hold off any closeness of that kind until everything was proven. I trusted you not to act. How far have things gone?'

'No further than what you saw. Adam and I are not close, not in *that* way, and I'm sorry if that's how it appeared. I've been prepared to wait very patiently, but once or twice, I admit, I've very jokingly kissed him and that is what you saw. But I'm asking you to see things from my point of view. I know you're convinced. It must be traumatic to lose a child – see! It's made you jump. I understand how the regret eating away for years could cause you to latch on to what you want to believe. But I'm asking you to understand that I've no such baggage from the past, which is why I want the certainty.'

'And he hasn't encouraged you?'

Helena laughed. 'No, he has not! – out of some strange respect for you, which I don't understand. You mustn't blame him for behaving as if he *is* your son.'

Elizabeth saw a rare thing then, a single quiver of Helena's lip, a blink of her eyes. She reached out across the table and wrapped her hand gently over Helena's fist. 'I know it's upsetting, Helena, but I'm sure we'll find an answer.'

For a few seconds Helena sat defiantly, her lips pursed, looking away to the window, but then she turned to Elizabeth with a smile and said, 'Yes, you're right, that's what we must do. Find the answer. We'll go and find Adam now.'

Elizabeth watched Helena walking ahead of her out of the dining saloon and along the passageway towards the cafeteria. Although much less violently than before, the ship was still rolling on the waves, yet Helena kept her composure despite the movement of the ship, walking almost straight when everyone else was stumbling. The spectre appeared again: the outrageous thought that Adam was not her son at all, forcing a war of carnal rivalry to break out between mother and daughter, an internecine pursuit worthy of a Greek tragedy. But instantly she recoiled in disgust, wondering whether anyone else ever had these momentary visitations that aimed to thrill – the most evil thoughts imaginable, menaces that had to be gripped and cast out to feel worthy and good again. Or the other tricks and questions that sometimes sprang to mind, such as whether everything in her past was merely imagined, her memories of Ralph weren't real, that none of the past was real at all; perhaps she'd never been in the war, had never been to Bayeux. And if Ralph never existed, she couldn't have had his child. All these things could be false memories that had taken root and haunted her for years.

Or, what if only parts of her memory had deceived her? That she had indeed been a supplies administrator in the stores at Bayeux in 1944. It was a tedious job at times. She checked the goods and checked the stock, keeping records, then checked them again. It was hypnotic, but she was good at it. Her checking and her counting were meticulous, which was why she was given more and more responsibility and she ended up at seventeen running the stores unit, giving orders to people twice her age. She wasn't fazed by it at all because she was driven by her devotion to Ralph, feeling invincible because her love of Ralph would drive her through anything. She had no doubts at that time – the war would soon be over; she and Ralph would settle in England for a new bright life. Could it be that up to that point her memories were intact, and the moment she sat in a chair to be told of Ralph's death, her subsequent memories had become unreliable? Maybe at that moment when her dreams were crushed and her mind was shattered, her memory became dismantled? Her utter helplessness may have made her memory play tricks on her; her mind may have subsequently constructed the experience of having Ralph's child as something to cling to as a form of homage. She may have merely imagined giving the child away.

As she and Helena walked into the cafeteria, Elizabeth saw Adam sitting at a table by the window staring out at the sea. The demons, the doubts, immediately flew out of her. They were exorcised; that *was* her son sitting there. She was confident it would be proved to Helena's satisfaction. She was herself again.

* * *

While Adam was banished to the cafeteria frowning out to

sea, he imagined what Elizabeth and Helena were discussing. Had Elizabeth sent him away to spare him the embarrassment of an angry dispute? It seemed unlikely because Elizabeth and Helena never argued as such; their conversation was always like some ancient dance or ceremony, circling around each other, testing their reactions with a knowing smile; even when in complete disagreement, they would fight it out without fighting at all. Whenever he witnessed the beauty of this ritual dance, he felt far away from them, as if he lacked a language in which they were fluent. Perhaps in reality he was purely incidental to them, outside the circle, looking in. But that surely was the difference between them: Elizabeth was already reconciled to him being part of the circle and Helena was not. Elizabeth talked to him and advised him now in that maternal way of hers, whereas Helena ... He thought of her again, languishing on his bed, daring him to respond.

Briefly the sun came out and lit up the sea, which was less violent now, but the waves were still big enough to cause a struggle for the little yellow fishing boat passing by, bobbing up and over the waves. He had grown used to the idea of Elizabeth being a mother, but it was impossible to think of Helena as a sister whenever the images invaded, the offered dress, the picture of her fussing over the clothes rack in his bedroom, the way she bit into an apple a few days ago, watching him watching her. The kiss on deck. They were all too painful and he wanted them settled one way or the other.

Drinking his coffee, he sensed people trying to guess his situation. They would be wondering why that young man was sitting on his own looking so forlorn. Is he French and returning home for some bereavement, or is he wounded in love? But then, as Elizabeth and Helena came into the cafeteria, all eyes were on them, admiringly, it seemed. As soon as Helena and Elizabeth spotted him and came towards him, all the glances turned away again, melting into the hubbub of conversation at each table, for the mystery was solved: the young man was merely being joined by members of his family for a hot drink now that the sea was calmer.

He stood up and started to ask Helena and Elizabeth what they would like to drink, but the Tannoy blared out again, announcing that car passengers should make their way to the car decks. Helena and Elizabeth raised their eyebrows and rolled their eyes at the unwelcome interruption. Then he realised he had joined them in unison with precisely the same expression.

Elizabeth led the way, followed by Helena, as they joined the crowd of people winding their way along the passageways and the flights of steps down to the car deck. There was a collective air of relief and joviality now that the ship was gliding evenly and slowly in the calm of Cherbourg harbour.

The queue came to a halt for a moment, and Elizabeth bantered with an officer who she must have met while she was on deck.

'I must say you look much better now, madam. Did you have some ginger biscuits?'

Seeing her confusion, the man explained that ginger was a long-established seafarers' cure for seasickness.

'Ah, yes, I remember that custom now.' She laughed. 'I suspect it's a gimmick dreamt up by those wretched advertising people to sell more ginger biscuits. Anyway, thank you for your concern, but I'm fully recovered. It was just a little queasiness, that's all.'

27

Adam sat in the back of the car as they drove off the ferry into the Normandy sunshine. At the customs booth, Elizabeth wound down the car window to give the man the three British passports. He asked, in faltering English, whether madame had had a pleasant crossing. Elizabeth replied in rapid French, which startled Adam. He had never heard her speaking French before; it made her voice sound even more elegant than usual, with the 'R's rolling and the vowels flowing softly in a song. He'd forgotten most of his O-level French, but he could tell that Elizabeth was joking with the flirtatious officer about the voyage over, because the flat of her hand undulated ridiculously to convey the picture of a bumpy sea. She smiled and said to him, *'Oui, la mer était un peu agitée.'* The man laughed while snapping the passports together and handing them back through the window.

As they drove out of Cherbourg into the countryside, Helena asked Elizabeth whether she had travelled along the same road during the war.

'No, I came across into the Mulberry harbours further along the coast. I remember it well …'

Because the road was in a terrible condition, Elizabeth drove slowly while she seemed transported into her past, giving her account of arriving in Normandy in 1944. To Adam, it was as if he was a boy being read a story; he listened intently to Elizabeth's part in setting up the supply lines after D-Day, describing vividly the landscape, the people she worked with and the work she did. As the Jaguar rumbled over the pocked road, Adam imagined her driving an army wagon in the war, ghosting it along. She would have been the same age as Helena now, causing an entire battalion amazement, no doubt. In those days, coarse innuendo would have been less prevalent – there was a war on and there would have been respect for the ring on her finger and the knowledge that her fiancé was an officer in the advance army. The car yawed over another series of potholes; he shouldn't be thinking of Elizabeth at seventeen, so he switched his thoughts to Helena and what she would be like when she was Elizabeth's age.

Helena interrupted Elizabeth's story and said, 'Oh! Look up there. What an adorable church! Can we take this little road towards the village so that I can take a picture?'

Once parked in the village, Elizabeth and Adam sat in the car watching Helena walk up the winding path to the church with her Minolta dangling from her shoulders.

They both walk in exactly the same way, Adam thought. It's not just a question of them speaking the same, dressing the same and sharing the same quirks – even the gait is the same too. He wound down the window to breathe in the heather and grass at the side of the road.

'That was a deep breath. What's the matter?' Elizabeth said, turning her head towards him.

In the quietness of the car he didn't dare meet her eyes, but looked straight ahead at Helena walking away. He knew what Elizabeth would look like fully turned towards him. For most people, it was not the most flattering position, the way the skin on the neck might crease a little – or was it ruched? – another of the words he'd learnt from her. But he knew that her neck would appear graceful despite the turn of her head, and he thought he could sense its fragrance. No, he wouldn't turn to look. 'I was wondering whether that camera might slip off Helena's shoulder. She needs to be careful.'

'Yes, she must be careful. She does walk beautifully though, doesn't she? I don't think I taught her to walk like that. She must have learnt it somehow. Anyway, I wanted to say thank you, Adam.'

He looked at her briefly and resumed his stare straight ahead.

'You see, I think I understand now. You seem to have behaved admirably. Helena assures me that you haven't been encouraging her. It must have been very difficult, so I just wanted to say thank you.'

Standing on a little mound, Helena raised her camera to take the photograph, but the breeze blew her hair in front of the lens. She shook her head and flicked her hair behind her, raising her elbows higher to keep her hair pinned back as it waved and flashed in the sun.

'Yes, it's been difficult. I just want it to be over. I want everything to be certain.'

'You're not certain?'

'I *do* believe you. But I need Helena to be certain before I can be certain. But then again, nothing can ever be truly certain. Even gravity's only a theory, you know.'

'You do say peculiar things sometimes. It's not always very helpful.'

'I'm saying that if Helena ... or *once* Helena is certain, *I'll* be certain, and then everything will be different.'

'Well, as you know, I'm already certain,' Elizabeth said, patting him on the knee. 'I too just want it to be over so that the three of us can be together, as a family.'

'And you've thought through how you'll deal with Magnus in all this?'

'Of course I have. Just as you must have thought about Constance and Arnold, surely?'

'Yes, I've thought about it a lot.'

Helena was walking back towards them, her dress flicking in the breeze. He tried not to think about the perfect mole he had seen that time when she was drying her dress, below her navel and down to the right. Elizabeth had one too, a smaller one, lower down, to the left. He remembered kissing it and immediately banished the thought with another sigh.

'Yes, it's been a very tiring day,' Elizabeth said. 'Thankfully, we're staying at a very comfortable hotel. It's surrounded by gardens and should be nice and quiet. Helena and I have rooms next to each other on the first floor and you have a room on the floor above us. We'll all sleep very well, I'm sure, after that stormy crossing – Oh, look! You were right. The camera nearly slipped off her shoulder.'

It was another of Elizabeth's foibles, Adam thought, listening to her kindly little laugh, that muffled, mischievous hoot of delight she occasionally let slip, just as had occurred earlier with the man at passport control. She seemed completely serene again now that she was on firm land, as if convinced that everything would be resolved now that they were in France.

* * *

In the morning, the three of them met in the reception area of the hotel and were ushered into the sumptuous dining room by an effusive maître d' who asked them whether they had all slept well and whether they were a family on holiday. Simultaneously, Elizabeth smiled and said yes, and Helena said no. The bemused maître d' chose to ignore the apparent confusion and led them to a table in the centre of the high-ceilinged room.

Examining the menu, Helena said, 'I'm wondering whether to have a nice, cooked breakfast. What do you think?'

'You have one, of course, Helena, if you wish,' Elizabeth said, 'but I'll stick to the croissants and fruit. When in Rome …'

'Are you joining me, Adam?' Helena said.

'It's a nice idea, but I think I'll have the continental breakfast for a change.'

Once Helena had finished her *oeufs à la coque,* they ordered more coffee.

'I've never quite understood,' Elizabeth said, 'why the coffee abroad always tastes much better than at home. It's made the same way with the same beans. I can understand why French patisserie is better than anything at home. It's because they use better ingredients and take more care with the preparation and the baking. It's the same with their bread.

I hope we have enough time today for me to find the *boulangerie* I used to go to in the war.'

Helena said, 'Our appointment at the *mairie* with Monsieur Denain isn't until eleven o'clock. Why don't we change our plan of getting the taxi to drop us at the edge of the town and walking in? If we go straight to the centre, we'll have time for you to find your *boulangerie* – if it's still there, that is. And Adam, you need to make sure you have that envelope containing all your documents. They'll want to see everything.'

Adam sat next to Elizabeth in the back of the taxi and Helena sat next to the taxi driver. When the taxi halted near the cathedral, Helena announced that she wanted to buy a street map of the town and made her best attempt to ask the driver where she might buy one. He raised his eyebrows and gave a little shrug as if he didn't fully understand. Elizabeth leant forward and spoke to the driver in a stream of French. The driver nodded his head in complete understanding and with much gesticulation provided directions.

'You did well, Helena. He merely has a different accent from the one you learnt at school. You see that little street straight ahead? Go down that and take the second left and there you will find a *tabac* that will probably have a *plan de ville*. You see that little café with the striped canopy? Adam and I will see you in there when you have your map.'

'What did you say to the driver?' Adam asked as he and Elizabeth crossed the street to the café.

'Much the same as Helena said, but languages are not just a question of stringing words together. With French, particularly, you have to speak with the eyes and the hands. Sometimes the words seem incidental. Technically, Helena's French wasn't too bad – it just needed to be more animated. It's impossible to acquire a new language properly unless you live in the place. She's probably just as I was when I arrived here in 1944, equipped with a lot of confidence but rather less French.'

At their table under the café's canopy, Adam and Elizabeth watched Helena walking towards them, waving her map in the air with great sweeps and a satisfied smile.

Elizabeth said, 'I'm very proud of her.'

'I know,' he replied. 'You're very proud of each other, though I doubt either of you say so very much.'

'And soon, *we* will be very proud of *you* – I'm sure.'

Adam was still getting used to the way Elizabeth smiled at him as if he was still at school.

Once Helena had sat down, Elizabeth said, 'We've still got an hour before we have to be at the *mairie*. You two can have a nice coffee here while I try to find my little *boulangerie*. I'm sure it's in one of the streets very near here.'

* * *

Elizabeth had only walked along three or four streets before she found the *boulangerie*. It now had a large window and a new red and white awning. The name was still the same, Chevalier, painted above the door. She was hoping Monsieur Chevalier would still be there and would recognise her, and they could talk about the town during the war and her visits to buy *ficelle* each morning. But he would be nearly eighty by now, surely.

Most of the bread had already sold out, but there were still a few batons left standing in a wooden bin and a single stick of *ficelle*. She spoke cheerfully with the two women running the shop, who became saddened when Elizabeth mentioned Henri Chevalier's name; he had died four months previously while serving in the shop. The two women were Chevalier's nieces temporarily running the place, which had just been sold to someone in the town who wanted to open a TV repair business. They talked at length about the funeral, for which it seemed the whole town had turned out – the passing of an era, it was said. But Elizabeth merely nodded her head politely as the two women spoke; her thoughts had been carried back to 1944, when Chevalier would smile and wish her a good day, chatting merrily as he handed the bread over the counter. Chevalier was gone and soon the *boulangerie* would be too. She bought the last piece of *ficelle*, bidding the women as cheerful a farewell as she could muster, taking the thin bread with a thin smile and walking out of the shop back to the café.

Buying the bread had let other memories flood in: the time she was advised to sit down before being given the news of Ralph's death, the words filling her with emptiness. She had wanted to know how Ralph had died. It would have made it easier somehow, but Jackson, the commanding officer, refused to go into detail, muttering that he believed it had been very sudden. She knew it hadn't been because he couldn't look her in the eye as he said it. So she had to imagine the worst instead and had done so ever since – the shooting to pieces. In the days leading up to the birth, the nuns in the convent tried their best to comfort her, but the grief simply accumulated as if stones were being piled on top of her. It was not only the grief of losing Ralph but also his betrayal. She had left that out of her account to Helena, Adam and Miranda because it made her buckle.

She was nearly back at the café in the square and stopped to regather herself, looking into the window of a haberdashery shop. She stood up straight, breathing in and pulling her shoulders back, looking at the array of brightly coloured reels of thread. She would be cheerful. They would soon be going to the *mairie*, where Helena would come to know the truth and so would Adam. The three of them would be happy.

* * *

Adam had assumed that their visit to the records office would be a dry affair. He had imagined a junior official sitting them down in a sparse room with bright lights and bringing them a dusty ledger to inspect, and that once they had looked at the birth records, the book would be snapped shut and they would be sent away.

Instead, Elizabeth, Helena and Adam were shown into a large and stately room at the *mairie*, where they were greeted by Bayeux's *officier d'état civil* himself, Pierre Denain, who shook hands graciously under the sparkling chandelier. He beckoned them towards a large desk, where three chairs were already set out for the visitors.

As Elizabeth broke into her fast-flowing French, Adam wondered whether he would ever get used to it. He had always been impressed at concert weekends when some unassuming music tutor would turn to an Italian or German and seamlessly switch languages; it was as if they had suddenly acquired a more dazzling persona. The same effect was true of Elizabeth. When she spoke in fluent French, her poise and electric directness became even more enchanting, putting a complete stranger at ease with her assured charm. He wanted to understand what she was saying and it made him wish he hadn't given up French so early at school. He gathered the gist of it; she seemed to be reminding Denain of the purpose of their visit. But he was clearly having none of it; he was not one to be rushed into the tedious business of searching for birth records – that was obvious from the way he raised his hand and shook his head. He appeared to be asking about where in England they had come from and the details of their journey. And, judging by Elizabeth's infectious laughter, they seemed to be sharing delight in something else. He turned to Helena next to him and whispered, 'What are they talking about?'

'They've really hit it off. He worked in the office here during the war and Mother has made the mistake of saying she was here at the same time.'

Now that he knew Elizabeth and Denain were reminiscing, Adam could piece together fragments of the conversation – how critical Bayeux had been as a supplies hub for the Allies after the Normandy landings ... the wonders of the road that was built around the town to carry the military traffic ... that once they may have stood in exactly the same bread queue at Chevalier's *boulangerie* ... and surely Denain had just commented on how young Elizabeth must have been at the time?

Eventually, Denain announced that it was time for them to attend to business and asked whether Helena and Adam's

French was as fluent as Elizabeth's. Helena said, in what seemed like acceptable French, that she understood some of what had been discussed, but was not as fluent as her mother.

Denain complimented her, saying that she was being modest as the British always are. '*Et Monsieur?*'

Adam attempted a few phrases before Helena said, '*Il préfère les sciences aux langues.*'

Denain laughed and clapped his hands, declaring that science was the future. He sank back into his high-backed chair, and in a more serious tone, seemed to be saying that it was fortunate that Elizabeth spoke such fluent French because the system for public records in France was quite different from Britain and his English would never have been good enough to explain all the details. Elizabeth became much more formal as well and the interview began, with Elizabeth describing what they wished to find out.

Adam felt as if he was a specimen of some kind. Occasionally, Denain cast him a glance when his name was mentioned during the rapid exchanges of French between Elizabeth and Denain. He asked Helena in a whisper what was being said and she hushed him. 'I'll tell you in a minute. I'm trying to keep up,' she said.

A few minutes later the conversation paused and Adam saw everyone looking at him.

'I think Monsieur Denain understands everything now, Adam,' Elizabeth said. 'He wants to see all your documents. He says he has to check that you're eligible to inspect the records and that you have a legitimate interest.'

Adam laid the documents out on the table and Elizabeth picked them up one by one, explaining the details to Denain.

Although he understood very little of the long conversation, Adam could tell that Denain was someone to be admired for his thoroughness; he seemed to be taking very methodical steps in his enquiries, pausing to think about Elizabeth's answers before asking the next question.

'*Bien! Tout est en ordre!*' Denain eventually said, beckoning the three of them to follow him into the records room. They filed in and then with great ceremony Denain leafed through the pages of a large ledger.

There was one birth entry for the twenty-fifth of January 1945. It was for a male named Raoul Pierre Philippe and was marked in the ledger with an '*X*' next to the words *père non dénommé* and another '*X*' next to the words *mère non dénommée*.

Adam looked at Elizabeth and saw her extraordinary eyes radiating towards him, her irises catching the light and pulsating with the same gentleness he had often seen her direct at Helena.

Helena looked on at this unravelling and smiled, but hesitantly. The smile was one of sympathy and kindness, but there was a tautness in her manner, something doubtful. 'It was a chaotic time in 1945. You said so yourself. We need to ask Monsieur Denain whether there is any possibility that the records were mistaken.'

Elizabeth didn't sigh or roll her eyes and did as Helena asked, questioning Denain. For the first time, his courteous manner slipped.

'*C'est tout à fait impossible!*' he said brusquely. He snapped the ledger shut and spoke in a torrent of indignant French.

When Denain had finished, Elizabeth replied very apologetically and turned to Helena. 'I have reassured Monsieur Denain that we have no intention of being disrespectful, Helena – and he understands. He's upset because for centuries the civic duty of keeping meticulous records in France has been beyond question and he has dedicated his life to the task. His long description was about the care he himself took during the war when every time the ink was dry on one of the records, it would be put into a steel box and taken down to the basement in case of bombing.'

Elizabeth apologised again to Denain, and Adam watched Denain's eyes, which were like dark olives, darting between Helena and Elizabeth, assessing the strange force that seemed to flow between them. Then Denain relaxed as if a storm had subsided. It was as if he finally understood the depth of feeling between mother and daughter about the significance of the birth record they had been discussing, or perhaps his breath was taken away by the sight of Elizabeth and Helena facing each other, beautifully poised, caught up in the fierceness of their silent duel.

Helena asked Denain a question, which Adam couldn't fully decipher, but it seemed to be about the way births were recorded in France. Denain's reply was long and full of technical terms, *actes d'état civil … acte de naissance …*

Adam sensed Helena and Elizabeth knew most of the details already, but they sat and listened patiently. Denain finished, and Helena said to Elizabeth, 'Please can you ask him more about the *Sous X* – surely he must know of some way that we can find out more about the birth of the … child … and the mother.'

Elizabeth had barely completed her question before Denain raised his hand and shook his head emphatically, and he started speaking very rapidly again. Adam was able to pick out certain phrases, '*absolument rester secrète*' ... '*l'hôpital de naissance*' ... '*la mère est autorisée à écrire une lettre*' ... '*les noms sur l'enveloppe* ...'

'You probably understood most of that, Helena? Under *Sous X* there is absolutely no way of identifying the mother ... other than if a letter was written—'

'Yes, I understood what he said. *Did* you write a letter? *Was* there an envelope?'

'Helena, please ...'

'I'm sorry, but we have to go through with this. I need him to explain how a letter can be claimed. What's the French for procedure?'

'*Procédure*,' Elizabeth said faintly, sinking her face into her hands.

Helena turned to Denain and asked him, very civilly, a series of questions, but he was having difficulty understanding Helena's phrasing and often had to check what she had said. Elizabeth had become pale and turned her head away to stare distantly at a large painting on the wall, excluding herself from the conversation.

Denain finished by saying, '*Ce n'est pas la mère, c'est l'enfant qui en fait la demande.*'

Adam shrank in the silence as all three of them turned to stare at him.

'Shall I explain, Adam?' Helena said. 'It appears that under *Accouchement Sous X*, before giving up the child for adoption, the mother is offered the opportunity to write a letter, which has to be kept by law in a sealed envelope by the birth hospital. The names the mother gives to the child are written on the outside of the envelope. You did write a letter, didn't you, Mother?

'Yes ... I did.'

'Why didn't you tell me before?'

'Because it's unbearable ...' Elizabeth hissed the words and then collected herself. 'I wrote the letter in despair. We already have all the proof anyone could ever need, Helena – the dates, the documents. We don't need a letter. It must never be found.'

'Can you remember which hospital it was?'

'Please, Helena ...' Elizabeth said.

They stared at each other, but eventually Elizabeth bowed her face into her hands and said, 'I don't remember its name. It was a small lying-in hospital not far from the convent. There were some steps leading up with tall black railings.'

Helena turned to Denain, attempting to translate what Elizabeth had said. She stopped halfway through and asked Elizabeth for the French word for railings.

'You could say *la rampe*,' Elizabeth said, struggling for words.

Denain listened to Helena speaking again and then interrupted her with immediate recognition, shouting the name of the place very rapidly and waving his hands in the direction of where it was.

'Yes, that was it,' Elizabeth said, looking down at the table as if she had just whispered a confession.

Adam could see that Denain was deflated now that the conversation had taken on such a sombre mood. Elizabeth had obviously also noticed Denain's disappointment. She stood up, making a great effort not to appear despondent, courteously shaking Denain's hand, thanking him for their meeting. The two of them led the way out of the room talking with a forced levity – sharing another of their wartime reminiscences, Adam presumed. Denain opened the front door to show them out into the street, pointing out the directions to the hospital in more detail.

They walked out of the *mairie* in single file, Elizabeth leading and Adam last.

As soon as Elizabeth was in the street, Adam could see she had regathered her strength. She turned her head and said, over her shoulder, 'We should be happy, Helena, but I can tell you are not. You want to go straight to the hospital and find the letter, don't you?'

'Yes. I mean no harm, but I need to go there straight away.'

Then, in the middle of the street, Elizabeth turned fully round to face Helena, resting her hands on Helena's shoulders. She said, 'Please, listen to me. If you insist on putting me through this – raking up the past with a letter I never wanted to see again, then I want you to promise to abide by the result. I've lived with this, or tried to, for over twenty years. Do you promise?'

'Yes … I promise.'

Adam turned away and looked at the high wall behind him because he couldn't bear to watch them burrowing into each other's eyes. Elizabeth's anger seemed to writhe in the air, but it was beautifully contained as her solemn understanding with Helena was reached. He relaxed his shoulders, relieved that there hadn't been a scene in the street. But there were no bystanders to witness Helena and Elizabeth's truce, and a passer-by would probably never have noticed that one had been reached. He himself was not a bystander; increasingly he felt he was being drawn into something he had never experienced before, this raw bond that seemed to flow between Helena and Elizabeth. It was almost terrifying, yet he ached to be part of its purity.

Having reached their perfect agreement, Helena and Elizabeth resumed their walk up the cobbled street towards the hospital, the sunshine glowering down on the grey stones.

Elizabeth said, 'You know there'll be nobody there to see us, Helena? It's lunchtime.'

'Let's find the hospital first, shall we? Then we'll see what to do.'

* * *

'Is this the place?' Helena said when they arrived at a stone building with tall black railings leading up to a heavily studded door.

Elizabeth stood and stared up, unable to speak. Her thoughts flooded back to when she had last staggered up these same stone steps, carrying a little suitcase that seemed heavy because she was hollowed out with exhaustion, gripping the balustrade to haul herself up. She remembered it exactly – cowering beneath the building above her and hearing the chimes of the cathedral clock that struck the hour and almost struck her down. Her contractions were tightening every few minutes, but her physical fragility was as nothing compared to her grief for Ralph, her despair in deciding to give up the child, the guilt seething inside her, the shame she would bring on her family if they ever discovered the truth.

'Yes, this is the place ...' Elizabeth said very faintly, looking up at the studded door.

'I do understand this will be unpleasant, I really do,' Helena said. 'But it has to be done. Why don't you two wait here while I go inside and investigate.' She walked up the steps and entered the hospital.

'We'll just have to wait here until she returns, Adam. I've learnt over the years that when Helena's like this it's pointless to confront her. I'm sorry if you find it all rather uncomfortable. You were very quiet just now.'

'It was very tense, and I didn't know what to say, but you seem more relaxed all of a sudden.'

'Yes, I've realised that if the letter I wrote is still there, the pain of it being read again will be worth it because everything will be finally resolved. When Helena first asked about the letter at the *mairie*, I hoped it might have been lost or destroyed. But it's clear now that the letter is the only means of bringing the three of us together. I remember the envelope very well. It was buff-coloured, and I wrote your three French names on the outside. The letter inside will be in my handwriting, which always causes Helena so much amusement. Even though I was trembling at the time, I'm sure she'll recognise it. And in that moment there you will both be. My children.'

Helena came out of the hospital raising her hands in exasperation, saying yes, all the administrative staff were at lunch, but she had found someone and arranged an appointment with the hospital's director for three o'clock.

'Then you two must have lunch as well,' Elizabeth said. 'Personally I'm not hungry, but you both must be. Why don't you find somewhere to eat and I'll meet you back here just before three. Here, take these francs.'

Elizabeth walked down the steps and sat on a metal bench that faced away from the hospital. She sensed the cold stone of the building standing behind her as she tore little pieces of *ficelle* from her pocket and ate them, absorbed in her thoughts about the letter, remembering the man who had brought her the ink, the paper, and the pen to write it. He told her that setting everything down might do her good – but in reality it was unlikely anyone would ever read it because, although by law the hospital was required to keep every letter, hardly any were ever claimed because they were so difficult to trace. That made her realise there was no point in writing down the reasons for giving the child up. Instead, she just poured out a lament, with barely the strength to move the pen – a *cri de coeur* that might cut her to pieces if she were to read it again.

* * *

She stood up straight and took a breath when Helena and Adam returned. 'Did you find somewhere nice for lunch?'

'We had a lovely *plat du jour* at a little bar full of locals,' Helena said. 'Why can't we have places like that in England? At first, they wouldn't serve us because they had finished serving lunch, but I persuaded them. Everyone was very friendly and it settled me for a while, but now I'm back here, I'm quite nervous about our appointment, aren't you?'

'I'm not looking forward to it, but it has to be done,' Elizabeth said.

Inside, they soon found themselves sitting in a stark and brightly lit office with the director of the hospital, a dour man called Heroux, who seemed to be the complete opposite of the exuberant Denain at the *mairie*. Heroux sat unsmilingly behind his desk with his hands clasped together on a leather-framed blotter beside which was a pen, a ruler and a steel paperknife.

Elizabeth let Helena explain the purpose of their visit, which she did in more fluent French than she had managed at the *mairie*, having covered a lot of the ground already with Denain. Heroux asked a series of questions and breathed out wearily each time Helena hesitated with her reply or had to repeat her answer in a different way to make herself understood. When Elizabeth had to intervene for the second time after Helena's French had become completely muddled, Heroux clicked his tongue and suggested that perhaps it would be preferable if Elizabeth replied to his questions instead.

Elizabeth merely stared at him for a moment. How dare the man try to make a fool of Helena! The room became very quiet. Elizabeth watched Helena and Adam lowering their eyes as if fearing an eruption, but it composed her, seeing them sitting together in harmony, with the same concerned expression. For a moment it took her mind away from the letter she did not wish to read. No, she would not seethe, or purse her lips. Instead, she replied, '*Mais oui, certainement, vous pouvez parler avec moi.*' She answered Heroux's questions very satisfactorily in her rapid French, and while he didn't exactly soften, he became less abrupt as he turned his attention to the documents Elizabeth handed to him one by one. As she explained each document to Heroux, he seemed to weigh the piece of paper in his hands before becoming engrossed. He said it was his duty to be fastidious – that for precise legal reasons he needed to be absolutely certain that Adam was entitled to claim a letter.

'*C'est très inhabituel,*' he said eventually, puffing out his cheeks, adding that he had never heard of any letter being claimed under *Accouchement Sous X*. He asked for Adam's passport and darted his eyes between the photograph and Adam sitting there. At last he snapped the passport shut, placed it on the pile of documents and declared that everything was in order.

'*Voyons, 25 janvier 1945,*' he said, walking over to a large steel filing cabinet, which he unlocked. He pulled out a drawer ceremoniously and flicked through the filing tabs. Eventually, he licked his finger to draw out a buff-coloured envelope.

'*Et voilà!*' he said, bringing the envelope to Adam and laying it on the table, smoothing it out with his hands.

Helena leant over and gasped when she saw the three names written on the outside of the envelope. 'The handwriting! The loops and the flicks!' she said.

Elizabeth's heart leapt then, seeing the sudden realisation light up on Helena's face. Helena asked Heroux whether she could borrow the paperknife and was already reaching towards it when he stood up and said that as far as he was concerned the interview was over. If they wanted to open the letter, they should take it away with them for he had nothing further to say. He had fulfilled his obligations. He was busy and had other things to do; it was a hospital not an archive. He said goodbye and walked out just as his assistant walked in to escort the three of them to the door. Adam thrust the letter into the flap of his jacket pocket and out the three of them filed, into the street, where the high walls were warm in the summer sun.

'What do we do now?' Helena asked.

'It's Adam's letter. It's for him to decide,' Elizabeth said.

'But it'll be in French,' Adam said. 'One of you will have to read it.'

'It's not in French,' Elizabeth said. 'Apart from the very beginning. You'll find that the first two lines are taken from Racine's *Andromaque*. The rest of the letter is in English. I suggest you open the letter and let Helena help you with the first two lines. And then I think we should leave you in peace for a few moments to read the rest of it, not that it'll tell you very much about what happened. I apologise for that. I want you to understand that I was desolate at the time, abandoned and completely alone. I was very young.'

Adam ran his thumb along the back of the envelope. As he unfolded the letter, Elizabeth recited the two lines.

'*Parle-lui tous les jours des vertus de son père,*

'*Et quelquefois aussi parle-lui de sa mère.*'

Looking round Adam's shoulder, Helena translated, '"Talk to him every day about his father. And sometimes speak to him of his mother." And yes, the rest of the letter is in English—'

But before Helena could read any further, Elizabeth took the letter from Adam's hands, folded it, and handed it back to him. 'Come, Helena, you and I need to take a little walk around the block while Adam reads his letter. No doubt your brother will show it to you when we come back.'

* * *

Adam wanted to sit down to read the letter, but an elderly couple had just sat down on the bench nearby, so he crossed the street and settled on the kerb.

> *My dearest,*
>
> *I'm too weak to write and too empty to move the pen in this grief and guilt, with its pain and shame.*
>
> *I have tried to fight the thought of losing you, but you deserve a better life than I can ever give.*
>
> *You have your father's names, you will have his strength too. You will be a wonderful son. I am certain you will be good every day. I can hear your voice and see you standing tall, even though I never saw you before you were taken away.*
>
> *I wish I could explain it all, but I beseech you to believe me when I say this is for the best.*
>
> *Your father is gone and you are now gone too. I will never forget you. You see, I cannot even write this.*
>
> *I pray for you to forgive me, but know I do not deserve it.*
>
> *I leave you with all my love and hope.*
>   *Your mother*

Adam swallowed and wiped one eye and then the other, not wishing to disappoint Elizabeth by making a spectacle of himself. If he read the letter again he would be unfit to look Elizabeth and Helena in the eye when they returned; he lacked their strength. There was no need to read the words again in any case because he could hear them in his head, spoken by Elizabeth, whose voice at seventeen would have been exactly the same as Helena's. He couldn't imagine Elizabeth, even a very young Elizabeth, pouring out her feelings. Had she, in the moment she had written the letter, resolved to be calm and poised for the rest of her life? He tried not to think about her distress, or he might unravel completely. He would think of something else, fixing his mind on anything to maintain his composure. He stared at the cobbles on the street, wondering what type of stone they were, then fixed his eyes on the balustrade running up the steps, considering the age of the iron. And what of Helena? When she read the letter would she finally accept the truth that Elizabeth had been right all along? It would be a great wrench for Helena because it was a wrench for him now, even though he had believed Elizabeth for most of the time. Already the warmth shimmered through him as the realisation struck. A mother, a sister; the certainty of it made him uncoil. But his neck immediately became taut again, thinking about his parents. How sad would they be? At which house would he now live? And then his thoughts drifted back, thinking about how his whole life would have been different if he had not been adopted. He let all these thoughts veer about, gripping the letter between finger and thumb. He would hold himself together by not reading it again, and folded it twice.

He looked up to see that Helena and Elizabeth had just come into the square from the opposite corner. He turned his head away to wipe his eyes fully before they were near enough to see him properly.

'Well?' Helena said when she was standing over him.

He stood up and said nothing, handing her the letter, which she unfolded and started to read. Elizabeth had once described to him how Helena used to read when she was very young; she would become completely absorbed, her little hands gripping both sides of a book, moving not just her eyes across each line, but moving her head at the same time, as if being hypnotised and lost in the story.

Helena was finally still and offered the letter to Elizabeth, who closed her eyes and shook her head very slowly from side to side. Helena folded it twice very carefully along the creases and handed it back to him. He slid the letter into his pocket.

* * *

It was a thing of beauty, Elizabeth thought – the way Helena embraced Adam with a slightly embarrassed sense of understanding. And then both of them turned to embrace her, and there the three of them stood, the tops of their foreheads touching, with their arms wrapped around each other's shoulders, rapt in silence.

'Now, Helena, really, there's no need for that,' Elizabeth said, handing her a handkerchief when they finally broke away. 'Well, perhaps just this once ... Now then, I think we need to find somewhere to celebrate, but everywhere will be shut. We'll have to have a celebratory dinner this evening back at the hotel. Let's go towards the cathedral where there'll be taxis. There's so much to talk about.'

She knew she was right. They had so much to talk about that even though the cathedral spires were in view most of the time, they took a very circuitous route, meandering calmly and aimlessly along the cobbled streets to the cathedral, laughing at some of the nonsenses from the day: Denain's joviality at the *mairie*, Heroux's clipped austerity at the hospital, the *ficelle*, and the fact that they hadn't yet seen the tapestry or the inside of the cathedral. Their words were the decorum of a game of chess as they trod along carefully, refusing to acknowledge that anything particularly momentous had occurred.

28

It was four o'clock when they got back to the hotel. When they collected their keys at the front desk, the receptionist asked them whether they'd had an enjoyable day. Had they seen the sights? Did they find somewhere nice for lunch?

Elizabeth, taking her key, smiled and said, 'Yes, thank you. It's very kind of you to ask. We've had an interesting day.'

The three of them stood in the middle of the foyer, holding their keys, making arrangements to meet for dinner at seven thirty. The keys had large wooden fobs that clacked while they waved them around, discussing what to do until dinner.

Elizabeth said she was tired and would go to her room.

Helena said, 'Well, *brother*, what shall you and I do? What do you say to a little stroll in the garden?'

Adam, taken by surprise for a moment, said, 'Yes … yes, of course.'

'Good. Shall we meet back down here in twenty minutes?'

Elizabeth wished them a pleasant walk and went up the wide stairs to her room. She closed the door and slumped into a *caquetoire* chair, which was uncomfortable with its wooden back, but she was too exhausted to find another.

Helena's ability to adapt was astonishing – to experience the high charge of the day's events and then to calm everything down by asking Adam so effortlessly to walk with her – just as any sister might with a few hours to pass the time. If nothing else, the events of the last few weeks had accelerated Helena's path to full maturity, her imperiousness catching up with her beauty. She would have to be careful though not to overreach herself. Being able to command the attention of the world was admirable, but being seen to mould it excessively to her needs was not.

But then Helena had always been quick to adjust. When she was about five, she had been playing in the large cupboard under the back stairs and the door had shut behind her. The McKenzie family had come to stay, and Elizabeth was entertaining them and some other house guests in the drawing room, so it was a good hour before Elizabeth had noticed that Helena was missing. Elizabeth excused herself and went on a hunt. When she turned to go up the back stairs, she heard Helena hammering the door and shouting frantically from inside the cupboard. But when the door was opened, Helena immediately found her equilibrium and said no, she hadn't been frightened at all of the dark or that she might be lost forever. In fact, she said, it was cosy in there. Elizabeth had to be very firm with her then, saying that Helena was never to go into cupboards again, or anywhere else where one might be locked in and suffocate. Helena promised, and the matter was never mentioned again.

It was too uncomfortable resting in the chair with its carved mahogany digging into the back of her neck and making her dizzy. Maybe it was hunger. Yes, it must be; she hadn't eaten properly all day, so she got up and dialled reception for something to tide her over until dinner. *Un croque monsieur*, she said, and no wine, just a jug of iced water.

While she waited, she considered standing in the bay window to look out over the large parterre in front of the hotel. She could wait and watch Helena and Adam walking out together, hand in hand. Not like *that* of course; they would be walking a few inches further apart than they had been recently, and their steps would be slightly more measured. But it wouldn't be wise to watch them; they might turn round and look up as they walked, seeing her peering out from the side of the curtains, an interfering mother. No, she must let them work it all out for themselves.

She went over to the four-poster bed, kicked off her shoes and lay down, propping herself up with the lace pillows.

Yes, Helena would manage the adjustment perfectly, the new circumstances, the recalibration. What a picture it was when Helena read the Racine, her face lighting up as the realisation sank in; she handled it very well.

And Adam's success in appearing to be unfazed by the afternoon's events was also admirable, although in his case it was his habit of bottling things up. When she stopped Helena from reading the English part of the letter, he slid it into his pocket as if it meant nothing more than a weather forecast. He would have to watch out too. Someone one day would find it annoying, this apparent ability to drift along, accepting things without question. Or was he calm because he had already been resigned to the truth, believing her all along, behaving like a dutiful son for weeks?

She must have fallen asleep because there was a knocking at the door. She sat up and swung her legs out onto the floor, realising it must be room service arriving. She called out, '*Entrez, entrez,*' in a sleepy, dusky manner. The lad wheeling in the trolley looked bashful as she stood in her stockings, arranging her dishevelled hair as best she could. He wheeled the trolley to the table by the window as she found her purse and thanked him, palming a five-franc note.

Having eaten, she felt restored and wondered whether she might take a walk around the garden herself, but it would be awkward meeting Helena and Adam if they were still out there, having so much to say to each other, coming to terms. So she sat and read, looking forward to dinner. She would phone down to reception and say it was a family celebration and could they do anything special.

* * *

Adam was in his room wondering why he had not questioned Helena about the need to wait for twenty minutes before their walk. If they were in reception wanting to walk, why didn't they just walk out into the garden instead of walking upstairs, only to walk downstairs again to go for the walk? It was exactly the kind of thing Elizabeth would have done. They were mysterious sometimes. He would have to set about assimilating their numerous habits, respecting the very specific ways in which they lived their lives, the way they conducted a conversation, the order in which things sometimes had to be done, indeed the very expressions one might use in different situations, everything fitting in. Elizabeth and Helena would never think of these things as foibles; they were foregone conclusions about the only sensible way to live. The thought of striving to become more like them made him smile. His first task would be to acquire their powers of adaptation, the rapid way in which they were both able to reconfigure themselves if circumstances arose beyond their control. Helena had demonstrated it with exemplary skill – in the space of reading Elizabeth's letter she had been able to shift her foundations. Now that she was certain of the truth and was already behaving exactly as a very confident sister might, he knew he would not be able to question her any more than he felt able to question Elizabeth. There would be no debate about when was the right time to go for a walk, for example.

He smiled again, feeling a surge of supreme warmth – the relief that everything was finally settled. The three of them would grow used to each other, the bond would become fast. It was no effort to idle away twenty minutes. He would think about a new future and not look back. Already his unmentionable obscenity with Elizabeth was so distant it was as if it had never happened. How his parents would react weighed heavily on his mind, but he would address all that when he got back to England.

'Shall we go then?' Helena said to him when they met in the foyer.

They marched out into the late afternoon sunshine and ambled in silence along a path leading to a sundial.

'So what do you think, Helena? Will it take you time to get used to all this?'

'No, I don't think so. I'm used to it already. Let's just say you and I had a misunderstanding, that's all. There's nothing wrong about a misunderstanding, as long as you clear it up, which in our case we have, so there's nothing more to say about it really. Besides, I've much to think about. First there's what to do about Father – and I'm sure you've been thinking about how to handle Constance and Arnold too, but all that can be sorted out when we're home. The more pressing concern is Mother.'

'Yes, she seemed exhausted today. It must have been quite an ordeal for her.'

'Which ordeal? The one during the war, or retrieving the letter this afternoon from the hospital?'

'Both, really. And she must have been worrying about *you* – the possibility of you not believing the result.'

'Oh, that's nothing, that's all settled! No, my concern is what happened in 1945.'

'What do you mean?'

'I simply don't know how she could do it.'

'Do what?'

'Give a child away! Give *you* away, in fact. Of course I worship her, but none of it fits. It's not remotely in her nature to abandon a child. It must have been a ghastly time, but I'm sure she was as tough then as she is now. However bad things were, she would know how wrong it was to cast someone off, to desert them like that. She would have said then – just as she says now – that you have to live with things through thick and thin, come what may. Surely you agree? I'm going to raise it at dinner.'

Adam almost tripped on the path. Was this how brazen life was to be? Previously, Helena and Elizabeth had made allowances for him, had softened and muted their bluntness because he was not part of their inner orbit. But he was becoming part of it now. Helena's abruptness made him flinch. The candour between Helena and Elizabeth was unbridled precisely because the tie between them was so sacrosanct – they could say whatever they liked, however they liked, with the complete understanding that their honesty with each other could never cause bitterness or resentment. He feared being a part of it. By confronting Helena now, telling her bluntly *not* to raise the matter at dinner, he would be taking his first step. But he didn't dare; he wasn't ready. He needed to learn the rules first, find the strength, become a part of it.

'Or, I suppose, you could let things lie?' he said. 'It was a long time ago. Will it do any good?'

'It will make me not feel ill of her.'

'Can I make … a request? That you don't raise it at dinner?'

'What a strange thing to ask! A *request*, did you say?'

'Yes, a request.'

Helena blinked as if trying to understand.

'I just thought we might all have had enough for one day. We could just relax and have a pleasant meal.'

'Well, we'll have to see about that …' Helena said, frowning and walking slowly for a moment. Then, as if she had decided something, she started walking more briskly and said, 'As for the meal, I'm sure it'll be perfectly pleasant because I know exactly what she'll have been up to. She'll have had words with the hotel manager, insisting that all the stops are pulled out for a celebratory dinner – a *family* dinner, no less. Come on, Adam, you need to cheer up! And you need to speed up too. I think we've finished with the garden. It's hardly spectacular.'

29

Adam took off his jacket and his shoes to lie on the bed with his hands behind his head. It was unusual for him to be ready so far ahead of time, but here he was, ready for dinner with fifteen minutes to spare. He didn't want to go down early and find the dining room empty and look empty himself. He had decided that Helena and Elizabeth would be down there at seven thirty precisely, but not until he had given it considerable thought: it was another of their codes that he was gradually learning to decipher. They were both very strict about the importance of punctuality, but the rules seemed to vary depending on the circumstances. For meeting someone outside a station, say, it was critical to be on time, and if one was late it was very bad form. But for social occasions, such as a dinner party, for example, being exactly on time would be a cardinal sin: it was impolite to arrive in good time because the hosts might not be ready. Manners were never whimsical, Elizabeth had said; they evolved for sound reasons. Helena had announced something similar once, although in her case she had said, rather confusingly, that manners were never fashionable. By which she meant, he was certain, that manners were a constant and not subject to the whims of fashion – rather than the alternative interpretation of her ambiguous expression, which was that manners were never *in fashion*, which she would never think.

What were the rules for being on time for a family dinner? Was it a form of social occasion or more like an appointment? He decided to go downstairs the moment the half hour struck on the clock in the courtyard, which had been interrupting his thoughts throughout the afternoon with its jangling chimes. He sat up to put his shoes on before lying back on the bed – that way he would be ready to go downstairs the moment the chimes struck. He had been looking forward to dinner, to seeing Helena happy and Elizabeth happy and being happy himself. But Helena had cast an ominous shadow over a potentially joyous evening by threatening to challenge Elizabeth about the reasons for having him adopted. Was it not sufficient for her that he himself – the aggrieved party, no less – had no desire to dig up the past? He brooded over it, but he certainly hadn't acquired the confidence yet to trip along to Helena's room and demand that she refrain from spoiling the evening – and besides, her room was next to Elizabeth's, so a quiet word with her might be difficult.

As the half hour began to strike, Adam darted out of his room and went down to the first floor, where he saw Elizabeth and Helena walking arm in arm towards the wide stairs down into the main foyer of the hotel. He calculated that if he followed them down several steps behind, they would not hear him on the deep carpet, and he would arrive at the foot of the stairs at precisely the right time. He could hear Elizabeth asking Helena about the walk around the grounds of the hotel and whether the garden was worth a look. He was close enough now to hear Helena whispering, 'I don't think it would be your sort of thing.'

'Ah!' Elizabeth said with a little guffaw of perfect understanding.

'Have I missed one of your jokes?' Adam asked with a smile as they walked across the foyer to the restaurant.

'What excellent punctuality, Adam!' Elizabeth said. 'I was just hearing all about your lovely walk in the garden. Let's go straight in.'

* * *

When the maître d' had shown them to their table, Elizabeth realised she had made a mistake. In booking the table and mentioning that it was a special occasion, she hadn't expected a fussy and reverential one. She took one step up into a raised area with a single table beautifully set for three. With great ceremony, the maître d' pulled out the chair for Elizabeth to sit and then did the same for Helena to her left and Adam to her right. The sommelier appeared, flourishing a tray with three glasses of champagne, which the maître d' insisted were *avec les compliments de la maison*. Elizabeth thanked him and he departed, leaving the waiter to step up, bowing with the menus. Elizabeth decided none of it would worry her, not the fuss, not the ostentation and not the glasses, which were flutes rather than the tulips she preferred. Instead, she would savour this moment that had lain as a dream in her mind for weeks – the three of them raising a glass towards each other to salute their sublime harmony. The pain she had felt from Adam and Helena's uncertainty was gone. She had even been spared the pain of reading the letter when Helena had offered it to her earlier; she had waved it away with a wince, knowing it would break her heart to read it. She had spent years confining her memories at seventeen to a distant past, treating them as abstract facts. Reading the letter would have forced her to relive the reality about Ralph and she would have broken down completely.

Then it was exactly as Elizabeth had hoped. The three of them had no need to clink glasses in the French style, overlabouring the significance of the moment. Instead, they raised their glasses with a little nod to each other, as if they had been family for years. She sat quietly, listening in reverie as Helena and Adam talked garrulously. They were teasing one another. Her children! Helena berating Adam for knowing so little French as they discussed the items on the menu, and he in turn reminding Helena that when she checked their bill at lunch her maths was far from good.

'Well, it's all right for you two – at least you *had* some lunch.'

'What are you talking about?' Helena said. 'You had your *ficelle*. You must have enjoyed that, munching away at it like a mouse, eating it secretly out of your pocket.'

'I like bread.'

'Oh, we *know* you do. Look! the waiter's coming. You'll be able to have *more* bread with your soup. Adam and I will hold back, so that you can have the whole basket if you like.'

* * *

Adam looked on in wonder as Elizabeth and Helena traded

their friendly insults for several minutes. Previously, he had always felt excluded from their cheery badinage. He had always seemed to be on the outside of it looking in, but now he felt the warmth of being almost part of it for the first time. It was like being borne along on a gentle stream.

But gradually he noticed a shift in mood as each course was brought to the table. He should have relished the fact that nobody else – not the waiters, not the maître d', not the people that now occupied every table in the dining room – none of them would be able to detect that Helena was becoming unsettled and that Elizabeth was becoming unsettled as a result. Although he was alarmed, he was proud that he alone was able to gauge the gathering edginess in the conversation, the lightness of tone no longer running away with itself as brightly as before. When Helena had fallen silent and lowered her eyes to sip the bisque from her spoon, Elizabeth stole a glance at her, as if wondering whether something was amiss. He could tell Helena was unsettled from the way she laid down her spoon very precisely and said the soup was rather good before sitting back in her chair, straightening her back with a little fidget. He knew she was thinking about the letter. Was she hesitating to talk about it because he had advised her against interrogating Elizabeth? His *request*? If so, then her hesitation might at least mean she cared about his opinion – that it might be worth considering.

Then, when the fish course arrived, he was certain that Elizabeth was fully aware of Helena's change of mood. She would know only too well that almost imperceptible frown Helena wore whenever there was something on her mind, something that needed to be resolved. Yes, he could see that

Elizabeth had latched on to it now, slicing her turbot with studied purpose, waiting for Helena to say what was bothering her.

Seeing them now, he knew he would never acquire their immaculate poise, their backs bolt upright, the chins set firm, avoiding eye contact as their polite conversation continued. When they did briefly look at each other while they spoke, they seemed to be conducting a conversation with their eyes in parallel with the flow of words across the ornately arranged table.

The waiter arrived and asked whether the food was good. Elizabeth and Helena thanked him very warmly as if there was nothing on their minds at all. The conversation resumed. Adam looked around the restaurant to see if anyone was remotely aware of the ritual dance that was taking place, Elizabeth searching Helena's eyes occasionally for clues as to what the matter really was, her knife sliding delicately on the china. It was like watching someone peering into a pond; it was only when you were very close up that you knew their eyes were not looking at its surface, but *through* its surface at the hidden life lying below.

Was he sufficiently accepted yet? Did he dare to intervene? Eventually he did, rather mechanically, suggesting they could visit a garden on their way to Cherbourg in the morning rather than visiting the tapestry.

Elizabeth seemed delighted by his diversion. What a good idea it was, she said, and she asked him about the hotel garden and what was wrong with it, because Helena hadn't really said what was wrong with it. He repeated some of the things Helena had mentioned to him earlier – that the formality of parterres made for an unimaginative experience; they were too organised, too affected and contrived. Helena listened while she ate, and scoffed a good-humoured laugh, teasing him about how quick he was to learn.

After the waiters had departed, having set down the plates for the main course, there was a lull in the conversation. Elizabeth picked up her knife and fork to begin eating but placed the cutlery down again without a sound of the silver on the china.

'What is it, Helena? You must tell me what's on your mind, the thing you want to say.'

Helena placed her knife and fork down very carefully as well and said, 'It's difficult.'

'I can see *that*,' Elizabeth said. 'We should be happy, Helena ... I hoped so much that we would all be happy.'

Adam looked down for a moment and saw a piece of cotton on the edge of his chair, which he tried to brush away until he realised it was a loose strand in the upholstery.

'We *are* happy, we *will* be happy once the letter has stopped eating away inside me. The letter doesn't explain anything. It doesn't explain why you would give a child away. You're too strong. I don't understand it. It's completely beyond me.'

'I see,' Elizabeth said, picking up her cutlery again. Perhaps it was convenient that the meat was not the tenderest – she sawed it deftly as if grateful for some time to think about what to say. She stared back at Helena, whose doe eyes continued to beseech an explanation.

'Of course the letter doesn't explain anything, Helena. I was beside myself. I could barely push the pen, let alone explain. Maybe you would have coped better than me. But I want you to imagine being seventeen, far away from home in a country lost in the destruction of war with all its death and chaos. You've been working twelve-hour days for months and you're breaking down with exhaustion. You love the father of the child you're about to have, but your dreams were shattered when you were told two days ago that he'd been shot to pieces. Barely able to walk, you stumble to a hospital, terrified, and there you'll have his child, completely alone. You think about the future of the child. Your parents will cast you out, furious about the utter disgrace of it. You have no money, you have nowhere to live. You're sick with grief, with guilt and with shame. You *do* care for the child, so much so that you know his best chance in life is to give him up …'

Adam watched Elizabeth bowing her head, unable to continue. She poured herself a glass of water.

Helena said, 'I do understand all that, and you're right, I don't think I would have coped. I don't think anyone would. But—'

'Please, Helena, is that not enough?' Adam said, stretching his hand towards Elizabeth's shoulder.

But Elizabeth pushed it back gently, 'Thank you, Adam, but no, it's clearly not enough. Is it, Helena?'

'Why couldn't you have gone to Ralph's parents? Surely they would have understood? You were a war widow. Well, not a widow exactly, you weren't married.'

'No, I wasn't. But *he* was. Oh, you may as well have it all, Helena! *You're* shocked? Imagine how I was. How could I have gone to his parents? Or his wife, perhaps? Oh, they would have all *understood*, make no mistake about that.'

Elizabeth picked up her cutlery and then placed it down again as if she was too weak to lift it. Then she spoke very softly in a whisper, close to tears. 'When Ralph was killed it was Sandy, Ralph's closest friend, who told me about Ralph's double life – the wife he had back in Cheshire as well as me. *That's* what finally broke me, Helena … it was not only the sheer exhaustion, the pains chafing inside, the shame and the guilt. On top of that was Ralph's deceit, his betrayal. Some anger might have helped me, but there was none because I was still grieving … I still loved him. I was alone and panic-stricken, knowing the world would judge my child forever. Things were different then. You must understand I was near collapse, destroyed by the thought of Adam discovering the truth and thinking ill of his father. *That's* why I gave him up. The agony of it all was greater than the birth itself. I heard his cries, but he was hurried away before I could see him. I was told the baby was a boy and that I would have some time to reconsider. But I was convinced adoption was his best chance in life, so they brought me some pen and paper to write down his names and anything else I wanted. I was torn apart when I wrote that letter. It's preyed on me for years.'

A waiter approached, seeming to be on the verge of asking whether there was anything wrong with the food because the three of them weren't eating. But he must have detected the grim silence and walked away hastily as if inventing some other errand.

Helena bowed her head, staring at her plate.

'You do understand now, Helena?' Elizabeth said.

'Yes, I do now. I'm sorry.'

'You forgive me?'

'Yes, of course.'

'Then we forgive each other.'

Adam sat back in his chair and breathed out. There was no kiss, no hug, to seal Helena and Elizabeth's understanding, not even a touch of the hand. They lived beyond the need.

Elizabeth turned her head towards him. 'I don't expect *you* to forgive me, Adam.'

'But of course I do.' It was all he felt able to say.

They ate without a word, exchanging occasional glances as if weighing the day's events and everything that had been said. Any comment to break the silence would have seemed banal.

The waiter arrived with the menus and to take away the plates.

'What an exhausting day! I'm afraid I've lost my appetite,' Elizabeth said.

Adam and Helena said they had too, and the waiter suddenly became very concerned again, asking whether there had been something wrong with the dinner.

In the rush of French that followed, Elizabeth reassured him that everything had been fine. Adam hardly understood a word of it, apart from the word 'Cognac', which was mentioned several times. He watched Elizabeth humouring the waiter and they started to jest with each other, presumably about the virtues of different brandies.

After the waiter had left, the sombre mood around the table disappeared as if spirited away by Elizabeth's light-heartedness.

'That sounded fun,' Adam said, 'what was it all about?'

'The waiter was upset that we weren't enjoying the food. But I explained that we had a small family matter to discuss and that everything was quite settled now. He was very sympathetic and insisted that if we were skipping the other courses, we should go to the drawing room and have some very nice Cognac instead. It caused him some amusement when I said I would do no such thing because I prefer Armagnac. We joked a little, agreeing to disagree about which is the better digestif, but we settled our differences and respected each other's opinion. I asked him whether he had an Armagnac from 1945 or the nearest year, and he's gone to have a look. I can't recall whether you've ever tried Armagnac, Helena?'

'No, I never have, but I'm looking forward to sampling it.'

'And you, Adam?'

'No, neither have I.'

Once they had sat down in the large drawing room and the Armagnac had arrived, Elizabeth explained how she thought its chewier texture and bolder flavour made it preferable to Cognac. It was as if the tense conversation over dinner had never taken place. It seemed to Adam that she began to uncoil, finding herself again with the calm enthusiasm he hadn't seen in her since they left Southampton. Her shoulders relaxed, and it relieved the tautness in his. The melody returned to her voice as she enlightened them softly about the joys of Armagnac, with that uncanny knack she had of imparting wisdom without being in the least patronising. He worshipped her serenity, and he looked across at Helena, listening dutifully and worshipping it too, it seemed.

There was a low cane table in the middle of the three armchairs where they sat. Helena leant forward and smiled. 'Thank you, Mother, that was very interesting,' she said, raising her glass for a toast. 'I think we can put 1945 behind us now.'

The salon had been almost empty when they arrived because they had been among the first to finish dinner, but as other diners came from the restaurant, the room filled with the hum of contented conversation, the day winding down in the firelight and the low lamps, the scent of logs glowing in the grate. The three of them sat back in their chairs and said little because there seemed little more to be said. Their tranquillity was as if a steady tide had flooded silently into a creek, and, finding its high point in the still of night, lay settled and complete.

Adam didn't want it to end. He watched Helena leaning forward again, twisting the stem of her balloon glass, deep in thought. He adored her differently now, just as he had learnt to adore Elizabeth differently. He knew Helena was about to speak, but it would not be one of her difficult questions, for her frown was gone and she was smiling.

'So when you got back to England,' she said to Elizabeth, 'you must have recovered very strongly. You've always said that you became a secretary immediately after the war.'

'Yes, the war was finally coming to an end and everyone was looking towards a brighter future. Lots of people starting new lives. I was told that with my experience in Normandy I would be in great demand as a secretary or an administrator. It may seem unambitious nowadays, but it was what I was good at. One of the officers I worked with here in Bayeux said he knew a friend in the advertising business.'

'Where you met Magnus …'

'Yes, a few years before he started his own agency. It was

very exciting and everyone was optimistic. Everyone wanted to rebuild and start afresh, putting the past behind them …'

Eventually their peaceful conversation started to flag, expiring out of sheer tiredness. They made their way up the grand staircase, and when they were about to go to their rooms, Elizabeth turned to Helena and Adam on the landing and said, 'We'll all sleep well tonight, I'm sure.'

Helena said, 'I'm sorry, I didn't mean to be mean at dinner.'

'You weren't. It was the right thing to do. It's always better to have things in the open. Good night, Helena.'

Adam watched Elizabeth and Helena hug in that brief, unfussy way that seemed unique to the bond between them.

Elizabeth then did exactly the same with him.

'Goodnight, Adam. You've been very patient.'

He wanted to embrace her acceptance for longer, even shed a tear on her shoulder, but she had turned to go to her room.

He called out goodnight to them both and turned away too.

30

'Now that you're family, you'll have to learn the sixpence game, Adam,' Helena said.

Elizabeth was not usually fond of the sixpence game. But here she was, about to play it with Magnus, Helena and Adam. It was a family tradition that had been kept up ever since Helena was three or four – her reward for being so well-behaved, sitting dutifully through a Sunday lunch as the only child among eight or ten adults sometimes. After the cheese course, the women would retire to the drawing room to drink coffee and the men would stay to drink port in the Tudor dining room, with Helena plumped up on cushions sitting next to Magnus at the head of the table. Elizabeth had disapproved of the tradition, mainly because Helena was too young to be breathing in all that tobacco smoke, which always made her eyes smart. Her little eyes would be pink for hours afterwards, partly from the fug of the cigarettes and cigars and partly from the tears of joy she shed because the sixpence game was her very favourite.

Helena must have been no more than six when she announced very proudly one day that she was always allowed a little glass of port during the sixpence game. Elizabeth asked her whether the men behaved properly when it was played and she said oh yes, always, because she was actually in charge of the sixpence game and was very strict about the rules, forbidding anyone to use bad language, even if they lost the game.

On the few occasions when it had been just the three of them for Sunday lunch, Helena would insist that the sixpence game still be played, so Elizabeth would sit on Magnus's left and Helena on his right, Helena relishing the fact that she was in command, deciding who would go first and ensuring the paper was wrapped closely around the glass – tight as a drum, she always said. Elizabeth noticed that when it was just the three of them playing, Magnus would forgo the port.

Now that there were four of them sharing Sunday lunch, Elizabeth thought the seating arrangements very uneven, with Adam sitting to Helena's right. It was wondrous to see them side by side, opposite her, her children. But it was decidedly uneven and she would have to suggest the seating arrangements were reconfigured. But how? A round table would make sense for family meals, but replacing the rectangular tables in the main dining room and also in the breakfast room wouldn't work because the rooms weren't the right shape. It was important to take things gradually and not change everything at once, but when the time was right, she would lay the table differently when the four of them were to dine together. She could lay the table for two each side, but how would that work? With Magnus and Adam opposite her and Helena? No, that wouldn't be right – it would be better if Adam sat next to her and Helena was next to Magnus. It would be more even. A nice family arrangement. But it might be complicated if Magnus baulked at the idea of no longer sitting at the head of the table.

Yet in fairness to Magnus, his reaction to it all had been surprising. When they were travelling back from France three months ago, Elizabeth had confessed to Helena that she had no idea how Magnus was to be told that Adam was her son; she wasn't sure how such news could be broken. In fact, she admitted to being frightened.

'Oh, I'll deal with that, don't you worry,' Helena had said. 'It's probably best you stay out of it. Father never argues with me, he has more sense. Leave it all to me. I'll sit him down and tell him to behave about it. It'll be fine.'

And Helena had succeeded – Magnus had indeed been remarkably civil about it all, accepting Adam quite gracefully, even welcoming him into the family once it was clear that harmony in his household was restored.

'What's the sixpence game?' Adam asked.

Helena got up to fetch an empty glass from the chiffonier, which she set down in the middle of the table.

'First,' Helena said, you take a glass like this. It has to be a Paris goblet …'

But, Elizabeth remembered, there had been a catch to Helena helping out with Magnus: she had asked Elizabeth to oblige with a favour in return. Adam had confessed to Helena that he was in a terrible state worrying about how to break the news to his parents, and Helena had insisted that it was only fair that the burden should be Elizabeth's – she was the cause of the problem in the first place and should therefore be the person to correct it, Helena had said. It was wonderful, of course, that Adam and Helena had taken so quickly to being thick as thieves, confiding in each other so readily. So she herself set about the task of explaining everything to Constance and Arnold, taking them to the Orangery and Privy Garden at Hampton Court. It had all been charming, and Constance and Arnold were becoming fast friends of hers. They had come to stay for a few days, and Elizabeth had been to stay a couple of times at the Holland Park house. Everybody was content with the arrangement that had been agreed – that Adam would spend his time freely between London, Durham and the Holt just as he wished.

'Then you take a paper napkin,' Helena said. 'The best ones are the cheap crinkly ones, but these will do for today …'

Elizabeth watched Helena place the napkin over the goblet and then wrap it very tightly around the bowl of the goblet and its stem.

It was often the case, Elizabeth thought, that dependable people had dependable names, such as Arnold and Constance; it was like dogs resembling their owners or the other way round. She already liked Constance and Arnold very much; they would never be the life and soul of a party, but there was no harm in that. Quiet sincerity was in such short supply these days, what with sham and shallowness creeping in everywhere and the desire for things to be shiny and plastic, garish and faux. She would take her time to show how grateful she was for Constance and Arnold's understanding – they were coming to stay again in a fortnight and maybe in time they might all go on holiday together.

'The critical thing, Adam, is to make sure that the napkin is tight as a drum over the top of the glass. Like this, you see.' Helena tapped the surface of the napkin stretched over the top of the goblet with a couple of rat-a-tat-tats.

It was silly to think of all the 'ifs', Elizabeth thought. *If* she had never met Ralph ... Or, *if* he had never been killed, she would never be looking at Helena now, with her delicate fingers doing their little drumroll on the paper stretched over the glass. *If* Helena had never met Adam ... Imagine mothering them both through childhood! There would have been tedious childhood squabbles, of course. Helena would have been six when Adam was eleven, but she would still have teased him mercilessly; he would have towered over her, but he would have been too gentle to defy her.

Turning to Magnus, Helena said, 'You need to give me a sixpence, please. Watch this, Adam, the sixpence is placed in the middle of the paper. Now, pass me your cigarette please, Father ...'

It was enough to make you melt, watching Helena explain the game as she had done at Sunday lunches ever since she needed to sit on two cushions, then one, then none. When they were younger, Adam and Helena would have squabbled over whose turn it was to explain the rules of the game; she could hear their voices chattering now. But it was sad that there were no photographs of them holding hands running up the beach, shrieking with joy, their little feet shimmying on the wet sand, the buckets and spades swinging, the toothy grins captured on the glossy Kodak prints heaped in a drawer in the drawing room or neatly mounted in a photograph album with the little corner things to keep them in place. Oh look! That was the Isle of Wight in 1956 – I'm sure there was more sand then and I know the beach huts have gone after that storm when the cliff slid down that winter.

'Then it's quite simple,' Helena said, 'we take it in turns to burn a hole with the cigarette wherever you choose in the paper around the sixpence ... like this. As you can see, that's quite a small hole and the sixpence is perfectly safe. But as we each take it in turns to burn a hole, the paper becomes less able to support the weight of the sixpence. The aim of the game is not to be the one who burns the last hole that causes the sixpence to fall into the bottom of the glass. Each hole can be as large or small as you like, but it must be *discernible*. It was the first long word I ever learnt ...'

Elizabeth remembered the occasion very well. The men had joined the women in the drawing room after their sixpence game and they were in wonder that Helena had used the word discernible when she had barely learnt to speak. She must have heard an adult using the word and soaked it up. Her startling confidence was a source of concern at first, because one had to find a balance. It was one thing for a child to be admirably assured, but quite another to be embarrassingly precocious. She looked at Helena now, handing the cigarette to Magnus, nodding her head without a word, signalling that he was next to burn a hole in the paper.

Helena was overbearing sometimes, but better that than to be too timid in this day and age. Adam wasn't timid exactly, but a little too tentative perhaps. Surely one would learn from the other? The forthrightness and the gentleness would converge between them and both would find a happy medium. The process might be a little painful at times, especially when the pair of them were in cahoots – as they were the other day. She had taken Helena and Adam to lunch in the restaurant by the river and they ganged up on her, poking fun at her, teasing her again about her liking for bread. The joke was wearing a little thin now. All she had asked the waiter was what kinds of bread there were. There was no malice in Helena and Adam's guffawing, and she had pretended to be most indignant about the two of them picking on her like that, and they had all laughed about it in the end. It was another step for her *children* – she still blinked at the word – coming together. Being the butt of their humour was a small price to pay for the harmony of it all.

Magnus took a puff of the cigarette and passed it to her. She burnt a tiny hole far away from the two that were already there – that way the game would last longer and she'd be able to study Helena's delighted face as she presided over the game, adjusting to the strangeness of playing it for the first time with her new-found brother.

Helena said, 'It's your turn now, Adam. How exciting! The first time you've ever played the sixpence game. It has started the usual way with three holes spaced around the sixpence. This is the simple part of the game because you can burn a new hole quite easily without the sixpence dropping in …'

Yes, *tentative*, that was the word, Elizabeth thought as she watched Adam hesitating before burning a hole very cautiously. She was almost burning herself with the pride welling up within her. *Her* son was already of the mould she preferred. Not for him the brashness and the braying and the bravado to impress. He was above all that. His strength was to be generous, to be concerned for others and not to cause offence. But she would have to help him adapt – to be more assertive in a world where kindness was mistaken for weakness, a world in which being understated risked being ignored, even trampled upon. It was her new project, a grand vision far beyond her garden with its terraces and its stone steps, the tall shrubs and the herbaceous magnificence in summer.

'You can imagine how tricky things become, Adam, when we've all had several goes and there are lots of holes in the paper. The sixpence will begin to sag a little into the glass, hanging by flimsy little bridges between the holes, hanging by a thread …'

Elizabeth was silent as the game progressed. She was transfixed watching Helena and Adam smiling and laughing as if they had been together since childhood.

Finally, on Magnus's turn, the sixpence tipped into the glass, deafeningly it seemed, like the crash of a cymbal at the end of a concert. After the hands had been thrown in the air and the little gasps had subsided, he sighed and said, 'It's a silly game really, Adam, but welcome to the family, nonetheless.'